Russian Crossfire

Battling a Common Enemy

Stephen L. Thompson

Russian Crossfire

Books by Stephen L. Thompson

The Crossfire Series

Colorado Crossfire
International Crossfire
Believer's Crossfire
Israeli Crossfire
Spirit Crossfire
Faith Crossfire
Chinese Crossfire
Texas Crossfire
Dark Crossfire
Island Crossfire
Jagged Crossfire
Violent Crossfire
Russian Crossfire
Nuclear Crossfire
End Times Crossfire
Revelation Crossfire
Gates of Hell Crossfire
Assassin's Crossfire
Albatross Crossfire
Global Crossfire
Far East Crossfire

The SFO Series

Station Force One - Onset

Russian Crossfire

To find and destroy the terrorist Sam Sturgis the Crossfire Team must invade the nation of Russia. This causes demonic repercussions that require Russia to ask them to come back and help save them.

-   Stephen L. Thompson

Russian Crossfire

Published by
Stephen L. Thompson
Facebook.com/CrossfireNovelSeries

Unless otherwise noted, Scripture quotations are taken from the HOLY BIBLE, NEW INTERNATIONAL VERSION®. Copyright© 1973, 1978, 1984 by International Bible Society. Used by permission of Zondervan Publishing House. All rights reserved.

ISBN- 978-1-943879-13-7

Published in the United States of America

Foreword

To my Christian readers –

The Crossfire series of action/adventure stories include depictions of violence which are unusual in Christian literature. It would be nice if there were no conflict or violence in our world. But we live in a time when evil is increasing instead of diminishing, when some men seem to be controlled by selfishness, madness, or evil forces. When the enemies of decent mankind are bent on subjugation of other men and women, righteous men and women must stand against evil. Please remember that the yoke of oppression is not lifted by prayer alone. God is our shepherd and we are his sheep. As long as there are wolves about, God will use some of us as sheep dogs to defend the rest of us. These stories are about people like that and the forces they fight against. The stories describe violence because it occurs in the real world and it is active in the lives of all people whether they recognize it or not.

To my non-Christian readers –

The Crossfire series include depictions of spiritual warfare and spiritual activity with which the non-Christian may not be familiar. These stories describe the realms and activities of both God and Satan because they are real and active in the lives of all people whether they recognize it or not.

Steve Thompson

CHAPTER ONE

Stan Hargrove held his wife's jacket as he reactivated the car's security system. As he walked back across the parking lot to the Mexican Cantina he felt a slight chill. It was an early October night in the massive, sprawling city of Aurora, Colorado. Butted up against the metroplex of Denver, Aurora was a growing city of its own. Glancing at the horizon he realized that he really liked the soft Lilac glow over the Rocky Mountains to the west as the evening darkened the sky over the city.

Senor Pepe's restaurant, just east of downtown Denver, was an easy drive from their home and tonight he had no problem with traffic getting to the restaurant situated on I-225 just south of 6th Avenue East. Scanning the area Stan noticed that all the professional buildings around the restaurant were dark, abandoned by the daytime workers and the major light in the sky came from Buckley AFB just to the east.

Seeing his reflection in the glass doors of the restaurant Stan checked himself out. He felt his six feet of height displayed his athletic body as lean and healthy. He knew he looked like he was in his early thirties even though his fortieth birthday was only two months away. He liked the small feathering of gray hair at his temples feeling it gave him a wise and authoritative look. He tried to stay in shape by working out, lifting weights, and running five miles daily. Yesterday, Debbie told him that she was impressed that he still moved with ease and handled himself in a commanding way. He wasn't too sure of all that but he was glad she was proud to be his wife and these days she was also happy to be his partner

Walking through the restaurant he made his way back to their table. Stan smiled and tried hard to look very relaxed. Actually, all of his senses were on full alert. As an ex-police officer he had seen the signs that indicated trouble. He was certain now that he and his wife were being stalked. Two of the stalkers had casually ignored him as he walked back in from the parking lot.

But, experience had taught him that they were trying far too hard to ignore him. The men definitely avoided any eye-contact even when he tried to bait them by looking directly at them.

The three men had come into the restaurant within seconds after he and Debbie had entered. The third man sat behind them and was chatting up the cute young server, but Stan was convinced that this man was also watching them while trying to act like he wasn't interested in them.

Stan's experience had been honed by years of teaching tracking, stalking, and surveillance to rookie cops. That experience showed him all the signs of a fairly inexperienced or untrained surveillance team. Either that or they just didn't care if he knew they were there. It wasn't hard to imagine the use of subtle intimidation to make him worried. Stan thought through some of the possible scenarios and didn't like where any of them led.

Deciding that the stakes involved could quickly become lethal, Stan decided to alert some heavy-duty backup. When he returned to his table he casually leaned over to say something quietly into Debbie's ear. While that motion would draw attention to their heads he slid his hand into his right pants pocket and triggered the small unit he always carried there. The Emergency Wide Area Notification system or EWANs alert unit sent an emergency 1.2GHz signal to a satellite which bounced it down to a receiver in a mountain on the outskirts of Denver.

Keeping his voice low Stan whispered, "Deb sweetie, I think we've attracted some heavy hitters that possibly don't have our best interests at heart. The two guys ignoring us over two tables to your left and the lover boy near the bar in the green suit."

Stan stepped around his wife and sat down. He knew his wife's real strengths and knew she wouldn't announce their interest in the men by staring at them. Stan almost smiled but it stopped before it got to his face. Debbie looked like a quiet housewife with brown hair and a slim figure who was pretty but not overly gorgeous. She acted fairly demure in her conduct because that was who she wanted people to see, and it really was her nature.

2

Behind that facade Debbie was a professional military-grade sniper for the U.S. government. Stan grinned inwardly because he knew she was combat-trained and mission-capable. Debbie had traveled widely and had taken a number of lives in the course of performing her duty for her country. Only the team she worked for and the President knew how many. Debbie leaned over to him and kissed him softly on the lips.

As she grabbed his hand she whispered quietly, "Yeah, I'd spotted Mutt and Jeff but, I hadn't seen the third one. They're definitely staking us out. I doubt that they'll make their move until we leave the restaurant. Otherwise it would already have happened."

Stan sat back in the comfortable vinyl seat and laughed a quiet laugh like he didn't have a clue as to anything around them. He continued to weigh their options as they ate slowly, drawing out the time before the inevitable confrontation. He noticed that the dinner crowd was starting to thin which would make it tougher for the trio of hardmen to hide their intent.

Stan's patience ran out and he decided to pay the bill and see what the men would do. As he attempted to get their server's attention, one of the men got a cell phone call. He signaled the others and all three of the men got up quickly and left money to cover their bills. Stan watched as they headed for the front door even though the young server called after them saying they had left too much money for their bill. As they hurried to the door they didn't stop to answer the woman.

Stan got a really bad feeling in his gut. Standing up, he also put money on the table and tipped his head towards the side door to the restaurant. Debbie quickly slid out of her seat and headed that way. Stan watched until she reached the side door, then he headed out the front door after the men.

Stan knew this could be a sucker play and they could be waiting for him just outside. His training made him unconsciously flex his arms and check the location of his pistol. As he exited the building the noise of the street scene invaded his senses. Stan felt three short vibrations on his right leg. The EWANs unit was signaling that their backup was arriving on site.

Stan took in the complete scene as he quickly went down the three steps leading to the parking lot. He saw the three men he was interested in now running full tilt out of the parking lot and across the street. But, what riveted his attention and made his blood ran cold was closer than the men. He saw a small, dirty white, economy car accelerating toward him down the main isle of the parking lot. Behind the windshield Stan could see a skinny man with a maniacal look on his face and his eyes fixated on the front of the diner. The front of the car came up as the man floored the accelerator. He looked as if he planned to drive through the establishment and out the other end.

In that instant, Stan's mind flashed back to his experience in Iraq during his time in the Marines as they battled IEDs and suicide bombers. The face in the little car reminded him of the many crazies and wackos who were intent on killing themselves and others.

Running quickly to his right to get some combat stretch, Stan upholstered his .40 caliber automatic from the holster on his right side. He stopped, turned, dropped into a Weaver stance to steady himself, aimed and fired as rapidly as he could at the left front wheel of the small car. Stan knew by shooting the wheel you could cause the car to swerve away from the target regardless of what the driver tried to do.

Stan watched the 160-grain bullets slam into the wheel and flatten the tire. The car swerved to the left and ran at full speed into the back of a Ford pickup parked in the front row of the parking lot. Stan could see the driver screaming something. Unfortunately, this swerve also caused the car to come closer to Stan.

As his gun locked back Stan threw himself behind an SUV to put it between himself and the white car. As he dropped to the ground he heard an immense sound and saw an incredibly bright light. As the SUV lifted off the ground in front of him Stan felt something like a giant hand slap him off the ground and into the air.

Sam's air travel ended suddenly by his body slamming, back first, into a billboard. Later, he realized that the billboard probably saved his life. As his body hit the billboard his weight and the blast snapped the two-by-fours holding the sign up. Stan felt the flexibility of the sign and the releasing of energy as the two-by-four uprights snapped and took the deadly force out of the explosion for him

As the sign tilted over, Stan felt himself slide down the sign on his back and come to a halt when his head hit the ground. While this left him upside-down in a very undignified position, he was awed by the facts that; one, he was still alive, two, he hadn't passed out, and three, he still had his gun in his hand, Stan used his heels to push his body to his right and it finally slid sideward until he fell to the ground. He used his free left hand to lever himself into a kneeling position. His left elbow sent a lightning bolt of pain through his brain but he forced himself to ignore it. He stayed on his knees while he quickly said a heartfelt prayer of thanks to Jesus for saving his life.

Now that the initial shock was wearing off he realized he hurt all over, some places worse than others but none that could keep him from heading back to the scene of the explosion. Having lived through several explosions in his various careers he did glance down to make sure his clothes were still on and intact. The other two times most of his clothes had been ripped off by the blast and left him either naked or barely covered. This time was better for his wardrobe and, although surprised, he was grateful for that. Things were very quiet, almost peaceful but Stan figured that he had been pretty well deafened by the explosion.

Standing on his feet he swayed somewhat as he ejected the empty magazine from his gun and replaced it with a full one from his left jacket pocket. Switching hands he used his unhurt right hand and arm to work the slide and put a new round into the chamber. He put it on safety and locked it back into the holster.

As he maneuvered in the silence around the burning cars and piles of debris which litter all such scenes he was happy to see Debbie coming towards him. She was apparently unscathed by the blast and that gave him a warm feeling in the midst of his other aches and pains.

Stan breathed the night air that was full of the smell of burning accelerant, gasoline, and rubber. He heard sirens approaching and realized his hearing was already returning. He also noticed that the car the three men had been headed for was gone. He then limped over to meet his wife.

Debbie's smile told Stan that she was happy to see him still all in one piece but she could also see that he was hurt. She came close and he quickly held out his hand to stop her. He softened this with a small crooked smile on his lips. Stan knew his wife's affectionate nature and he wanted to prevent any more immediate pain in his body. "No hugs, not right now, okay?"

She pulled out a Kleenex out of her purse and wiped off some of the blood on his face from a head laceration.

Stan felt pain lance through his left knee and it made him walk with a definite limp as his left leg hurt whenever he put weight on it. But, his mind reverted to the battlefield attitude he fell into whenever he was hurt and things still needed to be accomplished before he could rest. His sense of honor made it a higher priority to see to the people in harm's way first.

So, regardless of the ringing in his ears and the pains in his body he forced himself to lean on Debbie's arm and limp to the front of the shattered restaurant. There was the heat and smoke of fire but it seemed to have burned itself out quickly.

Stan could smell the residue odor of dynamite from the car bomb mixed with the wood smell from the charred front of the restaurant. He looked at the crater where the explosion had occurred and couldn't find anything of the little white car or the driver. He realized that both of them had been reduced to fragments by the explosion.

He let Debbie go first to find a way through the furniture and wall panels the blast had strewn around the lobby. Stan felt a headache begin as he eased his way through the damaged doors into the lobby.

As his eyes adjusted to the glare of the emergency lights he could see a dozen people lying or sitting on the floor and there was blood. Stan prayed another heartfelt prayer of thanks to Jesus that only two of the people looked dead and most of the blood on the others seemed to be coming from glass cuts instead of more serious trauma wounds.

Debbie was slightly ahead of Stan and to his left as they worked their way into the damaged main dining area. As they slowly walked in, a large man with blood all over his shirt got up from tending a child on the floor and charged at Stan cursing and yelling, "You rotten SOB! I saw you run out of here. You knew this was going to happen and you left us here to die!"

As Stan stepped back lifting his good right arm to fend off the man's attack. Debbie stepped in front of him and used an Aikido martial arts move on the man's outstretched right arm. She brought the man's arm straight up as she stepped behind his moving legs. She forced the arm backwards as she kicked her right leg backwards. This not only stopped the man's forward charge but threw him forcefully onto his back on the floor as his legs left the ground. Stan saw her as she held onto the attacker's arm so that he didn't injure himself unduly as he slammed to the ground.

Debbie quickly kneeled on the man's chest with her right knee and grabbed his lower jaw with her right hand. The sudden stop had taken all of the air and most of the fight out of the man and he didn't struggle as she leaned down and spoke to him from about four inches away from his face. Stan heard her tell him "You need to settle down, NOW! If my husband hadn't stopped the suicide bombers, car everyone in here would be dead including you. He put his life on the line to save you. Try not to forget that, okay?" She slapped him lightly on the cheek and stood up. Stan could see in the man's eyes as the no-nonsense words sank into his mind clearly.

Any fight left in the man drained out of his body at that point. As Debbie stood up Stan offered his good right hand to the man to help him up from the floor. Smiling at the bemused look on the man's face Stan whispered, "That's why I don't argue with her, about anything." The man nodded in understanding and mumbled, "Sorry." Stan patted him on the shoulder and turned to look around the rest of the room.

Paramedics seemed to suddenly appear everywhere to triage the wounded and help the less injured outside.

Stan noted the efficiency of several Denver police officers as they searched the restaurant for additional victims. One of the officers approached Stan and Debbie to ask them about the bombing. Stan felt a sudden weakness and that woozy feeling you feel just before you pass out. He grabbed a chair and sat down heavily and put his head down on the back of another upright chair back. He fought back the fog that was trying to engulf him in wet darkness and breathed deeply in through his nose and out through his mouth.

He felt blood began to run out of the cut on his head again. The officer called one of the paramedics over and she went to work on Stan's head as he described the action prior to the explosion. The officer was impressed by Stan's actions to limit the bombing. Debbie added what she could to the information. It looked like they would be held up for quite a while except that Jack Malone and Mark Connelly showed up to assist them.

The police had a good working relationship with the Crossfire Team and that long-term cooperation helped speed up things greatly when the officer found out that Stan and Debbie were members of the team.

Stan also noted the officer had been duly impressed by the fact that both Jack and Mark were in full combat uniforms and carrying M-8 assault rifles with grenade launchers.

After checking with his superior the officer completed his notes and released Stan and Debbie as he went to assist another couple. Stan felt stronger and staggered to his feet. The four of them walked out of the damaged building with Mark Connelly helping Stan by holding him upright. Stan was grateful for the assistance. At first it hurt to walk but Stan felt better as they moved out into the parking lot and around the emergency vehicles parked there.

Stan's body was definitely dwarfed by Mark's six-foot, two-inch physique that felt like solid rock. Stan looked into Mark's brown eyes as he asked to stand on his own. Mark released him carefully with concern on his face. The thought ran through Stan's mind that occasionally he wished he had a two-hundred and sixty pound body with less than ten percent body fat like Mark, but, God had dealt him a somewhat smaller and lighter frame.

As Stan stood in the parking lot of the restaurant he thought that Mark, dressed in black combat fatigues, looked like a Marine poster. Mark's massive arms and shoulders were obviously capable of breaking things and Stan knew that they quite frequently did.

Mark shook his head, "Two innocent diners dead, and a body count of three if you add the driver of the car bomb, dozens injured and hundreds of thousands of dollars of property damage, for what? Bad Mexican food?"

Stan smiled thinly at his good friend and boss, "I think it was to kill Debbie and me, that's what." Stan related the story of the three men and their obvious interest in the Hargroves.

Stan turned to the other tall combat-clad man standing next to Debbie.

Stan noted for the hundredth time that Jack Malone was a physical match to Mark except he was slightly less massive in the upper body. Stan knew Jack was a martial arts instructor and a match for almost anybody in hand-to-hand combat.

Stan always felt like he hadn't quite grown enough when he was with these two guys as Jack was a couple of inches taller than Mark who was already taller than Stan himself by two inches. Having watched the two men in combat Stan again felt glad they were on his side.

Jack was still on full alert watching the area with his trigger finger just outside the trigger guard of the M8 Assault Rifle. He glanced at Stan and asked, "After we get you patched up at the hospital, why don't you and Debbie join us at the Fortress for a while? You and Debbie were fortunate this time but they may try again. Also, I suggest at this point we all get under cover. One of the people that really don't like us right now is, or was, an excellent sniper."

With Stan leaning on Mark, the four of them walked quickly south for a block to a used car dealership where a fully armed Blackhawk helicopter sat with its main rotor turning between the rows of shiny cars. There were three wide-eyed teenagers on bicycles on the edge of the lot staring at the helicopter. Stan waved to the two soldiers who were standing guard on either side of the chopper.

All eight of the team boarded the chopper that rose quickly upward and then slid sideward to get clearance from power wires. Su Li as the pilot poured the power on and the black helicopter rose rapidly as it transitioned into forward flight at a street level to limit its exposure to any ManPad antiaircraft missiles.

Stan leaned back into the hard seat and found Debbie looking unhappy as she was buckling him in. He smiled at her and said, "Don't worry honey, our car was insured."

CHAPTER TWO

Sam Sturgis sat in his three million dollar luxury condominium suite drinking fifty-year old, three hundred dollar scotch in a crystal goblet that probably cost as much as a normal person's monthly income. None of it meant anything because Sam was contemplating a very short and dark future filled with pain. His focus was on the primary cause for all of his pain. Right now there were four significant pains.

First, his employers of the moment, the ASF, knew he had failed his last mission and wanted him to complete the tasks they had paid handsomely for or they would make him disappear. Second, any future employment was severely in doubt due to his disability. Third, the physical pain. His entire body, especially his left arm and shoulder gave him mind-numbing agony. The only way he could control the pain was through alcohol and drugs.

But, the first, last, and most important pain, was the fact that Mark Connelly, was still alive and had single-handedly given Sam all of his present pains.

When the doctor's drugs and a good helping of expensive booze made the pain go away and mellowed his mood, Sam could understand the "why" most of it occurred. He thought back over the sequence for the ten thousandth time.

Given an assignment to eliminate the Crossfire Team, Sam had set out to do the job. He thought he had killed Mark Connelly in an ingenious ambush in Washington, D.C. Then he attempted to kill the rest of the team at Mark's funeral. His planted explosives didn't detonate from his remote unit as he had planned and he had moved In to trigger them himself. In retrospect Sam realized that the team had been setting him up rather than the other way around. They had probably dampened any radio frequency signals in the area. It was obviously a trap for him.

They would of had him too, except for the timely intervention of a third force of mercenaries who also attacked the Crossfire Team at the graveyard above Denver. In the firefight a Crossfire Team sniper was revealed who turned out to be the not-so-late Mark Connelly on an adjacent hillside using a .50 caliber M500 Barrett long range sniper rifle. His contribution to the one-sided fight was impressive as the whopping 11,500 foot-pounds of muzzle-energy was knocking over the mercenaries with every shot.

Sam remembered being irritated that Connelly wasn't dead but decided to get as many members of the team from the back as he could while they were occupied with the attacking force from the other side. Then a smashing force slapped Sam ten feet backwards and left him bleeding. He now realized that Connelly knew where he had been and in the midst of the battle still kept an eye on him. When he saw Sam start to aim at his team he snap aimed and fired from three quarters of a mile away. That was the only reason Sam was alive today to suffer as he was. If Connelly had taken the time to carefully aim there would be no Sam today. Sam knew that because he was an expert sniper himself. Or rather, had been an expert sniper.

Not anymore. His left arm and hand were pretty useless. Sam contemplated the limb as it lay on the table in front of him. He tried to make a fist and was rewarded with spasmodic twitching and trembling.

Sam downed another gulp of the amber fire in his glass and wiped the tears from his eyes. He was ruined as a sniper, and as a karate contender, and just about anything else. Oh, he could understand Connelly's shooting of him although Sam wished the shot had killed him.

Sam yelled at the walls of the room, "Since I wasn't killed then I need to pay Connelly back for the hell he's given me!"

Sam tried to think but the booze and the drugs were dulling his mind to the point he couldn't stay on any one thought for very long. He decided to go to bed and struggled to his feet. Lurching into his bedroom he fell on his bed and passed out.

In the world outside Sam's carefully secure dwelling the forces arrayed against him were searching for him. Every department of the government wanted him for the assassination of a presidential candidate, the Crossfire Team was searching for him as their assignment to eliminate him, and the ASF was looking for him to extract revenge for failing his assignment. At least Sam didn't have lawyers after him for alimony or child support as he had never married or sired children. Sam had been too full of himself and his "missions" to waste time on women. He actually had no interest in sex in any form, too non-productive in his line of work. The wife and children could be used as levers against him. He knew that fact because he'd used a wife and children several times to manipulate targets of his own.

At the Crossfire Fortress outside of Denver, Mark Connelly and Charlie Wu were studying grainy electronic images from Mark's combat camera of the shot he took at Sam Sturgis from the hillside above the graveyard.

Charlie slowly advanced the video through the sequence one more time. "You definitely hit him in the chest area, probably up to his left somewhat. I'm sorry the picture is so bad, those cameras aren't set up for telephoto shots."

Mark was focused on determining what he could of Sam's possible current status. "Hmmm"

Charlie sat back and shook his head. "How the man could even survive a fifty-caliber shot is amazing. That's fifteen-hundred grains of solid steel traveling at over two-thousand feet per second. It should of blown his chest apart or separated his left arm completely."

Mark looked at the head of their security for the Fortress. Charlie was about five-foot, eight inches tall, Chinese heritage and powerfully built. He was an unassuming expert at all things computer and communications. As well as being a great warrior. Charlie knew all sort of spy stuff which he had used to help the team in hundreds of ways. Charlie's background as an agent for the Chinese internal security operation ended when he and his wife, Linda, who had also been a Chinese Internal Security spy, had found Jesus and became Christians. Fleeing mainland China they were given asylum and citizenship in the U.S. for their "contributions" to the West concerning their field.

Knowing the team's sensei, Jim Grady from earlier contacts, Charlie and his wife settled in Denver and quickly became involved with the Crossfire Team in its earliest operations. Now, as the head of the ComSec group of the Fortress Charlie was orchestrating the missions and resources of the team with a bay full of CRAY computers and an expert computer team to assist him.

Charlie was matched by his wife in sophistication and capability. They actually worked as a team and Linda ran the ComSec group when Charlie was in the field on a mission with the team.

Mark thought about Charlie's comment concerning Sam Sturgis' wounds. Charlie had a lot of knowledge but Mark was more knowledgeable about combat as he had been a U.S. Navy SEAL team leader for several years and had a lot of practical experience in the field of combat. "The probability was that Sturgis was wearing some really good body armor and the round expended a lot of its energy overcoming the armor. You can tell that it penetrated because of the blood spray when it knocked him backwards. He probably suffered a good deal of trauma in the left shoulder and arm area because I only can see blood on the front and not the back. I'd guess that the bullet splintered on impact with the armor and messed him up internally. With no sign of a through-and through shot the rest of the impact would have been to the internal muscles, nerves, and blood system. The fact that he was gone after the action indicates that he survived the shot but that he was hurt pretty bad. I won't count him out until I see his body."

Charlie knew that Mark meant exactly what he said. Mark had intensity in his blue eyes that boded no foolishness and the combat knowledge to back up his opinions. Charlie knew Mark to be very honorable and true to his word. A good man to have on your side in any battle.

CHAPTER THREE

Sam was sweating and hurting and having a horrible dream where he was begging on the street for enough money to eat. He was trying to figure out where his millions had gone when he suddenly sat upright on the bed and reached with his right hand for his automatic which he kept next to the bed for unwanted visitors.

He fumbled around and couldn't find the gun. He looked at the large dim form at the foot of his bed in the dark. Before he could move at all, a deep vibrant voice froze him in position.

"Sam Sturgis! Look at yourself. You are a wasted wreck of an invalid human. You can just barely keep yourself from wetting the bed right now. Where is the powerful killer? You had such plans. Look at you now."

Sam felt the tears filling his eyes because everything the guy said was true. "I am a wasted wreck and I don't have much in the way of a future, so, what do you want with me?"

The form seemed to grow taller in the gloom of the bedroom. "I want you to finish the job you started with the Crossfire Team."

Sam sighed, "How?"

"I will heal your wounds and give you strength like you've never experienced before. You will be more formidable than before. Are you interested?"

Sam was interested. "I might be but what will it cost me?"

"You will have to worship me and do exactly what I tell you to do and I can have your soul if you fail."

Sam thought about that. He didn't believe in supernatural beings or a soul and figured he didn't have anything to lose. "No problem."

"Then do it."

Sam slid off the bed and clumsily kneeled on the floor and bowed to the form. "What do I call you?"

"Just call me Lord, or god."

Sam said, "My lord, heal me of my wounds and I will serve you to accomplish our mutual desire to destroy the Crossfire Team."

The being produced a piece of parchment and dropped it in front of Sam, "Sign that."

Sam unrolled it and tried to read the words, but it was too dark. The being held out a hand and reddish light sprang forth. Sam still couldn't make out all the words but it seemed he had to trade his soul to the being in return for being whole and rich if he fulfilled his mission. Sam thought about it and still didn't think he had a soul anyway. Whole and rich had looked impossible before this meeting and he so wanted to be effective again. Sam looked around for a pen and the being offered him one. Sam signed the form and jerked when a splinter on the pen jabbed his finger. A large drop of his blood fell on the parchment below his signature.

The being reached over quickly and snatched away the parchment and pen and waved his hand. Sam suddenly felt too sleepy to care as he fell to the carpet.

Time passed and the sun rose in the East. The rays came through the window and stuck Sam's face where he laid on the floor. He tried to brush the light away with his left hand and suddenly sat upright and stared at his left arm. It was whole and unhurt and Sam didn't find any pain anywhere in his body. He stood up and realized the dream hadn't been a dream. He felt stronger than he could remember. His mind was clear and the drugs and alcohol were gone from his system. He smashed his left fist into his right hand and it was a good solid hit. Sam was elated and almost couldn't contain himself. He went into the bathroom and took a good, long hot shower.

Dressing carefully he started thinking like an assassin again. He donned a disguise and added a blonde hairpiece and moustache which changed his looks completely. He ventured outside and was full of new hope and strangely, at the same time, intense anger. He realized that he wanted to get on with his assignment and not goof off just because he felt good. He started thinking of how to extract revenge on the Crossfire Team, and his old employers for their lack of faith in him.

Everyone was looking for a wounded, crippled man. He was going to surprise them all.

CHAPTER FOUR

The two leading Arab Strike Force strategists in the United States lived in a palatial estate in Brentwood, near Los Angeles, California, Hakem Majd and Fariq Mundhir knew they were a cut above their fellow warriors. They lived a better life with more of everything and expected all men to respect them and their superiority.

Hakem had finally gotten permission from the high command in Iran to do away with the incompetent man they had hired to do their work. He had Fariq bring in one of their best assassin teams and carefully explained what they had to do and where to do it. Sam Sturgis may have thought his life was hidden but they knew where to find him. Hakem warned the six men to do the job properly and quietly so that there would be no involvement from the American police services. He finished his remarks with, "The clumsy fool managed to get himself shot by the leader of the American team and no longer has the use of his left arm. He is quickly becoming a hazard to us in his medicinal drug use and his alcohol consumption. Filthy habits! I want him disposed of before the Americans find him and make him talk about us and our plans. See to it then. Fariq will give you the directions to his hiding place. Any one of you are ten times the warrior this man ever was. Make me proud."

The men were about to leave when something fell from the ornate skylight above the room. They all turned to look at the gray sphere when a large charge of compressed air silently shot one hundred, nine inch long, solid-steel nails in all directions except straight up or down. All eight men in the room were hit multiple times by the projectiles and collapsed together onto the bloody floor.

A rope fell to the floor and a man slid down the rope. Setting down a four-foot tall bag he walked over to the suffering strike team. The man efficiently silenced their feeble cries for help or moans with a silenced round to the head from an automatic with a six-inch silencer tube on the end of it.

Walking over to where Hakem and Fariq lay he noticed that Fariq had taken a nail through the forehead and was already visiting his ancestors. Hakem had taken nails through both legs, his stomach, and four to his chest. He had punctured both lungs and was quickly bleeding out internally. He looked up at the man that had killed them all and realized it was Sam Sturgis. "He noticed the strong arms and hands on both sides and wheezed "How?"

Sam studied the dying man for a few seconds. "It was not nice of you to plan to kill me Hakem. I don't take that type of betrayal very well. I am better than anything you could have sent against me. I videotaped your little speech and my answer for your bosses. After this, I think they will back me in our mission to kill the American strike team."

Noticing Hakem's eyes glazing over, Sam leaned down and said. "Why don't you go ahead and die. I'll take it from here." Sam's grinning face was the last thing Hakem Majd saw in this world.

Sam put an insurance round through both of the leader's heads and prepared to leave when a side door opened and a woman dropped a tray of sweetmeats and started screaming as she saw the carnage. Sam calmly shot her through the heart and walked out of the room and out a side door of the building. He heard dozens of men running and yelling in response to the woman's scream. He counted to ten as he walked and then pushed the button on the little transmitter he had in his hand.

The explosion leveled a good part of the building and killed all of the rescuers, not to mention several dozen women and children in the building including Hakem's entire family.

Sam reached his car, looked back in satisfaction, savoring the death and destruction. He disabled the alarm and climbed into the vehicle. Carefully removing any sign of his assassination work, he started the car and drove away, gleeful that he had responded to the challenge. As he drove he uploaded the video of the event into his cell phone and emailed it to Ariq Salmante.

In Iran Ariq was the ASF leader who had funded the dead fools behind. Ariq Salmante was about to get an invitation to fund Sam's operations directly.

Sam figured Ariq would jump at the chance to use some real talent, especially now that the previous crew didn't exist.

Eight hundred and thirty-two miles to the northeast of Sam's car his target had pulled out all the stops in a dedicated search for Sam himself. Jack and Sarah were running down any clues from the last contact they had with him at the cemetery or any medical identifications for his injuries since then. David and Mark were seeking out any contacts for contracts or weapons purchases that Sturgis could have initiated in the last few weeks. Alexis and Laura were haunting Sam's known background contacts for any new information.

Carol was praying for guidance and understanding in the heavenlies when Charlie Wu hit the "all members" switch and requested a meeting in the war room in ten minutes.

When the troops had assembled in the combat control center for the team, Charlie told them to watch the main screen. They watched as a man lay on top of a dome in a building near a large skylight window. They saw him as he dropped a two-foot round package through a hole in the big window. This was followed by a flurry of activity that took out the entire skylight window and several of the windows around it in the dome from the inside. The man then stood up and dropped into the building on a belay line.

The scene shifted to the same man walking out of the building through a door and then a massive explosion happened to the far side of the building away from the mysterious man who walked to a vehicle and eventually left the area.

Jack knew that the video was taken off of a keyhole satellite by the optical clarity and the angle of view.

The man drove out of the picture due to the angle and direction of travel of the satellite. After the video stopped everyone started asking questions of Charlie who held up his right hand in a request for silence.

Charlie indicated the screen with his thumb and dropped the bombshell. "That assassin is our assassin. The man in the picture is none other than Sam Sturgis."

Mark shook his head, "No way after the shot he took is he able to work with his left arm like that in three weeks."

Charlie smiled a small smile, "True, but that is Sam. I took the time to carefully monitor this CIA feed and to isolate the man responsible and the techniques he used. Look at the screen again."

Charlie ran the video until the man stood up on the roof to jump into the interior. He ran the close-up capability and got a reasonably good face shot even though the angle was still high. He then superimposed two face shots of Sam Sturgis from the front and the side. He let Crayton run a facial identification application that identified thirty points on the faces and matched them perfectly. The he did it again after the man had walked out of the building and was walking across to the vehicle he escaped in, same results. Then he went back to the roof shot and zoomed in on the man's left arm and shoulder.

Mark carefully watched the video for any signs of bandaging or weakness in the arm. There was none. He shook his head. "Sam must of had one great set of body armor on and what we interpreted as a solid hit must have only been a trauma impact."

Laura had been watching the video and praying for guidance as was her normal method of understanding things. This time she was surprised at the revelation she received. As Mark finished speaking she stood up and pointed at the photo glaring back at all of them.

She used a laser pointer as she spoke. "Not necessarily the case Mark. Look at the definition of the muscles of his chest and arms. I don't remember him having a buff shape like that from the earlier photos, do you?"

Jack had been wondering about the differences between the Sam Sturgis they had known from before and this one. "How could he buff up so quickly? Is he wearing a muscle suit?"

Laura shook her head, "No, I believe he has been healed and improved."

Alexis asked her, "Why would Yahweh do that?"

Laura smiled, "Who said it was Yahweh's doing? No, I don't think this healing was from the light side of the universe. More likely it was from the dark side. He has too much agility and capability as shown in this video. I think we're looking at a new and improved assassin thanks to demonic healing."

David frowned, "That can't be good for us."

CHAPTER FIVE

When his laptop computer chimed to tell him he had an incoming email message Sam Sturgis used the touch mouse to click "okay". Reading the message he was somewhat taken aback. First, the response to his "offer" to Ariq Salmante was being answered in less than thirty minutes which was a really quick response was considering the change in terms his assassination of the previous ASF American team had handed the man.

Secondly, there was no righteous anger about the operation. Simply a message agreeing to meet with him and arrange for assignments and payment.

He carefully checked the backtrack on the message and was reassured when he saw that it came from Salmante's own computer and hadn't been compromised as far as Sam could see. And, he could see a lot.

The meeting place was a public restaurant and included guarantees of his safety. The only troubling point here was that they wanted to meet here in Los Angeles in less than two hours. No way the Iranian could get here that quickly. So it must be either a return of his favor with their own assassination attempt on him, or a actual meeting with people that report back to Salmante. Either way he had to attend, but he would throw a wrinkle into any setup. The response at three o'clock would determine what type of action this was.

At precisely three o'clock p.m. in the chosen restaurant, a cultured-looking Arab sat at the right table dressed in an expensive suit and tie and waited. One of the servers came over to the man and handed him a note and then walked away. The Arab opened the note and read it. Nodding his head he rose from the table and exited the establishment. Walking two blocks away he entered a book store and sought out the reading area near the magazines. Looking around he spotted Sam sitting alone at one end watching him closely.

The Arab walked over to the magazines and selected one at random and wandered slowly over to where Sam was sitting. Taking a seat he asked in a British accent if Sam was comfortable with these surrounding to conduct business.

Sam checked his tell-tales from the cameras he had planted nearby and nodded his acceptance. The Arab rose and told Sam to wait a couple of minutes. He then went twenty feet away and sat down to read his magazine. To his disgust he realized he had picked up a homosexual periodical. Sighing deeply he pretended to read it.

Sam was very wary at this strange action and was about to quietly disappear when two businessmen in suits left the bookracks and converged on his position. They had the look of low class hoods but dressed better and seemed sure of themselves. Before Sam could decide whether to kill them or not they sat down across from him and carefully opened their coats. They didn't display any weapons. Sam decided to go along with the play and see what would happen. "Can I be of assistance to you gentlemen?"

The man on Sam's right leaned forward and in a quiet voice said, "Mr. Sturgis, Ariq Salmante has acquiesced to our request to speak to you in his place. This is a white flag truce meeting to see if our goals are similar and a working arrangement can be established. We mean you no harm and will walk away if you are not interested in our proposition. Is that satisfactory to you?"

Sam realized they could have taken him out before he even knew they were there so there was no immediate danger from them. It also gave them high marks on Sam's professional scale. He might not grant them the same courtesy but he would wait to see. "Who do you represent?"

The same man said, "We represent the true power behind the ASF and Ariq Salmante's operation. Our operations are run out of Moscow and are a direct descendent of the Solntsevskaya Bratva group. We handle the worldwide network of "contract" workers needed to achieve our goals."

Sam nodded, "The Russian Mafia then."

The other man shook his head, "Nyet, we don't like that Italian name. We prefer to be known as. "The

Russian Organization". Please refer to us that way from now on."

Sam chewed on that concept and order for a few seconds, "fine". As I asked before, what can I do for you gentlemen?"

The man on Sam's right stared at him for a minute. "I am Oleg and I will be your contact. Make no mistakes, we will get what we want and have far more expertise than you do at this game." Sam doubted that but they certainly had more men.

Oleg continued, "Our offer to you is four million dollars U.S. and a premier position in our organization for the elimination of certain individuals. We will determine which ones and when. You decide how and carry out the operation within the time restrictions. Expense is not a problem on any scale. If you meet your end of our bargain then you will be respected and well-paid. If you don't you will die. Do I make myself clear?"

Sam smiled a small smile, "Oleg, if I may use your name, I am a talented assassin that works alone. I do not report to you or any other organization. Your threats do not concern me and I, in turn, will promise you that if you fail to meet the terms of our mutual contracts, I will eliminate your entire Organization starting at the top. Are we clear on that?"

The unnamed member of the group laughed softly. "We have heard of your ego and pride Mr. Sturgis. We have also heard of your miraculous escapes and recoveries from almost certain death. I think we can work together."

He took out a package and slid it across the small table between them. "Here is our first "request" and full payment. Do not fail us in this matter."

The two men stood up and left. Sam opened the package to find a cashier's check for the four million dollars made out to him. It was also made out to his, supposedly unknown, bank account which spoke volumes about their resources and professionalism. He looked at the pictures and paperwork pointing him at the Crossfire Team. He put everything back into the package and thought, "Hmmm, maybe we can work together."

Sam thought about the arrangements and decided he would go along with them for now. Maybe in the future he might change the deal.

As Oleg and Mishka disappeared into the late afternoon Los Angeles traffic Mishka asked Oleg, "Do you think he will be obedient?"

Oleg shrugged, "For the time being, yes. Later, we'll see."

CHAPTER SIX

Mrs. Cochran had been a citizen of the great state of Colorado for almost sixty-three years. She liked to consider herself a native Coloradoan but since her parents lived in Missouri at the time she was born that wasn't really true. Still, since she had lived almost all of her life in the state after the end of the big war, WWII, she felt it counted towards state citizenship.

Her husband and best friend for fifty years had passed away four years ago and, at that time, it looked like she was going to lose her property. After Bill's passing there was still several thousand dollars owing and she only had a small income from social security. Then the military moved in next door and made her an offer that saved her day. This nice young officer offered to pay off the rest of her mortgage including the back taxes and provide her a reasonable monthly rent if they could use three acres of her property to put a road in leading up to the mountain a mile away.

She realized it was an answer to her prayers and she agreed. The monthly stipend was three times her social security check and it was not like she was going to do anything with that piece of scrub land at the end of her property anyway.

There had also been some additional support for her when she called the number the nice young officer had left her. Mrs. Cochran told the soldier about a man who had come onto her property and threatened her. He told her that if she didn't sell her land to him he would cause her untold misery and harm. The crude bully told her that he was going to block the road to the mountain no matter what. Glaring at her he implied that all sorts of bad things could happen to her and her house if she didn't sell it to him.

The young soldier asked for the man's name and told her not to worry about it anymore. He must of been telling the truth because the mean man never came calling again.

She was very happy with her military neighbors because she had always had a special place in her heart for soldiers. Her husband had been a soldier in both the big war and the Korean thing in the 1950s. Now, when she saw the soldiers practicing on the mountain and the helicopters going to and fro they gave her peace instead of bothering her. It was like having a bunch of big brothers next door.

But they needed to know about this new thing that was happening on her property immediately. It wasn't right and she was going to see that it stopped right now.

Mrs. Cochran had been walking her dog, Betsy, in the woods behind her house this morning. She still liked to walk, called it her "constitutional". Betsy was good company and always stayed with her, never running off. Mrs. Cochran heard a radio or something back on her property and walked back towards the new road. She found a van in the trees that must have run across her property without her permission. It was on a rise close to the new road. "Well!" They can't do that. She marched up to the big van and used her walking stick to beat on their driver's door.

The man that opened the door had a earpiece and a microphone on his head and a big pair of binoculars in his other hand. He looked upset at Mrs. Cochran and asked rudely what she thought she was doing beating on the van door.

Mrs. Cochran was not intimidated in the least. "This is my property you're on and I want you off of here right now."

The man made a face and breathed a big sigh. "Ma'am, this is government business and I'm going to have to ask you to leave us alone."

She thought that over and said, "All right, but turn your tom-fool radio down." She then marched away from the van back towards her house.

The man watched the old woman walk away and considered simply killing her to keep her quiet. But, that would have consequences too. She seemed to buy his government story so he dismissed her from his mind and went back to what he was being well-paid, to do.

As Mrs. Cochran walked back towards her house in the brisk early October morning she thought about what had just happened. She didn't like the idea of that man being on her property and she knew how to get rid of him. She let herself into her house and went to her bedroom. Opening the top drawer in her dresser she found the card right where she had left it.

Carefully punching in the numbers she waited until she was connected to the young officer she had met two years before. Major Gary Danning heard Mrs. Cochran's voice and knew that it was Divine Intervention that he was in his office each time she called. He had just been excused from a three day meeting, still in its first day, to handle an important call from Laura Malone. He was about to pick up the phone when it rang and the Communications Tech told her that Mrs. Cochran wanted to speak to him.

Gary listened to the kindly old lady as she described the man and the van on her property and about the binoculars and the supposed "governmental" business. The Major asked her to hold for a few minutes and called their Homeland Security liaison in Washington. No operations were being run near the Fortress by any of the American services. Gary thanked the man and told Mrs. Cochran to pack a bag for a trip. He would arrange for a cab to pick her up and take her to the airport. Gary was going to pay for a vacation so that she could see her grandchildren in California and coincidently get her out of the line of fire at the same time. He thought they might need some combat stretch.

He then made his call to the Fortress but spoke to Charlie Wu first before he talked to Laura. He brought Laura up to speed on Mrs. Cochran's unwelcome visitor. Laura typed a short message and pushed it to Mark and Jack's cell phones as urgent. Laura told Gary that they would take care of the situation and thanked him for the information. She then told him about the need for living quarters for an ex-president and his family that might be needed at the Fortress. Gary thought about the ramifications and told Laura that he had just the thing they needed. He would work it out and have it ready by the end of the year.

Meanwhile, Charlie had a mini-predator drone made ready and released from the helicopter base. He watched the crystal-clear optics on his screen as the almost totally silent, very small autonomous drone overflew the position of the parked van. Surveying the area he devised a plan to counter the threat. He created a order for men and material to place a full-time audio/visual/telemetry monitor on the van without the user or users being made aware of the emplacement.

As a distraction Charlie had David and Alexis take a combat car out of the entrance the van was watching and stop in view. Alexis would then keep the man's attention on them while the military put the monitor in place.

As the combat car drove out the eastern portal to the Fortress two hours later the sun was perfect for their purposes. This put the observer the observers in the van in the dark shadow of the hill behind them while the gate and the combat car were in bright sunshine. This made it easy to see them and much harder to see anything around the van due to the contrast of bright light to dimmer darkness.

The huge gate lowered itself to become a bridge over the twenty-foot gap that acted like a modern day moat without water. As he drove along David caused the military vehicle to jerk several times and then die. He coasted to a halt at the desired location on the road from the gate. He and Alexis got out of the car. David opened the hood and fiddled around with the engine while Alexis climbed up on the bumper and leaned into the engine compartment to watch and see what David was doing. Even though she was wearing fatigue pants and a light shirt her figure attracted the full attention of the man in van as it was supposed to do.

Two U.S. Army Rangers in black outfits and camo face paint slid up from behind the van and quietly attached the monitor to the frame of the vehicle. Completely self-sufficient, the small unit hid nicely inside the framework above the rear axle. As the two Rangers slid out from behind the vehicle and disappeared into the woods they sent the mission accomplished signal to the command room of the Fortress with an unexpected addendum.

Mark got the call from the Major in charge of the Rangers. "Yes Major, what's the flap?"

The Major had met Mark and liked him. "Our men spotted several more quasi-military types trying to hide in the woods behind Mrs. Cochran's house. They only saw three and made sure the three didn't see them. How do you want to handle this?"

Mark told the man, "We'll get back to you in a few minutes."

When David got the signal he and Alexis climbed out of the engine compartment and she stood there while he tried the engine. Getting a thumbs up from David, Alexis walked around to the passenger side and climbed in next to David. He did a quick U-turn and headed back into the Fortress as he normally would if there were problems with his vehicle.

Charlie in the meantime was able to determine the frequencies of the two-way radio communications and the man's cell phone and easily overcame the simple encryption they were using to communicate. He began to record the conversations and began backtracking the rf signal.

Thirty minutes later he called Laura to report on their progress. When she answered she put Charlie on the multi-position speaker phone so everyone could listen.

Charlie was pleased with his results thus far. "I've been able to determine the number of watchers, their organization, their names, who they're talking to, and, best of all, their intent."

Laura laughed, "In thirty minutes?"

Charlie laughed back, "Yeap, and had time for a cup of coffee while Crayton verified everything.

CHAPTER SEVEN

While Charlie was having the Army bug the van, Jack and Mark prepared to take six of the ex-SOG soldiers now living at the Fortress with them on a "training mission" to ensure that Mrs. Cochran made her exit without interference and find out what the mercenaries were doing on her property. Mark was fairly certain what group the watcher and the mercs represented; either the resurgent Sam Sturgis, leftovers from the Omicron Cartel, or the ASF. Mark wondered if the invaders would have some kind of a multi-level operation in process.

After hearing about the additional troops Mark decided that this might be the prelude to that all-out attack on the Fortress that Carol Moffet had warned them about involving Sturgis, Mark decided to set up the operation as a full-court press and included the Army Ranger and Marine units presently training on the mountain. Throwing it together quickly would add realism to the operation.

On Jack's warning about the additional troops near the house, Charlie went to full combat mode in the computer center and started using both Predator and satellite assets to analyze his data and he focused on combat research and tactics. He liked to think of Crayton, his computer alter-ego, as a ground-based AWACs for the Crossfire Team.

Charlie launched a program on the CRAY array for all birds (satellites) with present or recent coverage of the target area. He got intel from a Quickbird, two KH-13 Keyhole-class satellites and a Lacrosse-class Radar Imaging satellite. He also asked for and received permission to interrogate the computers at the NRO (National Reconnaissance Office) and the NGA (National GeoSpatial-Intelligence Agency). He got the usual limited access which was sufficient for his needs.

While the computers were correlating the images and information Charlie tapped into two Chinese IR satellites and one Korean radar-imaging satellite that were in the area. Using overrides that wouldn't identify himself nor get the attention of the other nation's satellite controllers he searched their image bases for intel on the area outside the Fortress.

His main screen lit up with a dozen different images that gave the ex-Chinese agent a great deal of information about the present situation outside Mrs. Cochran's home. He put the information into coherent order and sent it to Mark's tablet PC.

Mark received the information and analyzed it in less than twenty seconds. He was used to this type of information download from his days as a SEAL team leader. He whistled when he finished. Jack Malone looked at the raised eyebrows on his friend's face and asked, "What's up?"

Mark pointed at his tablet and said, "We've got a real combat operation here instead of a training mission. There are approximately sixty people within a mile of Mrs. Cochran's house and none of them are neighbors or our people."

Jack took the tablet and tried to make sense out of the data. Handing it back to Mark he told him, "Okay, if you say so. You run the operation, I'll back you up."

Mark nodded. He was used to this role anyway. He used the combat communications system to contact the Crossfire SOG soldiers, the squad of Marine Force Recon, and the Army Ranger group. "Gentlemen, we have a Class Three, aggressor situation at hand presently. Please bring your forces up to full attack strength for a force of sixty unknowns, probably heavily armed terrorists. ETA twenty minutes at coordinates Alpha Alpha Zulu Tango Beta. Bring the forces in under cover." Looking at Mark he said, "We need to move it to be there in time without alerting the enemy."

Gathering up their body armor and weapons they ran for the ground transportation where their entire contingent of twenty-four SOG soldiers were either climbing into or running to the vehicle. Some of them were also putting on their body armor or checking their weapons. Jack contacted the office of the Chairman of the Joint Chiefs of Staff in Washington, D.C. His Alpha priority call was answered by General Miles himself.

Jack filled the General in on the impending attack and requested permission to use the training troops in the operation. Getting an okay and a "Go with God" for success Jack broke the connection and hauled himself into the troop carrier. Mark went to the driver and gave him the specific location and the additional need for stealth.

Back in Washington, General Miles set several operations into effect that would authorize the use of the forces on domestic soil, restrict any press knowledge of the event, and set up a team to handle the watch for the battle if there was one and the resulting fallout.

Eighteen minutes later, one by one, Mark, the SOG and Jack exited the vehicle as it slowed going through a long corner. Falling back into the tree line next to the road they formed up quickly. The team met the Army Rangers and the Force Recon Marines a quarter mile from the positions Charlie had given them for the concentration of enemy troops.

Since troop vehicles commonly traveled through the area there was a good chance that the enemy wasn't aware of the massing of American troops as yet. Seventy percent of the troops involved were seasoned men and women with combat backgrounds. They had been training with new troops on the mountain that surrounded the Fortress and welcomed an actual test of their capabilities, especially against real enemy troops.

The individual troops had jumped or rolled out of slow moving vehicles and melted into the trees and grasses around the enemy positions. This allowed the vehicles to keep moving and lessened the chance that the enemy could spot a congregation of military transport vehicles in the area.

Mark Connelly and the two commanders conferred and used combat communications to move their troops into attack positions.

Just as they were getting ready to move, a taxicab came along the highway and swung onto the dirt road leading to Mrs. Cochran's house. Mark made a command decision and had two troopers stop the cab. They removed the driver and replaced him with one of their troops who took off his combat gear and assumed the role.

Using the arrival of the cab as a distraction, the American forces moved up on the enemy troops. Their scouts had identified the positions of the troops, their strength, and the weapons they had with them. It was an impressive list which included RPGs, heavy machine guns, and what looked like a truck mounted rocket launcher with rockets the size of ground-to-air, anti-aircraft missiles. Mark's command was to not let the vehicle acting as a rocket launcher be used. If the missile missed the Fortress Mountain no telling how much damage it could do to the general population. He cautioned the troops not to move unless the enemy tried to stop the cab from leaving.

The trooper pulled the cab up to Mrs. Cochran's house and got out. He had on the cabbie's jacket and hoped the camo pants and jungle boots he was wearing didn't alert the watchers. He went to the front door and rang the bell. Mrs. Cochran opened the door and the soldier took her bags to the cab. Feeling lots of eyes on his every move the soldier fretted quietly while Mrs. Cochran carefully locked up her house. He then helped Mrs. Cochran into the cab and headed back for the highway.

The enemy troops were good enough that there was no sign of them as he wheeled the cab off her property and back to the highway. Since they didn't try to stop him on the property, he stopped where the cabbie was waiting and gave him back his fare. He quickly grabbed his gear and ran to his unit. As soon as the cab disappeared over a hill, Mark gave the "go" signal to the troops. In less than twenty seconds there was a full-fledged firefight in progress.

The Army Ranger unit assigned to the rocket truck moved first and took out everyone in, on, and around the vehicle and secured it so that it couldn't be used. As soon as they attacked, the other enemy units realized they were being attacked and started shooting at anything they thought were the advancing troops.

Due to surprise and much better training, not to mention lots of experience, the battle quickly became one-sided and was reduced to pockets of terrorist soldiers defending themselves against the onslaught of the American Military.

Jack, Mark, and the expanded team of twenty-four ex-SOG soldiers moved to protect the northwest end of Mrs. Cochran's property and ran into heavy resistance. One group of the terrorists had a heavy machine gun embedded in a secure ditch. When the Crossfire warriors approached the terrorists opened up on their attackers with the machine gun. Jack took a round to his chest and went down, along with three of the soldiers with him.

Jack later recalled the incident. He was moving forward through the trees when a force slapped him backwards and knocked the wind out of him. He had never heard the round that hit him and hadn't seen the muzzle flash. He passed out for a few seconds from the violence of the impact. He came to lying on his back with the whole front of his chest numb from the strike.

Checking quickly he realized his trauma plate in his body armor had taken a high-powered heavy machine gun round and while it prevented the round from penetrating it translated all the power into force which threw him backwards. He wanted to jump up but he was still winded and couldn't get any energy. He tried rolling to his right and was rewarded with a little more success.

Mark used his M-8's grenade launcher and took out five of the enemy ahead and their machine gun position. He didn't have time to check on Jack or the others because there were bullets were flying everywhere, hitting trees and people indiscriminately. There were all of the usual battlefield sights, sounds, and smells. The smells never changed, sweat, fear, coppery smell of blood, the smell of emptied bowels and bladders.

A round smashed downward through the bush right next to Mark's helmet and another one whizzed by his head going at ninety degrees to the first one. Mark realized that there were at least two enemy snipers working on the American troops and tried to spot them in the melee. Both shots had come from on high, angled downward.

The group of terrorists ahead of them had them pinned down and that gave Mark time to locate both of the shooters who were in trees. Carefully aiming he shot one out of his tree and turned to the other. The second sniper had seen Mark take out his buddy so he concentrated his fire on Mark's position.

After several near misses by the sniper Mark tired of trying to get a good shot and used his grenade launcher to blow the persistent man out of the tree along with a good part of the tree at the same time.

A flying squad of Marines to the right of Mark's position waded into the Crossfire Team's opponents from the terrorist's left flank and decimated them. After that the action was simply mopping up until the remaining enemy troops were dead, wounded, or had surrendered. The entire firefight had lasted less than fifteen minutes.

Mark helped Jack to a standing position and checked to see that his body armor had adequately stopped the incoming round. Jack winced when Mark pressed on the area of his chest the bullet had struck. Mark smiled, "That's going to hurt for a few days but at least you're still here to talk about it. Most people hit by a machine gun don't get that option."

Jack grimaced as he looked at Mark and said, "You know, I really miss having a force generator at times like this."

Mark agreed and helped the other wounded troops get the medical attention they needed. There had been six American troops killed and eighteen wounded. two of the wounded and one of the killed were the Crossfire Team's SOG personnel. The terrorists only had three surviving, unwounded men out of sixty troops. Their wounded were attended to by the medics and twelve of them would live to explain their heroics to their fellow prisoners.

The Marine Force Recon commander called Mark and asked him to come to their original muster position and speak to the local authorities. Apparently the neighbors although remote had no trouble differentiating the grenade explosions and automatic rifle and machine gun firing from normal hunting and had called the police.

Jack called Charlie and asked him to come to the scene and question the prisoners.

An hour later the surviving terrorists were turned over to Justice Department agents for arrest, detention, and trial. After the DOJ personnel left the scene Jack asked Charlie, "What did you get?"

Charlie frowned, "Not as much as you'd like. These were just grunts doing what they were told. Apparently they were troops organized by Sam Sturgis to test our defenses."

Jack looked around at the large number of body bags stacked to one side. "I think the test was successful from our viewpoint, maybe not from his. But he definitely got a measure of our response to his attack."

CHAPTER EIGHT

The military regrouped and returned to the mountain or the Fortress. The one SOG member, Jerald Howland, who had been killed, was taken to the military morgue at Peterson Air Force Base in Colorado Springs. The wounded were being treated in local hospitals.

After a shower and a change of clothes the Crossfire Team met as a group with the SOG in their quarters and prayed for the wounded and the lost. The entire Sensitive Operations Group, or SOG, were spirit-filled Christians as well as top tier military personnel. They knew the chances of being killed in the line of duty and while they would personally mourn the loss of Jerald they knew beyond a doubt that Yahveh knew it would happen and was there with him to take him to heaven as the bullet took his life. They would raise a glass to him this weekend on leave, if they got one.

One of the men, Sergeant Morris, got Jack and Mark's attention. Stepping aside he brought up a question they had been throwing around in the ranks. "Sirs, we have more than two hundred requests from service men and women to join the SOG even though they know they have to leave the service to do so. How do we determine who we should interview as replacements for the three personnel we've lost?"

Jack nodded, "That is a reasonable question Sergeant. The way we picked each of you to begin with was at the leading of Yahveh. Only the people we selected came forth because they were called by Yahveh to this duty. How many of the new applicants expressed a leading or direction from God to join us?"

The man looked a little confused for a second. Then he squared up his shoulders and answered. "All of them did, Sir."

Mark looked at Jack as a suspicion crossed both of their minds. Jack addressed the Sergeant. "Give me the list of all two hundred applicants and we'll pray about each one. Yahshua will direct us to bring in who He wants us to have, okay?"

The Sergeant took a list out of his jacket pocket and handed it to Jack. "I somehow knew you'd want this."

After the core team retired to the war room Mark tipped his head to one side. "Are you thinking what I'm thinking?"

Jack nodded, "Probably. I think that this is Yahveh's second wave and we're going to need more barracks space here in the Fortress."

Laura had been listening to the discussion. "How many more?"

Jack handed her the list. Her eyebrows climbed as she counted the two hundred names. "WOW! Are we starting our own army?"

Mark laughed, "Maybe. If Yahveh wants us to take on the additional troops then there is a good reason and we will probably need them soon."

The door to the war room opened and Carol Moffet let herself in. She smiled at everyone. "HI! You've all been so busy I haven't had a chance to tell you the latest multi-dimensional prayer results."

Laura laughed, "Okay, what's going on that we need to know?"

Carol had just been welded to the team by the Father in the last month. She had been a young programming manager for a geothermal extraction facility in Phoenix, Arizona when the mercenaries of OC had tried to take over the plant. They had been warned by Charlie Wu, whose computers had ferreted out the information. The six member Core Team of the Crossfire Team had gotten there first and were able to defeat the attackers and coincidently save Carol's life at the same time.

Carol had been brought to the Fortress to familiarize the team about geothermal power. During this period, the entire core team and Carol had been transported to a position in heaven by Yahveh through the angel Rose and had seen eleven dimensions and understood how they all interacted on events that were both heavenly or spiritual and Earthly. The Father had used this method to explain the capture, torture, release, and healing of Jack and

Laura without trying to reduce the explanation into four dimensional terms. Our terms would have been woefully lacking in understanding and things would have had to be taken on faith only. This way the whole team got a chance to understand clearly from Yahveh's perspective.

After the team was returned to the normal world, Rose announced that Carol would be allowed to pray when Yahveh wanted to reveal things to her and the team and she would be able to temporarily see, and understand all the dimensions as she prayed. Yahveh had given her two symbols to indicate when she was functioning as the visionary for the team. Two small white diamond-shapes, one at her forehead (for her mind) and one at her throat (for her voice) would glow with the white fire of Yahveh's esteem. This sign was the same as the Sword of the Word wielded by Laura when she was praying and battling evil spirits that entered the human world without Yahveh's permission.

Carol was dark-haired young lady with a trim build and a intense focus concerning the matters of God and a set of intense brown eyes set into a cute face.

Jack nodded, "Please tell us what you have gleaned."

Carol smiled and it lit up her face. "Talking to Charlie and Linda Wu I believe you have already experienced an attack about to be launched against this facility by Sam Sturgis. Right?" Seeing the nods she continued, "The next thing Yahveh brought my attention to was the need for additional troops for the next stage of your fight with him. Oh yes!, You have learned that Mr. Sturgis was demonically healed and is now empowered by Satan himself. He has literally sold his soul for the healing and the chance to kill us all. The only other thing I am sure of is this. Look to Gog for the solution to these troubles."

Jack blinked, "You mean Gog as in Gog and Magog?" Carol nodded her agreement.

Mark frowned, "Russia, now what?"

Sarah raised an eyebrow. "Maybe they want to get their money back from the time we got paid but didn't have to do the work." She was referring to their honeymoon trip to that geopolitical part of the world. The new bosses who had just forcibly retired Mark's hiring group didn't want them there to do the investigation and told them to leave immediately, which they did. When dealing with shaky governments though, Mark always made sure he was paid up front. So they had over eight hundred thousand dollars (U.S.) of Russia's hard currency that they didn't have to work for.

Mark shook his head, "No, this is about Sturgis but I can't see the Russian government being involved. It's either a splinter group or something else."

CHAPTER NINE

As Carol was leaving, Linda Wu let herself into the war room. She walked quietly over to Laura and laid a piece of paper in front of her. She then turned and silently left the room.

Laura studied the paper for a few seconds and then pulled herself up to her workstation. Putting the paper in front of a lens she captured the image and threw it up onto the main screen.

Speaking softly she explained it. "It seems that since he had to coordinate the latest battle Charlie gave Linda the project to find Sam Sturgis. Linda ran a new program she had written with Carol's help and I think we've got a lead on the elusive Mr. Sturgis. Linda's program extrapolated the use of the credit card he used in LA to rent the car he had when he killed the ASF leaders. She found that he also had three other cards with that company. She tracked their usage and determined he uses a card once and then waits at least a month before he uses it again. But he has been cycling the use of the three cards one month at a time."

"He just used the second card in London, England and it was for food to stock a larder. This indicates a safe house or dwelling he is at and plans to stay at for at least two weeks. He used the third card twice in the same area for other necessities. She ran the addresses on the cards and they were of course, fakes. But, she was able to triangulate the area the three cards have been used in and has narrowed the dwelling to a four block area unless he is throwing us a red herring."

"Linda has put a spybot program on the credit card company's files for these three cards and when he uses another one it will alert her right away. Charlie added to her efforts and has piggybacked onto the street cameras in that area with a silent copybot that is undetectable by the British law enforcement. He has also instructed the computers to isolate the next credit card usage in real time and use the cameras to spot him and where he goes or get a license number if possible."

She looked at the two leaders of the team and said, "I suggest we wing over there and be ready when the killer comes out of his hidey-hole. We could take him down and end this game of assassination football we're in with him."

Jack thought for a few seconds. "Won't the devil let him know that we're headed his way?"

Laura rolled her eyes. She had dropped back into the physical and forgot the spiritual aspects of this operation. "True, sorry I slipped there. We need to pray for concealment from the enemy for all of our movements and operations."

Mark slapped his hand on the desk in front of him. "Then, let's pray and get over to good old England before he moves on."

He thought for a second and added an insightful comment. "You know, Sturgis is too smart to leave such an obvious trail. I think it is probably a lure to get us into a trap of some kind."

Jack raised his eyebrows. "You think we'll get any farther if we ignore this chance?" Mark grinned, "Nope, let's go visit the spider in his web."

Laura asked the computer where Su Li was at that moment. She was in the gym working out with Carol Moffet and Debbie Hargrove on martial arts and sword practice. Laura interrupted them and gave Su Li a heads up on their immediate travel plans. Su Li told her "Okay" and headed for her room to clean up, gather up her helmet and flight suit for the trip.

Carol and Debbie continued to work on their swordsmanship.

One hour later Su Li had completed her preflight of the Shrew. She really admired the CIA aggressor version of the traditional Citation X private jet. It was actually more of a fighter aircraft that carried passengers than a passenger jet that could fight. From startup to shutdown the operation was completely military. She had weapons stores and could use up to four air-to-air missiles as well as three chain guns that were hidden in the fuselage of the sleek aircraft. The helmet control system was as high-tech as it gets with almost thought control for combat flying and weapons usage. There were many signs of the modifications; the most notable was the large air scoop running the width of the airplane at the wing roots rather than two engines mounted on pylons on the upper part of the plane.

The fact that this plane had the engines from the F-22 Raptor and could use supercruise would only be observable from the performance and not just a visual inspection. She had asked for some combat capability since they were being attacked sporadically while in the air. What she got was far more than she had hoped for in her wildest dreams.

The fact that each plane was two hundred million dollars and the CIA didn't have the funds after they'd ordered them was the only reason the Crossfire Team had even heard of them. Their U. S. Air Force contact, Major Mike White, brought them to Su Li's attention and then trained her after the planes were purchased by the team. Actually the funds came from Victor Chamberlain, one of the richest men in the world who had become a Christian and a part of the team after being rescued by the Malones and the Connellys from a hostile takeover of his island and his businesses.

Su Li pushed the start button and watched the power up for thirty seconds. The plane was ready to taxi and take off at that point. She gave the command over her helmet microphone and the doors on both ends of the hanger were opened by the Air Force Special Forces personnel who had been added to the Fortress teams as training operations both at Denver International Airport and at the helicopter flight hanger at the top of the mountain.

Su Li hit the intercom and told the eight person team in the passenger compartment to strap in. She then concentrated on not revealing the true potential of the aircraft as she taxied out and got permission to use runway 16R after three heavies. As she watched the first plane, a Boeing 757 roll out and climb into the air she recalled that this airport had roughly fifteen hundred operations in a twenty-four hour day and there was always traffic. She didn't like sitting out in the open with this plane considering the severe penalties for revealing its true nature. Also, she was eager to get airborne and flying.

Finally she was cleared to roll and she carefully used a minimum of power to bring the plane off the ground after a lengthy acceleration run. She could have lifted off in half the distance if she had pushed the throttles forward, but she played the game and climbed into the pattern slowly and carefully to maintain the image of a normal biz jet. The hidden F-22 engines still emitted a staccato crackle and rumble that didn't sound exactly like a commercial craft but that couldn't be helped.

They had added the pylon mounted wing tanks which increased their distance to over thirty-two hundred miles. But even with supercruise they would be running on empty by the time they got to England and Su Li was quite sure that the Shrew would fall like a rock if it ran out of fuel. She had contacted Colonel White and explained their mission. He arranged for a mid-air refueling over the Atlantic. Su Li had trained on the flight simulator extensively concerning the refueling procedure and was sure she could handle it.

As they reached the assigned military flight corridor at 38,000 feet and Su Li put the aircraft on computer control. This military version of the usual cruise control was more precise but also controlled by the threat board. If an enemy action was detected the plane would defend itself even if the pilot was unavailable or unconscious.

The supercruise capability let them economically fly faster than sound. They were moving at Mach 2 which is the equivalent to either 1325 miles per hour or 823 knots per hour. They had to be in a military air corridor or risk catching up with commercial jets moving at subsonic speeds and that might get them noticed. As it was they were leaving a supersonic boom in their wake but at 38,000 feet it didn't affect too much on the ocean.

The mid-air fueling was handled adroitly and with no excitement at all. That came later.

An hour out of Britain Su Li took a call and listened for several minutes. She then slid out of the command seat and walked back into the darkened interior of the main cabin. Tapping Jack on his arm gently Su Li woke him up and had him come to the cockpit. She sat down in the command seat and indicated Jack should sit in the co-pilot's seat. Jack sat down and put on the headphones. Su Li connected the call to him.

"Jack Malone" was all he said.

"Mr. Malone? My name is Wasson, Charles Wasson; I'm your contact for Interpol and the British MI-5 organization concerning your target. I have some news for you that you probably won't appreciate. It seems that when our chaps were notified that your team was coming in to apprehend your target they contacted your FBI because that is the way things are done around here. It seems your FBI wants you to step aside and allow their people to capture Mr. Sturgis because of the warrant for his arrest is a United States Federal Arrest Warrant and it is in their authority."

Jack thought for a few seconds. "Mr. Wasson, do the FBI contacts realize that there is a demonic aspect to Mr. Sturgis? Perhaps they need to check with Joe Sobbel before they lock down the investigation. Check with Mr. Sobbel and get back to me please." Jack ended the conversation and sighed a large sigh. "It's back to territorial one-upsmanship again."

Su Li rolled her eyes which didn't come off too well with them covered by the helmet and reticule.

CHAPTER TEN

The Shrew was routed to a British Military Airfield thirty miles north of London that they had flown into several months before in the hunt for the Omicron Cartel. The team was met again by David Thornton, an MI-5 operative they had worked with before.

As the doors on the hanger were closed the team disembarked and Su Li finished her shutdown and post trip inspection. She then exited the aircraft and put the unique security system in the armed mode. Outside there were four British security men from the military. Their job was to make sure no one tried to test the security system on the aircraft.

Jack and Mark asked David what the latest ruling was concerning the arrest and jailing of Sam Sturgis.

The Londoner shook his head. "Not good. The FBI has gotten the Prime Minister to back their demand to give them the authority concerning Mr. Sturgis. As of right now, your team is to stand down and not interfere with the FBI operation."

Jack looked a number up on his tablet PC and punched the number into the phone. Joe Sobbel answered on the second ring. "Mr. Malone?"

Jack answered, "Yes Mr. Sobbel. I don't understand what your organization is doing in taking over this capture of Sam Sturgis. It was my understanding that you were put in your position because of your ability to understand and respond to spiritual angles in FBI cases. There is a definite spiritual angle to Sam Sturgis. If you've read our reports then you know he was permanently disabled by Mark's sniper shot in Colorado. Since then he has returned stronger and completely healed. This was not done through the power of Yahveh but through the power of Satan."

Sobbel responded, "Jack, I know what you're saying is the truth. I sought the Father over this and the understanding I got is that Sam is pulling out all the stops and running a bear trap for your team. I therefore recommended that we allow you to capture him, or kill him. But, I was overruled by the Director himself. He feels that our agency, with its greater resources and manpower can more effectively capture this man who has earned the top spot in the nation's ten most wanted fugitives."

Jack sighed, "Joe, it won't work. Do you know why it won't work?"

Joe sighed back, "Because Satan will work with Sam to prevent his being captured?"

Jack laughed a short dry laugh. "Sort of. Our team has worked in the spiritual field for several years now and we have spiritual resources your agency doesn't have. But, with that aside, I'll bet you dollars to doughnuts that there is no spiritual protection or covering for your team. If that's the case then the enemy will warn Sam of the impending operation against him and he will probably make things go horribly wrong. We're pretty sure he has deliberately exposed his whereabouts to draw us into a trap. We have heavenly help that could allow us to circumvent his tricks and traps.

You've got to warn the Director that Sam has demonic support against which a secular crew doesn't stand a chance. Not against that combination."

Joe was silent for a few seconds. "All right Jack, I'll try to convince the Director that there's more than meets the eye with this character. Although, I doubt that I will change his mind."

Jack frowned, "Okay, then tell the Director this. As soon as I hang up with you I am going to contact the President and give him our side of the picture. If this bust goes bad, as I am sure it will, the loss of Sam and any collateral damage will be laid directly in his lap."

Joe really sighed this time. "Okay, I'll tell him but I may be looking for a new job soon."

Jack shook his head, "Possibly, but I think it will be the Director who's about to put himself out of work. If he does come down on you or fires you give me a call. We can always use another good man."

Jack called the President but had to relay the message because the President was in conference at the time. As a backup, Jack called General Miles, the

Chairman of the Joint Chiefs of Staff for the military. Getting through to the General, Jack outlined what was going on and asked for any prayers the General had time to lift up to the Father.

Jack called the team together and told them about the FBI situation.

Mark was alarmed because he knew better than most how Sturgis worked. He shook his head and turned to David Thornton. "David, can Scotland Yard or the London Police quietly evacuate the people anywhere near Sam's location once we determine where it is?"

David thought for a second, "Wouldn't that warn your suspect that something is going down?"

Mark shook his head, "Don't worry about that, he'll already of been warned by the devil. What I'm concerned about is that he might leave a deadly package for the FBI that could have bad collateral consequences for your public."

David pulled out a cell phone and walked off to talk to his boss.

Jack's cell phone beeped and he answered it to hear Charlie Wu's voice. "Jack, I've got Sam's hideaway location. It's the third building on Hawthorne Road, first door to the West. I'm sending the location to your tablet right now."

Jack thanked Charlie and broke the connection. He showed the map to Mark. Mark called David back over and showed him the map.

David relayed the information to his department head and hung up. "It'll be the devil's job to get that warren cleared out. A lot of those people don't trust the Police and won't evacuate even if they knew a bomb maker lived in their building. But, we'll try. How long do we have?"

Mark shook his head, "I don't really know. But, we have to give this information to the FBI or risk being labeled as "obstructionists". I'd guess it would be about two hours if their team is on the ground here in London."

David agreed and hurried off using his cell phone again.

Jack's phone chimed. "Jack Malone"

The President was on a short break and wanted to find out what Jack needed so urgently. Jack explained the situation and the possible danger to the FBI and the people in the area. The President said he would look into the problem but it was fairly late in the game and he would not be able to handle it personally because of the meeting priority. "I'm sorry I wasn't informed about this earlier." Jack thanked him and broke the connection.

Jack and Mark just looked at each other. Jack called the team together. "Guys, we need to pray for Yahveh's protection for all the combatants as well as the innocent neighbors."

The next hour and a half passed quickly as the team prayed together and then individually for Elohim's protection for his children.

Jack's cell phone beeped and he answered it quickly. It was Charlie again. "Jack, I'm so sorry. I'm getting preliminary reports that the FBI team went in and surrounded Sam's place and forced an entry. The resultant explosion destroyed that building and the four buildings around it and severely damaged a four block area around the building. Apparently all the FBI agents were killed along with eighty to ninety civilians in the area."

Jack thanked Charlie and asked him to keep monitoring the situation.

Laura came over to Jack and rested her head on his shoulder. "I know about the explosion and the body count. Any ideas about where Sam is headed?"

Jack shook his head. "No, I just hope that we were able to reduce the death toll by getting David's group to try and evacuate the surrounding area."

Mark walked over to the Malones. "Guys, I just got a call from David's superior in the Scotland Yard. David Thornton was killed in the explosion trying to evacuate the neighbors. He and a dozen officers of the London Police had already convinced several hundred other people to leave when David went back to make a last sweep."

Laura felt hot tears run down her face as she sent a prayer for David heavenward.

CHAPTER ELEVEN

A new detective was assigned to work with the Crossfire Team and he came to the airport to see them. His name was Michael Allard. He introduced himself to Jack and asked if there was anything he could do to help them. He conveyed Scotland Yard's gratitude to the team for helping reduce the death toll by over eight hundred souls who escaped Sturgis' bomb.

Jack looked at the ruddy-faced young man and shook his head. "I'm sorry that our internal politics allowed Sturgis to kill so many, especially David, and get away Scott free."

Michael agreed and shook Jack's hand and left after telling him to contact the Yard or himself directly if they needed additional information or help. He gave Jack his card.

Jack told the group to reboard the Shrew for the trip home. It had been a wasted and futile trip. Now they were back to square one on locating Sturgis.

Twelve miles from the airport, Sam Sturgis was listening to Oleg describe the action as they saw it. "Apparently the Crossfire Team was able to track you to the location you were in and were coming to get you rather than you get them. Is that the case?"

Sam snorted, "Not likely. I purposely used credit cards associated to the one I used in Los Angeles because I knew the team would pick up on them. I then used one twice more and walked openly to the building I had selected. I had a fertilizer bomb set up and armed for the team." While knowing the truth from his "contact" Sam lied to the Russian. "Apparently either the local police or Scotland Yard preempted the team and got killed instead."

Oleg was impressed. "So that was a trap you set and baited to get the Crossfire Team to bite on? Oh, that is very good. But, you have now set yourself up as an international terrorist by killing half a neighborhood in London not to mention a lot of cops. I suggest that you move your base of operation to a secret, remote location in our country. We will make sure that you are safe and we will allow only the Crossfire Team to approach you. We, of course, will warn you if they attempt to do that. We will also grant you full freedom and control of your affairs. Do you want to do that?"

Sam thought about the offer. It would get the international heat off of him and give him the protection he needed. And it would allow him to strike when he wanted to without a dozen organizations attempting to stop him. He realized that the Russian Mafia, oops, Organization, would use his being there to exercise some form of control on him but he could blunt that as needed.

Thinking about the warning he got about the FBI from his "lord" he decided to see if the communications worked both ways. He closed his eyes and asked, "Lord, is it a good thing for me to relocate my operation to a central Russian position?"

The voice that he heard in his head was oily, superior, and arrogant. "Of course it is. I told those fools to invite you!"

Sam thought, "Well, I guess it's a done deal" Over the phone he gave his agreement to the switch in bases. Oleg said that they would see that Sam got a Russian flight without giving any information to the authorities that he was travelling. The flight was to leave in six hours from Heathrow Airport.

In Washington, D. C. the President summoned the Director of the Federal Bureau of Investigation to his office. The President wasn't happy about the international furor over the incident. There had bettered be a very good reason for the debacle that took so many lives when they had been warned of the danger by the Crossfire Team and their own internal management in advance.

Director Foley showed up at the allotted time and was shown into the Oval Office. The President and the Director of the Department of Justice were waiting for him. The DOJ was the parent organization of the FBI.

Director Foley had been embarrassed by the London operation and knew he'd stepped in it badly. Figuring his best defense would be an offense he first asserted his objection to being called on the carpet by the President over an operational directive. "I seriously doubt that there is any validity to this hearing. I made a tactical decision on my authority based on a federal warrant for Sam Sturgis' arrest. Why am I being interrogated about my doing my job?"

That was precisely the wrong note to strike with either of the other men in the Oval Office. Don Wessley, the head of the DOJ, cleared his throat to tell the FBI Director that it wasn't his choice to decide if he wanted to come to this meeting. But, his comments were cut off by the President's dry comment. "Director Foley, based on the information I have been given by Scotland Yard, you personally authorized the removal of the Crossfire Team and substituted your agents to make this arrest, is that right? And you did this without consultation with Scotland Yard?"

Foley frowned, "I authorized this raid and don't see where a private, non-governmental group has any right to stick it's nose into government business."

The President shook his head. "Tom, just answer my question."

Tom Foley took a deep breath and said, "I dismissed the efforts of the Crossfire Team as unnecessary as it was only based on religious reasons. Our teams are specifically trained to handle these take-downs. That is why I made my decision as I did."

The President nodded, "Okay, but, if you'll remember, after the nuclear attack on Denver, you and I agreed that if there was a demonic, or spiritual, element involved that the Crossfire Team would have the option to be primary in any operation due to their successes to date. Why did you change that agreement unilaterally without consulting me first?"

This rendition of facts which did not support his position rattled and irritated the Director. "I ignored it because they're a bunch of religious, quasi-military types that have no oversight control and no responsibility to me. It is my sworn duty to enforce the laws as they are written, not give in to special interests!"

The President took notice of the heat behind the Director's comments but declined to match it. "Tom, you violated our agreement and as a result you got twelve of your agents and almost a hundred British citizens killed in what seems to have been a trap set by Sam Sturgis, probably for the Crossfire Team. Jack Malone was trying to tell you that. Scotland Yard tried to tell you that, General Miles tried to tell you that. Still you insisted on doing it your way. I seriously cannot see that you acted properly or insightful in this matter."

The President was about to continue when his phone chimed. "Excuse me for a second gentleman."

The President listened for several seconds and then hung up. Looking at Director Foley he asked, "Did your Western Director, Joe Sobbel, also meet with you and ask you to reconsider your decision?"

Foley frowned again, "Frankly Mr. President, I don't know if he did or not. It wasn't a decision on his level and whatever he would say wasn't going to reverse my directive!"

Don Wessley had heard enough. "Director Foley, you're embarrassing me taking such a impudent tone with the President of the United States! He is my boss as I am yours." Don shook his head and looked Foley in the eye. "Tom, after that mess in London and your performance here today I have lost all confidence in your ability to run the FBI as directed. I will expect your resignation on my desk by four o'clock this afternoon. I am hereby suspending your authority and will communicate that to your organization immediately. If you wish to argue with my decision you have the normal channels to file a grievance. Do you agree to step down?"

The reality of the situation rolled over Tom Foley with the impact of an ice storm. He nodded, "I agree and you'll have my resignation on your desk by four o'clock. But, I can also guarantee you that the next president of these United States isn't going to kowtow to the wants of special interest groups like the Crossfire Team!."

At that Foley got up and stalked out of the Oval Office without asking permission to leave.

Don Wessley picked up his cell phone and punched in a preset number. When the security director of the FBI answered the head of the DOJ made it clear that Foley was no longer the FBI director and he was to be accompanied to his office to write his resignation and pack his, and only his, effects. The security man was to change all the passwords, key codes, access codes, and permissions before Foley arrived back at the FBI Headquarters. Don Wessley ended with the caution. "If you or any of your men grant him any access I will prosecute anyone personally and it will be a federal felony. Am I clear on this?"

The security man's answer left no question in the DOJ Director's mind.

He looked at President Bollen. "Who are you going to nominate for Foley's position? You still have time to get it done before the elections."

The President thought for a few minutes. I think I'm going to nominate Joe Sobbel to take over the Directorship. He has the ability and the training and the required years of experience. And, he was willing to stand up for what is right even if it meant his career."

Don Wessley thought about the nomination. It could be the best nomination the President ever made.

CHAPTER TWELVE

On the flight back to the Fortress Jack and the team prayed and sought Yahweh as to what to do to find Sam Sturgis before he could strike at them again.

In the midst of his prayers Jack had a sudden thought of Charlie and Linda Wu. He shook his head and tapped Mark on the shoulder. When Mark looked up Jack pointed towards the rear of the plane.

When they were both seated in the back of the plane where their conversation wouldn't interfere with the other people's prayers, Jack told Mark about the sudden thought he'd had. Mark thought about it and said, "Maybe Charlie and Linda are going to locate Sam."

Jack nodded, "That's what I thought too. The reason I called you back here to discuss it was because I normally think things through in a systematic manner. This thought came like it was shoved into my mind in the middle of other thoughts. Now, did the thought come from Yahweh or from Satan?"

Laura's soft voice came from behind Jack, "It came from heaven because I got the same thought and I tested the spirit and I believe it was confirmed in my spirit."

Jack looked back at her and smiled. "I forgot that we're spiritually close and if it was Satan one of us would have picked up on the source."

Laura laughed, "Maybe, maybe not. Old Nick has been fooling Christians for thousands of years. What makes you think he couldn't fool us?"

Jack was about to answer when his cell phone beeped. He looked at the time and it would be close to three a.m. in Colorado right then. He smiled at the other two, "I'd guess It would be Carol."

He opened his phone and saw that it was indeed Carol Moffet. "Hi, Carol, what's got you up so early today?"

Carol's cheery voice came back, "Well, when Yahweh wants me to pray, it really doesn't matter what time it is does it? Anyway, he had me look at the heavenlies and focus on a particular event which bothers me. You and Laura are going to be in an extremely dangerous situation soon and it is because of a leading from Charlie Wu. I can't tell if it is a good leading or a bad leading, only that you two are subject to extreme peril and are alone against many enemies."

Jack told her, "Thanks Carol, try to go back to bed and get some sleep, okay?"

Carol said she would and rang off. Jack put his cell phone away and explained the call to the others. Laura nodded her head and Mark, being the hyper practical one said, "I guess we'd better get hold of Charlie as soon as we can tomorrow."

Both Jack and Laura said together, "No, he'll call us first." They looked at each other and laughed.

Mark didn't want to wait but knew it would be counter-productive to bother the computer guru before he was ready to talk to them. "Do we know when we should expect him to call us?"

Jack yawned, "Easy, let's go get some shuteye. I expect he'll call as soon as we're asleep."

Laura raised an eyebrow at that. "How pessimistic, true, but pessimistic."

The three of them walked quietly back to their seats in the now darkened aircraft. The others had turned off their lights and were sleeping as best they could.

Mark excused himself and went to the cockpit to see if Su Li needed any company to keep her alert during the night shift flying the plane. He slid into the co-pilot's seat and asked the young Asian how she was doing.

Su Li quickly glanced at Mark and made a small smile. "I'm a little tired but not too tired to get us back to the states. But, you drive home from the airport and nobody had bettered wake me before two p.m. tomorrow afternoon!"

Mark talked to her for a few minutes until he realized he was distracting her from her piloting. He slid out of the seat with one last comment. "If you feel like pulling over and resting for a while, buzz me. I'm in seat three-cee. Okay?"

Su Li nodded and said, "Go, get some sleep. I couldn't sleep while this beauty was in the sky anyway. I'll be fine."

Mark went out of the cockpit and closed the door. He then sat down quietly so as not to wake Sarah. He was asleep in two minutes with the blanket covering him from foot to shoulder and the seat reclined into a flat bed surface. The last thought he had was a surprise. He hadn't realized just how tired he really was.

The Shrew continued to bore a hole in the sky at fourteen hundred miles per hour in Supercruise.

CHAPTER THIRTEEN

Su Li had gradually decreased the speed of the CF-88 "Shrew" until it matched the operational envelope of the normal Citation X so that when they started hitting commercial traffic they would not look out of place.

It was a beautiful dawn coming from behind the aircraft as she neared the eastern seashore of America. Su Li had adopted the land as her own and thought of herself as an American these days. She had fought many times for this new homeland of hers and she was proud of it and the fight needed to keep its image bright.

She checked the passenger compartment and saw that the ten people back there were comfortably sleeping. That made her yawn and sigh. Her turn to sleep was coming soon and... The alert board lit up and the aircraft went through several configuration changes in preparation for possible combat. One of the configuration changes was the automatic release of both the pylons and the under wing fuel tanks.

Su Li frowned at that. That was twenty thousand dollars worth of hardware that was headed for the bottom of the ocean. She was glad that she'd used all the fuel in the drop tanks first but they'd have to modify that response and let the pilot determine if it was truly necessary to drop the tanks.

She had been scanning her threat board and her instrumentation and determined that there were three military aircraft, fighter configurations homing in on her aircraft. She keyed the communications and challenged the approaching aircraft. "Military aircraft on heading due east of New York City on a vector of ninety three degrees, you are on a collision course with westbound traffic. Please identify yourself and your intentions."

Her radio squawked back with the power associated with combat aircraft transmissions. "Crossfire Team, we have been assigned by ADC to provide air cap for your flight due to possible bogeys in the area. Please continue on your flight path and we will form up on you."

To Su Li there were so many things wrong with that statement she didn't give the courtesy of an answer. She pushed the button that sounded the combat alarm in the passenger compartment, brought the engines up to full power and extended the forward pointing canard wings at the front of the fuselage.

Changing frequencies she contacted the civilian Air Traffic Control center and told them she was deviating from their approved flight pattern due to an attack by three or more aircraft.

Mark dropped into the copilot's seat and strapped in quickly. Su Li got a heads up from the rear gun positions that Jack and David were in position and ready to use the chain guns as necessary.

Su Li used a coded frequency to contact Air Defense Command and used Mark's "General Connelly" persona to get quick response. "Air Defense Command, this is Crossfire Flight One, General Mark Connelly commanding. We have three fighter aircraft closing on our position thirty miles east of New York City. These aircraft claim that you have sent them to provide protection for our flight. Is that true?"

ADC came back immediately, "Crossfire Flight One, be advised that we have no knowledge of those aircraft or a request to provide protection for your flight. We have you on our screens and are scrambling ADC fighters to your position with an ETA of fourteen minutes."

Su Li acknowledged the message and switched off. "A fat lot of good that will do us. This will be over in the next eight minutes. Su Li watched as the additional speed of the Shrew threw off the initial attack pattern and forced the other aircraft into a tail chase position. She centered her emotions and focused her attention strictly on the battle about to happen. She prayed that Yahveh would give her the ability to avoid destruction and to protect the other people in the plane.

She saw the indication when the following fighters went into afterburner by the change in the closing rates which caused them to quickly close on the Shrew's position. "Hold on!" she announced to both Mark and the people in the back. Su Li's mind ran over her training in the application of the energy-maneuverability and variation steepest-descent optimization techniques typical of a multipurpose tactical fighter aircraft. Picking what she determined to be the best alternative given the number of enemy aircraft, relative speeds, and probable weapons to be used, she didn't second guess her gut instinct.

Rotating the controls, kicking the rudder pedal, and tipping the aircraft into a rolling dive she quickly escaped from the attack parameters of the trailing aircraft by increasing her dive speed to well over Mach two and essentially reversing her course without losing any time or speed. This is a maneuver that few military aircraft could do without losing wings, let alone a civilian plane so it was totally unexpected by the fighters.

Taking full advantage of the canard wings at the front of the airframe Su Li pulled the nose up hard. This was so far outside most aircraft's abilities that the enemy couldn't believe it could be done. Essentially she was flying forward and to the right, side-slipping actually while at the same time the nose of the aircraft lifted unnaturally above the line of flight. This pointed the front of the Shrew at her opponents. The maneuver allowed her to paint two of the attackers with her attack radar. She got an acceptable firing solution from the computer and she didn't hesitate but fired two of their radar guided air-to-air missiles from the hidden compartments at the bottom of the body.

Continuing the technique she'd started she rolled the Shrew to its left and maxxed the engines. The plane went straight up and then rolled over its right side. The third attacker had tried to follow her dive and had chickened out which required him to pull up. This put him directly in Su Li's attack pattern and she fired a third air-to-air missile. These missiles were "fire and forget" types that weren't easily confused by chaff and radar jamming. When the target aircraft attempted to jam the radar signal with a more powerful signal the missile switched to "jam tracking" and homed in on the signal being sent by the target.

Chaff would distract and fool a normal missile. Not so these advanced packages. The compact computer inside the missile tracked only solid signals that continued to move under acceleration, which meant the evading aircraft and not the radar reflecting chaff. She noted the destruction of the third attacker by the explosion and falling debris.

Su Li's threat board showed that even though she had destroyed the first two attackers they had each fired two missiles before being blown apart. The designers of the Shrew figured that since we had advanced missiles it was probable that the enemy also had advanced missiles and that chaff and jamming would not deter their missiles either. The Shrew's computer tracked the position of the oncoming missiles and at the right time launched four small rear facing missiles whose only job was to intercept the oncoming Mach eight missiles.

This all happened horribly fast to our senses but to the computer it was only a chess game and the right piece at the right time would take care of the problem. The nice thing about the anti-missile missiles was that they didn't have to compute a lot of data since they were starting out from where the enemy missiles wanted to be and only had to follow a direct collision course. This all happened so quickly that the enemy air-to-air missiles were destroyed before Mark was aware that the defensive missiles had been fired.

Su Li slowed down the engines and retracted the canard wings as she did a lazy circle to the left. The big black clouds of the three explosions each had descending smoke trails where the debris that had been three fighter jets only minutes ago fell towards the ground. The missile explosions had been smaller but brighter and were quickly being blown away by the upper level winds.

The whole battle had taken less than seven minutes from first contact to full destruction of the enemy aircraft. Su Li looked at Mark, "What type of birds were they?"

Mark shook his head, "Don't know, you didn't leave enough to identify. Oh, by the way, thanks! That was some of the best flying I have ever seen and you were so cool it was excellent lesson in combat flying."

Su Li smiled. Praise from Mark Connelly was indeed rare. "It's really this amazing airplane. Oh! Mark, I do like it!"

ADC interrupted their conversation, "Crossfire Flight One, Please confirm that you're resolved your problems."

After Su Li confirmed the downing of the three attackers ADC added, "We will investigate and try to determine who, why, and what was involved in the assault on your aircraft. Can you state your aircraft type?'

Su Li keyed her microphone, "ADC, thank you for your assistance and we will be looking forward to the results of your investigation. Our aircraft type is CF-88, civilian light aircraft. If you need additional information please contact base command at Groom Lake."

There was a brief pause during which Mark could imagine the raised eyebrows in Cheyenne Mountain, ADC command's location. All they got was a "Roger that."

CHAPTER FOURTEEN

After they returned to their hanger at Denver's International Airport the rest of the team congratulated Su Li on her victory not to mention for saving all of their lives in the process.

Su Li was grateful that the others appreciated her talent to fly. She decided to check the aircraft after the stress of combat and see if there had been any damage or flaws that could compromise future flights.

Sarah had a strange feeling, like a catch in her spirit that it wasn't right to leave Su Li there by herself so she opted to stay and see if she could help her in any way. Su Li was very focused on her inspection and at first didn't notice Sarah's presence. So Sarah decided to work on the paperwork demanded by the airport administration for their use of space at the airport.

Almost four hours later one of the Air Force Special Services personnel walked into the hanger and saw Sarah was sitting at a work bench watching Su Li. The Sergeant indicated the door to the hanger. "General Connelly? There is a full bird Colonel and his aide at the guard shack demanding entrance to the facility. He's from Cheyenne Mountain and has credentials in the training squadron there. Since we're technically training here at the air field he says he has authority over us and is getting pretty hot about not being allowed in here. General Connelly's orders were to let no one but Crossfire personnel and our staff in here. How should we handle it?"

Sarah thought for a minute. This could be a problem. She pulled out her cell phone and hit the button for Mark. When he answered she explained the situation and asked for his thoughts.

Mark told her to get the Colonel's name. When Sarah asked the Spec 4 he nodded, "Yes Ma'am, it's Dunning, Colonel Dunning."

Sarah passed it on to Mark. Mark came back with, "I've heard of this guy, he is an efficiency expert and, of course, the troops aren't too fond of him. But, in this case he is being too nosy for his own good. Go out and explain to him that this facility is not in his need-to-know and thank him for his interest but he doesn't have the chops to get in there."

Sarah sighed, "Mark, that's great to get rid of him this time but he'll probably keep digging and trying to get authority until someone gives it to him."

Mark became very serious. "No he won't, I promise you that he'll leave us alone after this. Go tell him what I said."

Su Li walked away from the Shrew wiping her hands on a towel and came over to Sarah. "What's the problem?"

Sarah gave her a recap of the visitor problem and headed for the guardhouse. Su Li finished wiping off her hands and tagged along to see how things worked out.

Sarah led as she walked across the tarmac and out through the gate to greet the Colonel. "Hello, Colonel Dunning, I'm General Connelly. I understand you are requesting access to this facility. May I ask why?"

The Colonel looked at the tall, pretty, black haired woman and almost sneered, "I'd like to see some identification if you don't mind ", General"."

Sarah reached into her pocket and produced the identification card with her title and authority on it.

The Colonel looked at it for a second as if he thought it was a fake. But he wasn't sure. It didn't really matter. He was going to see this mysterious, "civilian" aircraft that had just beaten three fighter jets. He came to attention and saluted the woman. Sarah returned his salute.

The Colonel repeated his request. "Fine, General, I'm requesting admission to this facility based on its use as a training facility and I am in charge of all training west of the Mississippi River. I believe that Denver is west of the Mississippi these days."

Sarah kept her cool and nodded, "Yes Colonel, the Mississippi is east of Denver. But, this is a restricted facility that is off-limits to anyone who does not have a Beta-level clearance need-to-know, and a pre-approval authorized by the Chairman of the Joint Chief of Staffs,

General Miles. You do not have that need-to-know and you're not on the list of approved personnel. Therefore this facility will remain off-limits to you at this time." Sarah had handled tougher men than this Colonel in Israel during her military service there and she wasn't about to back down.

The Colonel took a determined stand and fired back, "Regardless of Beta-level need to know and approval lists I have access rights to all bases using our people as training security. I respectfully demand my right to enter this facility or I will eliminate their use by your organization!"

Something about the man's insistent behavior bothered Su Li. Also, something about the movement of the traffic outside the gate area gave her a bad feeling in her spirit. Su Li tried to pin down what was bothering her but it elusively stayed just out of reach. She stepped into the guard shack and asked the Spec in there to bring Colonel Dunning's file up on the screen. When the man hesitated Su Li leaned down and spoke softly in his ear. "I have authority and several General staff members to back up this request but since time is of the essence I'll give you five seconds to comply or I will render you unconscious and do it myself."

The Spec 4 had heard tales about the fighting capabilities of this Asian pilot and he believed that she could do exactly what she said. He coded in the correct sequence and after several seconds the Colonel's file appeared on his screen. This didn't help anything because it was an empty file with the large, red-letter warning blinking on the screen. This file is restricted to Alpha three level personnel. This attempt to access this file will be recorded for investigation and resolution.

Su Li asked the Spec to contact Cheyenne Mountain immediately and let her talk to the base commander. This was an Alpha request. Two minutes later she was still watching Sarah and the "Colonel" sparring over authority when she talked to the Base Commander.

After she explained who she was and who she represented, she asked the Commander to describe Colonel Dunning to her. Taken aback somewhat the Commander described his subordinate. Su Li thanked him and suggested that they see if they could find him because she had an imposter at the guard shack using the Colonel's identification papers.

She saw the Spec start to go for his sidearm and put her hand on his arm, "Don't." We'll catch him off guard. Call for backup because there are at least two other men in his staff car and there is something else is going on out in the parking lot. Sarah and I will handle the "Colonel" and his "aide". Be very alert. But, try to act nonchalant because I'd be willing to bet that they won't hesitate to gun all of us down if they think we're on to them."

Su Li told the man to give her a high-five to confuse the watchers and then left the guard shack and went back to the gate where Sarah was beginning to tire of the man's insistence.

Su Li tapped her on the shoulder and led her to one side. Su Li whispered in Sarah's ear. Sarah looked at her and nodded. Sarah walked off towards the hanger and Su Li opened the gate to let the Colonel and his aide in. "I'm sorry Colonel, we're just a little too careful here sometimes. She pointed towards the door Sarah was walking towards and waved them on. The man with the Colonel's identity smirked and strode off like a winner.

Su Li saw the thumbs up sign the Spec in the guardhouse gave her as she followed the Colonel and his aide to the building. The aide entered the door in front of Su Li who closed the door behind her That's when the phony "Colonel" pulled an issue 9MM automatic out from under his uniform jacket and pointed it towards Sarah. Sarah had expected some mischief and was watching the "Colonel's" reflection in the window to her left. When he pulled out the gun she bent at the waist and did a roundhouse kick that knocked the gun out of his hand.

The "Colonel" jumped back and pulled out a medium-sized combat knife as Sarah came around toward him. She spun to her right and swung her right arm down to block his thrust. Caught off guard by her sudden movement the man countered her block with an upsweep of his knife. The blade sliced the flesh on Sarah's arm and caught her chest and shoulder before she could knock it far enough away from her.

Blood flew from her wounds and the pain caused a sparkle effect in her vision but, her focus was on the battle and she drove a full power left hand palm heel strike to the man's face. Sarah was well trained in how to apply power in her blows and the fact that the man was driving towards her in his knife strike just amplified the power in the blow.

Sarah's counterattack smashed the man's nose to pulp and straightened the "Colonel" out parallel to the concrete floor as his feet kept going forward as his head suddenly reversed direction and travelled backward. He fell the three feet to slam onto the hard floor. The blow had knocked the sense out of him and the fall drove him into unconsciousness as his head slammed onto the concrete.

As the Colonel attempted to stab Sarah the "aide" spun on the ball of his left foot as he pulled out a handgun. Su Li snap kicked at the man's head but he leaned backwards and took the blow on his chest. Knocked backward he cushioned his fall and rolled to his right to get away from Su Li. As he completed his roll he pointed the automatic towards Su Li and fired three rounds. Su Li had seen the move develop and had thrown herself behind a tall metal file cabinet to her right. The man then swung more to his right to fire at Sarah. This was a professional fighter and knew what to do and when to do it.

Unfortunately for him the two Crossfire warriors were his equal and more. Sarah saw the movement and threw herself backwards so that she rolled over the large, heavy metal desk and dropped behind it as the man fired. The gunshots were deafening in the small office space they were in. All three rounds slammed into the desk which stopped them short of hitting the ex-Mossad agent. As the man turned back to his left he saw Su Li throwing a metal wrench at him. As he focused on her throw he missed the fact that Sarah had also brought out a handgun. She lined up on the aide and fired three rounds of her own.

Apparently sensing the threat the man squatted as he turned back toward Sarah. This left an opening and Su Li dodged Sarah's bullets and rushed at the man. Caught between deadly forces the aide tried to aim across his body at the rapidly approaching Su Li. Sarah's fourth shot caught him right above his right ear. The hydraulic pressure of the 158-grain HydroShock hollow point travelling at 1200 feet per second blew his brains out the other side of the man's head, ending the battle.

Sarah felt the blood running out of her arm and down her chest and slumped to the floor dropping her gun. Su Li ran over to help her stop the bleeding.

As they crouched on the floor behind the desk suddenly a large volume of rifle rounds pounded through the wall and door and hit everything in the office. Su Li threw herself over Sarah as the firepower ripped up the office and pounded the desk and the metal wall to the hanger behind them. Glass shattered, wood splintered, and the noise was deafening.

The fire eased off and Sarah grabbed her cell phone with her right hand. Batting some of the floating paper debris away from her face with her good left hand she hit the EWANs button which sent the emergency alarm call to the rest of the Crossfire Team requesting immediate assistance.

Outside the office three of the Air Force Special Forces were attempting to hold off thirty or so heavily armed attackers. Each of the Special Forces men had found cover to fight in a crossfire arrangement which kept the attackers from rushing the office door. The Spec 4 at the guard shack had tried to stop the troops as they rushed the gate and died in the effort. The high chain link fences with the razor wire on top kept the attackers from doing an end around the AF Special Forces but, the number of the attackers flowing through the open gate would soon overwhelm the defenders when their ammo ran low.

A fresh volley of rifle or machine gun rounds slammed through the wall and Su Li thought furiously. They had two handguns which were probably useless against the firepower outside. The people out there were going to probably kill them and steal the Shrew unless she did something. She remembered that there were eight M-8 assault rifles on the Shrew in two special compartments. But, one rifle against the number out there would be suicidal and she doubted that Sarah would be in any shape to handle a second rifle. Su Li didn't know what to do as more bullets smashed through the office, smashed against the walls, and pounded the desk.

Su Li turned to the only source she knew could save them; she prayed that Yahveh would help them to live through this onslaught. A thought came to her mind and her eyes widened at the implications. She handed her handgun to Sarah who obviously was not up to running at the moment. "I'll be back in a minute after I get rid of the crowd outside!"

Sarah looked at Su Li with a questioning stare but she wasn't paying attention. Su Li waited a few seconds until the firing slowed down again and crawled over to the door to the hanger. Opening it slightly she crawled through it and closed it again. Coming to her feet she sprinted to the lowered stairs at the passenger door of the aircraft.

Racing up the stairs at a dead run she hit the retract button which started raising the stairs and closing the door. Not slowing down. she made her way to the cockpit and dropped into the pilot's seat. Hitting the start sequence button she left the computer to start the engines while she strapped on her helmet and lowered the reticule. The weapons systems came on line as the engines came up to power. Su Li hit the remote control button to open the hanger door and at the same time selected the front chain gun. The hatch snapped open on the right side of the fuselage and the M-134, six-barreled "Gatling Gun" lowered into firing position. Su Li had seen what the 4,000, 7.65 mm rounds-per-minute firepower could do and it was awesome.

As the hanger door opened sufficiently Su Li brought the throttles of the Shrew up slightly and rolled the aircraft out of the hanger. Turning left as she passed the corner of the hanger, she let the nose command the area in front of the office and then hit the landing lights.

The intense light split the night and showed all the details of the dozens of men with rifles moving towards the office. Su Li didn't give them a chance to find cover or fire at the aircraft. She used the reticule and voice command to open up with the M-134. The flame from the Gatling Gun reached out ten feet as hundreds of 7.65mm rounds decimated the area in front of the plane. As Su Li looked from right to left the six-barreled machine gun followed her direction. In only a few seconds she had cleared the area of anything standing and she turned her attention to the gate area where there were muzzle flashes. The Gatling Gun chewed up several trucks and other vehicles, the gate and guardhouse.

The rate of fire was too immense for any defense and by the time she had run out of ammo and the M-134 spun down into silence there wasn't anything left to shoot. Su Li was mad enough to spit nails and by voice command selected "Missiles" and saw the tell-tales that the firing bays were open. If anything out there moved she was going to blow it away.

In her helmet she heard Mark's voice, clear and commanding. "Good job Su Li, we've got it from here."

Coming in above the Shrew two fully armed Air Cobra choppers lit up the area in the parking lot and all the way to the hanger as they hovered above the Shrew.

A Chinook troop helicopter settled down to the ground and the SOG troops led by Jack and David started advancing over the area of combat.

Su Li keyed her microphone, "Mark! Sarah got cut by that phony Colonel. You need to get her some help. She's in the office and bleeding. I'd go in carefully, she's armed and angry."

Mark replied in gratitude and one of the attack choppers settled briefly to the ground and Mark jumped out and ran to the battered office door.

Su Li cancelled the missile activation, shut off the landing lights, and reversed the engines on the Shrew. She backed it up enough so that she could steer it back into the hanger and shut the door.

CHAPTER FIFTEEN

Mark called out at the door of the office, "Sarah, it's Mark. Don't shoot!." He eased open the heavily damaged and bullet hole-riddled door to find Sarah with a little smile on her face as she sat on what was left of the splintered desk that had saved her and Su Li's lives. Her right side was covered in blood.

She had gotten the bleeding to stop with towels from the riddled rest room but still it looked gory. Mark went over to her, gently touched her cheek, and asked her how she was doing.

Sarah winched in pain as she tried to shake her head. "I'm okay, a little worse for wear but nothing some stitches won't fix." She looked at the floor where both the "Colonel" and the "Aide" were lying. Both men had been hit dozens of times by the incoming rounds and were very definitely dead. "I can't say the same for these guys."

Mark walked over to the "Colonel" as he used his combat microphone to call for medical aid for Sarah. Using his foot he moved the man's head so the one still functioning light in the office showed his features.

Walking back to Sarah he frowned and gritted his teeth. "That's Robert LuCay, a French paramilitary buddy of Sam Sturgis. Now, it's time to kill that unwanted spawn of Satan. He's..."

Sarah interrupted him. "You're right; we need to end this thing now. He almost had Su Li and me cold. I didn't even guess that they had troops in the area. I was just bringing the phony Colonel in here to interrogate him and his "Aide". Sorry Mark, I greatly underestimated the situation and should of called for backup before I brought them in here."

Mark nodded, "Yeah, well, that happens. Still, I was confused by this guy's attack on you and the major attack on the office. If Sam wanted you dead he would have had a sniper in the parking area take you out. This whole attack was just weird." Mark considered what he knew of Sturgis' techniques and he got an idea. "But, I think I understand it now. The plan was probably to get you two in here, out of sight, away from the Air Force guards, where LuCay and his buddy could take you down or kidnap you both and then take the Shrew as a bonus. When you and Su Li foiled that plan it threw them off and they went all-out to eliminate you and Su Li." Mark realized he needed to be in prayer because the black anger he felt at Sam wasn't from Yahveh. "Oh yeah, it's time we concentrate on eliminating Sam and his entire operation!"

Sarah saw the flashing lights from an ambulance pull up outside the open door and told Mark. "I can get these injuries patched up. Check on Su Li for me. She really saved our bacon this time."

Two medical corpsmen came into the office and helped Sarah out to the waiting military ambulance. Mark detailed a five man squad to accompany Sarah to the civilian hospital and make sure she wasn't attacked again. He walked over and took some of his anger out by kicking the office door to the hanger open. It had taken enough abuse from the bullets that it flew off its remaining hinge and slammed to the floor of the hanger. Mark stalked through the door in a really dark mood and went to find Su Li.

He found her checking over the plane. She looked up at him and made a little face. "I think she took some rounds and may be out of operation for a while until it can be repaired. Sorry."

Mark put his arm around the small Chinese woman and hugged her to him. "Don't let that worry you. You did a smart move. I owe you a big debt for finding a way to save Sarah and yourself against heavy odds. The details aren't important."

Su Li sighed, "Thanks, but it was Yahveh that put the idea in my somewhat addled mind at the time."

Mark smiled down at the shorter woman. "Okay, you were obedient as well as efficient. I don't think there's anything taller than two inches standing out there. The troop trucks they brought the troops in were turned into scrap metal along with the guard shack. We may never identify some of the mercenary troops after that Gatling gun riddled them. Good call using the Shrew as an equalizer when you were so out-classed in firepower and numbers."

There was a commotion at the hanger door and Su Li went to the wall controls and shut off the hanger lights except for one above the personnel door effectively hiding the Shrew from sight. She then activated the motors opening the personnel door set into the big hanger door. Mark automatically swung his M-8 into firing position as he walked to the door and didn't lower it until he could identify the various law-enforcement and military personnel coming in through the opening.

The Denver Police Captain approached Mark with some trepidation considering the firepower he saw the man was carrying. "Mr. Connelly? I'm Captain Peters of the Denver Police Department and I'd be very grateful if you'd enlighten me as to the reason there is a war zone in my airport here."

Mark nodded and lowered the M-8. "That I will Captain, that I will. By the way, it's General Connelly and I do hope you can give me some idea how thirty or forty heavily armed men could roam around "your" airport until they could affect a full-out military attack on our facilities here."

Su Li thought to herself, "This is going to be a really interesting discussion tonight." She caught the attention of one of the Air Force Security group and made sure that he got the covers over the Shrew and kept everyone except for the Crossfire Team away from the plane.

Twenty minutes later, Mark and the Captain reached agreement concerning the action at DIA and how to present it to the press. No mention would be made of the Shrew, the Air Force personnel who were killed or the vast amount of collateral damage done during the firefight. One errant burst of the M-134 took out seventeen civilian vehicles so badly that they would need to be replaced.

The Captain became far more cooperative when the Governor called and asked him to extend all possible help to the Crossfire Team. Mark figured that General Miles knew the situation and had the President call the Governor. The firefight was played down as gang activity attempting to steal aircraft to use in drug running operations. The few people that survived the fight weren't going to talk to the press about the Shrew or the battle.

Mark called Jack who contacted their insurance company so that the damages could be covered.

Things wound down and the Crossfire Team went home to the Fortress.

The next morning a patched up Sarah came back to the Fortress and got the royal treatment for two weeks as her wounds healed. She brought the news that the Air Force had found Colonel Dunning's body stuffed in a culvert on the air base near Cheyenne Mountain. She also let everybody know that she had been given two units of blood to replace what she had leaked all over the hanger office and that made her officially an American since it was American blood.

Carol sought her out and apologized for not being able to warn either of them about the attack. It simply wasn't foretold in the patterns in heaven. Carol looked at her good friend with concern. "I have prayed for hours about the lapse that caused this attack to be without warning until Yahveh had Hugo tell me what actually was supposed to happen."

"Apparently Sturgis' men were supposed to simply case the place and see if there were any of the team available. If they weren't there then they were supposed to steal the new corporate jet that they'd heard had defeated three fighter jets sent to destroy the team. Apparently surprised by the appearance of the General in charge who was a member of the Crossfire Team, you, they improvised and attempted to take both you and your "pilot" hostage and still steal the plane. The heavily armed troops were simply a backup for the original theft."

When you wouldn't let the imposters in and their demon couldn't influence you because of your closeness to the Father and the fact that Yahshua is in charge of your life, the demon told the two men to kill you both. When you foiled that plan, the demon told the other troops to attack the hanger and kill you both. The whole deviation was because the local demon lost his head in anger and took matters into his own hand. In other words, it wasn't planned at all."

Sarah nodded her head. It suddenly all made sense. She looked at Carol, "Any indication where Sam Sturgis might be found?"

Carol shook her head, "Not yet. But, I have a feeling we may be getting a clue to his whereabouts soon because he is now supported by a demon to maintain his physical health and that has a way of showing up in the demonic plans in heaven."

In the next week Su Li had a team of specialists from Groom Lake flown in to the airport to repair the Shrew. Thirty days of hard labor later a new double row of security fencing surrounded the Crossfire property and hangers. The concrete barriers, solid fencing and the posts supporting it could stop anything short of a tank and there was a lot of razor wire capping the fence to compliment the new video surveillance equipment and sensors. The new fifty-yard long gate isolation area and armored guardhouse would give a suicide bomber heartburn trying to figure out how to attack it without wasting his life uselessly. The whole setup, to any experienced observer, indicated that an attack would not be successful without major weapons like a tank.

At the Fortress Mark used the President's name and that of the CJCS to generate a great amount of interagency cooperation while Jack drove the team's assets to the max to locate Sam Sturgis and his mysterious backers before they attacked the Crossfire Team again.

CHAPTER SIXTEEN

Exasperated by Sam's ability to stay hidden regardless of the amount of effort spent to find him, Charlie Wu decided to drop back into his history somewhat and go at the search from the Chinese Agent methodology.

Charlie took everything they knew about the old and the new Sturgis and mulled it over trying to put himself in the assassin's mind. He knew that all the western governments were actively searching for him so it would profit him to seek the less democratically leaning countries such as the Middle East, China, Russia, or possibly Cuba. While Sam was quite capable of considering the double-blind option and hiding in the west, the odds were too great of accidental discovery.

But then, even dictatorships would profit from selling the west information about such a highly wanted assassin and so he wouldn't want them to know he was there.

Charlie thought, "How do you hide in a dictatorship or a religiously controlled country and still run such high-priced operations like fighter jets or armed attacks in America without irritating the ruling party?"

Charlie remembered a similar case in China several years ago when a French assassin was on the run from Interpol and British MI-6. The man had aligned himself with one of the Tong gangster organizations and was allowed to serve their purposes while still doing high-priced assassinations in western countries. The Chinese government found out about the arrangement and decided to remove the possible embarrassment to their country. Charlie clearly remembered that assignment as it fell to him to bag the assassin.

The thought of that particular man brought back a rush of memories.

------------------------******------------------------

Charlie had been one of the top Chinese internal security agents at that time. It was just before he got promoted and met Linda. He had been given the assignment with the knowledge that he would be going up against one of the most vicious territorial gangs in the country. He realized that it would take subterfuge and great wisdom to move in their world and quietly remove one man that they were protecting.

He had studied all the files on both the Tong and the assassin who was code named the "Scorpion". He locked onto the one weak point the man had. His only vice was gambling. He would go to a local underground casino twice a month and play until he had won a significant amount. The Tong ran the casino and made sure the Scorpion always came away a winner after several hours of play. It was their insurance that he remained away from other Tongs and the government who watched those places.

Charlie was able to get an invitation to the casino on one of the nights the Scorpion was to be there. After waiting four hours without sight of the man, Charlie called it a night and went back to his cover story apartment. He reported in through a dead drop on the way home.

He learned through his control that the assassin had been out of the country doing a job and would be back tonight. Since the man had missed his regular fix of gambling he would most likely show up that evening.

Again Charlie waited and played the roulette table. He had actually won three times his investment when his target came into the room. Charlie was careful not to show any interest in the man but to watch him carefully out of the corner of his eye.

The Scorpion had a serious taste for American poker and spent his entire time at the major player poker table. After winning a considerable amount he cashed in his chips and headed for home accompanied by three of the Tong's enforcers.

Charlie continued playing for over an hour to throw off anyone watching him to see if he had any interest in the assassin.

Back at his apartment he considered the best way to kill the man and still not get caught. The Tong ran the casino and owned the dealer. So there would be nothing doing there. They were in charge of surveillance and protection of the patrons at the casino so it was unlikely Charlie could do anything one-on-one with the Scorpion without paying the price for it. He didn't have a death wish so he needed to be more creative, his specialty.

The concept came to him suddenly. It was brilliant and daring and it was a perfect way to accomplish his goal without having to kill a lot of extra people in the process. He had two weeks before his next encounter with the assassin which should give him the time to prepare his attack.

Over the next twelve days he obtained a particular briefcase along with specialized parts and pieces and worked feverishly on his concept. It suffered several setbacks requiring new parts and a completely new software program which Charlie wrote himself. The program was not something you'd want an independent contract programmer to handle. Several test runs worked flawlessly and he only needed one more unique biological agent and he got that by stealing it from a member of the Tong itself.

The night the assassin was to gamble Charlie arrived at his usual time. He was greeted casually because of his earlier visits and his penchant for spending lots of American dollars. It had been raining and he hurried over to the coat rack on the wall. He put his briefcase on the shelf above the coat rod and carefully positioned it so that the front of it faced the poker playing area. He then hung his wet coat and umbrella from the rod along with the dozens of other coats and umbrellas.

He played quickly this night and kept checking his watch. He continued to do that even after his target had arrived and sat down at the poker table. After losing several hundred dollars Charlie cashed in his remaining chips and collected his coat and umbrella. As he left the casino one of the goons stopped him and asked him why he was leaving when the evening was still young. Charlie told the man that he had an appointment to get more money and would be back later. The goon smiled and opened the door for him. Charlie bowed to the man and put up his umbrella. He then walked down the street in the pounding rain.

After reaching his car he drove around several blocks to ensure he wasn't being followed. He parked several places down from the front door of the underground casino. He donned a large pair of goggles which were in actuality small CCD chips. It was like looking at a movie screen and no one outside the vehicle could tell he was using video gear.

He activated the remote control and the inside of the casino sprang to life on the little screens before his eyes. He pushed the second button and a cross hair appeared on the screen. He moved a small control and the cross hairs moved across the casino until they were locked onto the assassin's neck right at the base of his skull.

Charlie pushed the last button and watched the dart fly true to its target. The man jerked upright and stiffened. He then fell face forward onto the poker table and stopped moving.

Charlie sent one more signal and killed the transmission unit. He then shut down the video gear. He pulled out of his parking place and left the town behind him. The Tong would never use his equipment he knew. That last signal activated a small Thermite fuse which fused everything inside the case in less than twenty seconds. He arrived back at his base in time to report his mission accomplished to his superior.

The Colonel that was his boss asked him how he had accomplished the task. Charlie explained. "I realized he was at one place outside of his armored compound every two weeks. It was a gambling casino that was owned by the Tong. After looking at all angles I decided to use a poison dart fired remotely from a briefcase I had left in the place before the target arrived. The dart hit the assassin right at the base of his skull in the back and he had time to jump slightly before the toxin killed him. He fell to the table dead."

His boss asked him if he wasn't worried about retaliation by the Tong.

Charlie shook his head, "No, I used a briefcase and equipment that are current items the Tong uses. Then I obtained a poison which is very unique and only belongs to a rival assassin also working with the gang. They will quickly determine whose poison it is and settle the matter themselves."

His superior chuckled and noted the file that Charlie had potentially eliminated two assassins at the same time. He congratulated Charlie on a job well done and closed the file on the Scorpion. He then sent a message to his superiors recommending a promotion for Charlie due to his intelligence and resourcefulness.

-------------------------******------------------------

Thinking again about Sam Sturgis Charlie decided he would start checking the underworld connections for any indications of Sam's whereabouts.

Three hours later he had a definite hit from a Russian government camera located in Serov, Russia. After several minutes researching the city and its inhabitants he called Jack Malone and Mark Connelly to a meeting at his office.

After they were seated he brought up a map and gave them the information about the town.

"Serov, pronounced sye'ruf, is a small city with a population of approximately 184,000 people. It is located in Eastern European Russia, in the eastern foothills of the Urals, on the Kakvy River. A metallurgical center, Serov produces cast iron and quality steel and has lignite, iron, bauxite, and gold mines. The town was founded in 1894 in connection with the building of the Trans-Siberian railroad. At that time the city was called Nadezhdinsk. That was until 1939 when it was renamed Serov. Due to its remote location it has attracted the attention of the wrong crowd. The latest addition to the city is a large collection of villas and townhouses in a private, gated community. This new community is owned by the Russian Mafia or as they like to be called, "The Russian Organization". Cameras in Serov have given me several views of Sam Sturgis along with the date and time of the picture. Sam moved in there about three weeks ago. Right after the British bomb he set to kill you guys. My latest satellite surveillance has him living at a villa which has a lot of communications antennas on the roof and a serious number of fixed and roaming guards."

Mark asked, "What is the weather for October in Serov?"

Charlie checked his notes. "It will be chilly to downright frigid in the last half of this month. Temps will run in the low forties during the daytime to a nighttime low of something in the teens. That's absolutely balmy for Russia."

Jack and Mark studied the pictures and the map. Jack congratulated the computer expert on his discovery and decided they needed to brainstorm how to get at their nemesis to eliminate him and his demonic vendetta against them.

CHAPTER SEVENTEEN

The girls were taking a break and discussing life and things that women discuss everywhere. It was a scheduled "venting" session they found to relieve their personal stresses and realign with the others on the team.

Sarah thought to herself, "As an adult I've never had girl friends I could let my hair down and talk to without worrying about security or politics." She made a little face and kicked the informal session off. "Everyone looks in good health. I have my little momentous of the airport battle. But, generally this lifestyle certainly provides sufficient exercise and limits eating out or snacking on the job."

Su Li barked a one note laugh. "That's true, I've lost eight pounds in the last month." She sized up the other women in the group. "And, comparatively speaking, I probably don't need to lose any more."

Laura chuckled and wrote in her "unofficial" log of these meetings. "I'll make a note of your dietary deficiencies and see if I can't increase your caloric intake on missions."

Su Li grinned, "So, you're going to fatten me up?"

Debbie chuckled, "I don't think you'll get the chance to fatten up on this job. You're flying so many hours you probably just break even with a better diet in the air."

Laura looked at Su Li. "Mike White should be here next week with the other Shrew and that should take some of the load off of your back."

Su Li thought about the man that had taught her to fly modern fighter jets and helicopters as a part of his role in the Air Force. Jack Malone had made him an offer he couldn't refuse and he retired from the service and would join the Crossfire Team in a few days. She was looking forward to his guidance and council as the newest pilot in the fledgling Crossfire Air Wing. She broke out in laughter when she realized what the acronym would be.

"You do realize that the Crossfire Air Wing would be "CAW" like the crow speaks. "

Everyone stared at her and she realized her laugh seemed to indicate that Mike's presence wouldn't ease her burden. She hastened to explain her thought about the name.

Carol then laughed in turn. "You could name it the Crossfire Reserve Air Military Indigenous Team or CRAM IT!" That brought down the roof and everyone let a lot of tension go in the hilarious laughter that broke out.

Sarah wiped the tears of laughter out of her eyes and added her comment, "How about "Super High Air Force Team"? Short for SHAFT?"

There was more laughter and a plea to stop there because it was going to cause a mass exit to the bathrooms if it kept up.

Sobering up somewhat, Laura asked if there were any comments, complaints, worries, or concerns they could address.

Debbie spoke up first. "I'd like to talk to Jack and Mark about equipment for sniping. There has been some major improvements in the field in the last two years and I'm not one that wants to fall behind. I can call in a marker or two with my old director and see if he can either bring us up to date or make some of the new things available."

Laura wrote in her log, "I'll talk to Jack and have him get in touch with you on the matter."

Sarah's interest piqued because of her training as a sniper in the Mossad. "Debbie? What new things are you talking about?"

Debbie described some of the newer mods. "I read an article by Victor Epand who is an expert consultant for WarGear.info which carries some of the best military clothing, war gear, and combat accessories on the market including sniper gear. This is a civilian company but they're pretty plugged in and have a good record of being on the leading edge."

"Victor explained about some of the newest things in the field. Modifications that include a cryo-stress relieved heavy barrel, a composite dimensionally stable stock with aluminum bedding blocks to "free float" the barrel which means the barrel is not touched by the stock, so that there is no stress placed on it, and each shot is allowed to harmonically resonate without interference."

She looked at Sarah. "As you know, each rifle is an individual, but I have seen some capable of shooting into a 1/4" bulls eye at 100 yards if the operator can do his part. Operating parameters when I was active were that our military generally did not use night vision scopes. Rather, they used night vision headgear through which they look when operating at night."

Debbie looked around the circle of women, "Scopes don't make rifles accurate. They don't help you shoot better. They help you see better and seeing can be an aid to shooting. But people who don't know how to shoot won't be helped much by any scope, regardless of the cost. Some years ago the military was experimenting with propriety technology in regard to a sighting system, but to the best of my knowledge, the project has been abandoned. The cost was very prohibitive, and somewhere along the line someone figured out that seeing better does not equal shooting better."

Debbie continued, "Although the military has experimented with other cartridges, they still find the .308 or 7.62mm, which has been in use since Korea, to be the most common "sniper" cartridge. It is a good cartridge, but it has more to do with the fact that we have guns chambered in it, and more data on the effects of wind and drops than for any other cartridge. The army sniper school requires shots to 800 meters with this rifle. The U.S.M.C. sniper school requires shots to 1000 meters."

Realizing that most of the women didn't have a intimate knowledge of these things she elaborated, "Those are extraordinarily long shots. If the average rifle can shoot into 1/2" MOA which means a target grouping of your shots in a 1/2" group at 100 yards, then you could shoot very accurately at 1000 yards. Beyond that distance, bullet drop and velocity become such a factor it makes the round fairly ineffective. Above those ranges, say a three thousand to ten thousand foot shot, is typically done with a .50 BMG sniper rifle. Normally these huge cartridges and projectiles are not anti-personnel rounds. Rather, they are used to take out equipment like communications, truck engines, or helicopters. But occasionally they are supremely effective as anti-personnel weapons as Mark proved at the cemetery recently."

Debbie added, "The mission of the military sniper is different from that of the police sniper. The military sniper often looks for targets of opportunity; the police sniper usually has a specific target. The military sniper tries to take his shot from as far away as he can because once he gives away his presence by the shot, the enemy will be looking for him. The police sniper tries to get as close as he can; the military sniper operates in less than ideal conditions; the police sniper usually has a mat to lay on, a flat surface to shoot from, and lots of backup. The military sniper is at the mercy of his environment; while the police sniper is normally in control of his environment. A miss by a military sniper usually causes no immediate harm; a miss by a police sniper means likely that a hostage will die. The roles are significantly different and that is why we have to be super careful because of the vagueness of our authority in some cases within the various countries we have to work in."

"Because of their different operational situations, the military sniper's equipment will trade some accuracy for ruggedness and dependability; because the police sniper shoots "on his terms" his equipment can be the most accurate available, and ruggedness is not an issue. For example, until very recently, U.S.M.C. snipers had fixed power scopes, because variable power was just too fragile for the field).

Debbie tipped her head to one side and looked at Sarah. "Then there are the "rumored" new advances such as the SLRTS or Super Long Range Targeting System that is supposedly capable of compensating for wind, range, drop, movement, and weather. I believe it is a super powerful laser dot backed by some major computer power that gives the sniper the same capability as a handgun laser. You put the dot on the target and that's where the bullet hits."

Sarah blinked at that one. "Wow! Everyone could be a sniper then."

They both laughed at that.

Debbie grinned, "Then there are more secret items that we need to find out about. Such as a new electronic camouflage that makes the sniper completely blend into his background without having to mess with grass and bushes to hide your shape or color. There's one other one I'd like to see if it is real and or available and that is a new .50 BMC cartridge that is not only metal piercing but explosive too. Lots of new things we need to be up on as soon as possible."

Sarah nodded, "One new thing you didn't mention is being developed by Israel. They have been working with several American firms such as Motorola and Texas Instruments on a super secret sniper device that uses several stealth technologies and merges inputs from satellites, ground transmitters, and heat sensors. The device will give a sniper super accurate positioning for targets including true distance to target, tangential angling, and complete darkness sighting including anticipated positioning based on movement and rate. The whole thing can be hand held or attached to the rifle on one of the accessory rails."

Laura ruefully smiled, "I guess we really need to look into the future of sniping. Okay, I'll get on it as soon as I see Jack. Any other comments or concerns?"

The meeting went on for another hour and concerns were voiced and either solved or listed for solution.

After the other women left Carol approached Laura and asked, "When you have so many beautiful and highly talented women in such a high-stress environment how come there aren't little spats and confrontations or complaints?"

Laura grinned, "Carol, this is your specialty. Because we each pray and follow Yahveh as faithfully as we can we avoid ego spats or interpersonal rivalries or even dissatisfactions. Prayer gives each of us the time to express any frustrations or irritations and deal with them honestly. That way they don't become big, ugly, confrontations or arguments. Since we each realize we are walking the path that Yahveh wants us to at this time none of us are dissatisfied with our lot. Plus there's a lot of respect for the talents each of us brings to the table in this war we're in at present. Each one of these women have had their lives saved by one or more of the others and those type of battlefield friendships are much deeper and more meaningful than comparisons on any level. When you know the other person would absolutely give their life up to save yours it makes for real friends."

Carol thought about it and realized that what Laura said was true and she was again grateful that she had been chosen to live and fight with these people.

CHAPTER EIGHTEEN

Jack called all the members together including David's two-man support team and eight of the Crossfire SOG.

He looked around the room at the people assembled and was proud to be associated with such a faithful and talented group of individuals. "People, we have a location on our attacker, Sam Sturgis. The good news is that we have a pinpoint location on the man. The bad news is that he is in a Russian criminal underworld stronghold in the middle of Russia. We need to figure a successful way to neutralize Sturgis and his operation before he kills some of us."

Jack sharpened his tone. "Don't be fooled by him. This is life and death and only one winner will step into tomorrow. Literally, it's him or us. Now I will let Charlie define the problem and then I want solutions, or possible solutions to the problem."

Charlie covered the same data he had for Jack and Mark and then sat down.

Mark got up and ticked off the limitations they had. "First, this is Russia we're talking about. They aren't on good terms with the west especially America. They are in a terrible condition due to lack of services and money. The mass of Russians are poorer than when they had Stalin as a dictator. One of the major reasons is their version of the Mafia or Russian criminal class. The Mafia has taken over the banking system in Russia and controls the money. They are also fully in control of the usual sins, prostitution, gambling, wet work, alcohol distribution, and of course, drugs. The crime syndicate is very strong in Russia and has contacts everywhere. They will not tolerate our entering their country in force or armed to the teeth to exterminate someone they have given sanctuary to for their own purposes."

Mark paced a little, "Sturgis isn't an idiot and knows if he leaves Russia he'll probably be spotted and arrested or killed. His profile is too high and the price on his head is even higher. Therefore, we have to get him where he is regardless of the criminal army and the Russian military inadvertently protecting him. Are there any suggestions?"

The first four suggestions were identical. "We need to pray for Yahveh's will in how to achieve His command in the elimination of Sam Sturgis." So Mark agreed and everyone began praying, alone, or in groups for guidance and direction in this matter.

A short time later a group approached Mark. He noted dryly that it was an all female contingency. "Yes?" He asked with a small smile on his face.

Sarah waved her hand to include Laura, Alexis, Su Li, Linda Wu, Debbie, and Carol as well as herself. "We have gotten a leading that we may be able to pull off. We will join a women's group that wants to tour Serov because there is a popular hotel and wine cavern there. I checked on my pocket PC and found that there is a tour of an all-women's group scheduled to leave four days from today. We'd like to try and join this group and search out Sturgis in our downtime. I'm pretty sure we could find a way to revoke his existence if we were close enough. I can probably get a weapon that Debbie could use to eliminate the man."

Mark furrowed his brow, "Wine Cavern? What is that?"

Sarah shook her head. "Apparently they discovered a group of huge caverns in the hills near Serov that hold a perfect temperature, year round for storing and aging wine both in casks and bottles. Three years ago the world found out about the caverns and with the price so low due to natural refrigeration they send their wines there to be aged naturally. It has become a huge business and offers tours of the caverns and, of course, free wine tasting of hundreds of kinds of wine."

Mark asked her to wait for a few minutes. He took the time to seek the Father himself as to the women's plan. He had learned to distinguish Yahveh's voice from his own or that of the devil and realized it was the Father's will to let them attempt their assassination plan, But, there needed other involvements to assure the completion of their plan. Yahveh just didn't tell Mark what other involvements were required.

Mark felt a finger of dread as he realized he was sending the woman he loved into a very major dose of harm's way. Still Yahveh was in favor of the action and he didn't know of a more capable spy. He looked at his wife and told her, "Okay, set it up and make it work. I expect you home in two weeks. One change though, I believe that Yahveh needs Carol here, at the Fortress."

Sarah could see the concern in Mark's eyes but saw that he accepted the Father's will regardless of his worry. She suddenly got a lump in her throat as she realized that when they left for this trip it might be the last time she saw her husband. She nodded her agreement and turned away as much to hide her tears as to start getting the ball rolling.

Jack came up and watched the women walk away talking excitedly to each other. He turned to Mark. "Okay, what have you done now?"

Mark gave Jack a quick outline of the women's plan and added, "You know they're onto something. For one thing, this women's group they want to join has probably had their plans in place for months. Since it was arranged before Sam got there, the Mafia won't be looking too hard at it."

Jack nodded, "That's true, but as a male I'm not happy with all the women going into deepest Russia to accomplish an assassination. My problem is that I don't know that I'm not happy because they will all be in danger or if I'm worried that they could pull it off, making us guys look bad."

Mark laughed at that. "But, Yahveh says that there need to be other involvements required to make their ploy work. Do you have any ideas?"

Jack nodded, "Yeah, how about you, me, David, Stan, Charlie, and Mike White pulling a HALO invasion of Sam's place and killing him? I'll let you figure out how we get out afterwards."

Mark thought about the plan for a minute. "It may not work for three reasons. Number one is the very good and very real Russian radar network. Unless we can come up with a good reason for a plane to be flying across that part of Russia we will be spotted and probably iced on the way in. Number two is lack of Intel on Sam's hideaway. If the Mafia designed it then we may not have the time to find Sam before the entire Russian army drops in to express their lack of enthusiasm for American commandos. Last, but probably most important is that none of us has Laura's spiritual warfare capabilities. If Charlie is right then Sam is backed by some heavy demonic spirits and with Laura somewhere else we might be in over our heads."

Jack nodded, "All good points. But, we may have an answer. Ex-General Serakov."

Mark's memory flew back to the time that never existed when they and the General had stood together against all odds to save Russia and the world from a demonic invasion. They had all made it through a harrowing experience that Yahveh eliminated from time after they had obeyed his command to stop the nuclear amplification of a demonic rift. That event taught Demetri Serakov that God was real and the General had left Russia and was now working undercover for the U.S. military.

Mark nodded his acceptance but asked, "While that's a good answer for one and two, what about three? We still don't have a demon buster without Laura."

Jack frowned, "Okay, you're right. We need to seriously pray about that."

CHAPTER NINETEEN

While the men were working out a plan of their own, the women refined their scheme with several phone calls and trip details. They knew they had to look like suburban housewives with no hidden agendas to pass as part of the woman's tour of Serov, Russia.

At the same time they needed to have, or acquire the tools to complete the mission. Sarah assured them that they would start from scratch in Serov and do the job. She ought to know, she'd done it dozens of times before while working for the Mossad, several times in Russia.

That thought train reminded her of one memorable trip to Russia in her early years as a Mossad agent.

----------------------******-----------------------

The gray, overcast skies cast a pall over the neighborhood that Sarah was walking into that afternoon. The temperature hovered around ten degrees F and a stiff wind sent chills through her flimsy cotton coat. The overall scene was depressing with old buildings in poor repair, trash blowing in the wind, and the smell of the automobile tire factory a mile away mixing with the smell of sewage and unwashed bodies floating in and out. Everything was shades of gray with no color anywhere. Many windows in the cinder block tenements had no curtains and stared out like glassy eyes from the frayed cinder blocks holding them in place. She used her training to calm down the fear that tried to make her avoid the upcoming conflict.

Sarah kept her head down and acted as hopeless as she could. She knew there were people watching her as she headed home from some obscure job that paid so little it was almost not worth doing. Her head was encased in a shawl that mostly covered her face. Her shoes were worn half boots with dirty socks sticking out of them. She wondered just how these people could face each unrelenting day after day like this. No hope of improvement and no hope of escaping the life-sucking poverty.

Her target was just ahead of her on the right. There was only one guard who wasn't openly displaying any weapons. He looked as poor as her and just as cold and miserable. She knew better. His name was Boris Tradkey and he pulled down over three thousand American dollars worth of pay each month. He was just blending in and acting innocent. His file included the three Israeli agents he had killed six months ago. All three shot in the back by the supposedly trustworthy Boris. But he wasn't her target, just a means to acquire the weapons she needed to take down the Russian Mafia leader and the Israeli traitor. They were meeting in the first floor apartment right now to give Hiram his blood money. Not if she had anything to say about it.

She turned into the walk leading to the apartment house and shambled up to Boris as if she was going to pass him and go into the building. She was counting on Boris being the putz he normally was according to his file.

Boris stepped in front of her bringing her to a halt with an upraised hand palm outward. In Russian he told her that the way was closed unless she had some Rubles for him.

She stared at him as if she was in a fog until he repeated his demand in a louder voice. She slowly took out a small coin purse that was so worn it looked like it couldn't last much longer. She opened it and took out three rubles and held them out to the heavy-set thug.

He grinned and reached out to take the money. Sarah let her hand shake until the coins dropped to the concrete between them. She let fear show in her eyes and put her left hand to her mouth in astonishment at what she had done.

Boris got a mean look and pointed to the coins and told her to pick them up. She squatted and reached for the coins with her left hand. Boris tried to stomp on her hand with his right foot as she groped for the coins.

This was the opening Sarah was waiting for. She let the eight-inch sharpened metal peg slide out of her right coat pocket into her right hand and slammed it into Boris' groin so quickly he never saw the movement. His face turned ashen as the pain surged through his body and he gasped in a big breath. Sarah continued with her strike and pulled the stake out of his groin and rose quickly and then rammed the peg up through Boris' throat and chin, effectively shutting off any shout he wanted to release. His eyes got big and the look of fear was a tangible thing on his face. Blood squirted and ran everywhere from his wounds. Sarah continued her movement of the steel spike up through Boris' head until it came out the top of his head switching off his brain. She caught his dead body and pushed him back into the covered entry way.

Sarah quickly took the MP-5 submachine gun he had slung over his right shoulder and checked it for a full load and a live round in the chamber. She also took the Marakov 9MM pistol from his belt holster.

Rising to her full height she walked carefully to the door to the first apartment and listened at the door. She heard Hiram counting in Hebrew and the other man telling him in Russian to hurry up because it was the full amount.

She carefully and slowly opened the door and saw the two men at the desk in the middle of the room. Checking for any other guards and not finding any she pushed the door open and emptied the submachine gun into both men with no warning. The bullets punched into Hiram's back and the other man's chest and flew out the other side in major blood splatters. The Russian fell backwards in his chair and his legs stayed in the air. Hiram slammed into the desk and fell backwards onto his back as money flew everywhere in the air.

Sarah walked over quickly with her hearing stunned by the loud reports of the submachine gun. Dropping the empty submachine gun she held the pistol at arm's length and stopped over Hiram. He hadn't given up on life yet and he looked sadly up at Sarah with the word "Why?" on his bloody lips. Sarah looked at him with no pity. "Because you had three of my friends killed!" She pointed the pistol at his forehead and triggered one round, sending Hiram to Sheol where he belonged.

She turned to the Russian and gave him the same security shot even though he looked dead. One never knew.

Throwing the pistol on the desk she grabbed the bag full of money off the desk and lightly ran to the back of the apartment. Checking carefully outside, she shed the cotton coat and the shawl. Then she kicked out the window. She crawled out and ran quickly to the end of the building. She pulled on a bright blue hooded jersey which she had hidden by wrapping it around her waist under her flimsy coat She walked on the concrete in her shoes until she came to the main door in the next building. Her footprints had dried from the snow by then. Holding the bag of money like a purse she turned and ran quickly to the street. She started jogging away from the scene of the shooting. No one is going to try and escape dressed in bright colors and she knew the police would know that.

Sarah tensed as she heard a car pull to the curb right behind her. The car idled up next to her and a voice in Hebrew asked her if she would like a ride. She turned and looked at David Zahavy and smiled. "Sure, sailor", she said in Hebrew.

Sarah had never regretted her occupation and thought that she had completely forgot the death she had dealt that day after she was debriefed.

-----------------------*****-----------------------

Today it was the same thing but with a different agenda and a different target. She wasn't going in alone this time and in her world that meant that she had more people to take care of during the operation. She smiled; she knew that Yahshua was really the one that was watching over them. She would do the best she could with her training but now it was lead by prayer and her path was guided by angels.

CHAPTER TWENTY

Roseanne Taylor was very intelligent and not just in finance and economies either. She had grown up during her early years on some rough streets and in a hard neighborhood. She had street smarts and knew that there was a lot more to the request from Sarah Miller than met the eye.

The inclusion of six additional women into their depleted group was actually a Godsend. The original trip had been arranged and paid for to include fourteen women and those flight and hotel accommodations had been made three months ago and were non-refundable. The loss of four members in a single car crash last week would have pretty well scrapped the trip because they couldn't meet the quota requirements for the group rates. But, then to make matters worse, two other women were lost to the trip, one to illness and the other to nerves. That had led to a very glum travel group meeting last night.

While they were deciding how to give up the trip and accept the financial losses the phone rang. Roseanne had taken the call from this Sarah Miller asking if they could be included in the trip and offering to pay, not only their own way, but the entire cost of the trip, with the exception of drinks or shopping. The four thousand dollars each person had already sunk into the trip would be able to cover a lot of shopping and drinks. That would make this trip one of the most memorable in their history.

The meeting had been suddenly turned into a frenzied generation of packing lists and trip preparation sessions with more details popping up constantly. They adjourned after two a.m. That night, as she laid in bed next to her husband who was snoring lightly, Roseanne wondered just what the new people would be like, if they would fit in, or would they think they were better than her and her group because they were paying.

Shaking her head she knew that it was her own insecurities talking. The new members would be just fine. She drifted off to sleep dreaming of the trip to come.

Laura and Sarah were looking over the files on each of the eight women they were to join up with for the trip to Russia. The files weren't complete because of the short notice and investigators had not had the time to dig into their histories deeply. But the files were still fairly detailed after Charlie Wu and his complex of CRAY computers had pulled all known and public information about each woman.

Sarah closed the last folder and smiled. "Nothing here to worry about except that they don't have a clue that their Russian adventure is sponsored by, facilitated by, approved by, and will be overseen by a Russian criminal cartel."

Laura prayed quietly about the danger they could be putting the civilians in by going as a part of their trip. "You know, we could endanger these ladies if we get caught and are identified as a part of their tour. They could be either arrested and detained or taken captive by the Russian Mafia. Neither one would be a fun experience if it didn't turn out to be fatal."

Sarah sighed, "Yes, I know that. We must make sure we don't get caught or killed so as to not draw attention to the club."

Laura laughed, "Is that like the man who went to the doctor and told the doctor that if he raised his left arm it hurt. And the doctor told him not to raise his arm so it wouldn't hurt?"

Sarah grinned, "Right, keep them out of harm's way, don't get caught."

Laura flipped open one folder and pointed at the history in it. "This Roseanne Taylor, the one you talked to, she has a gang background and looks to be pretty smart. I don't know if we can fool her completely."

Sarah shook her head. "It is in her best interest to not know what we are doing. That way she can honestly say she wasn't involved."

As the women continued to prepare for the trip that they had to leave for in less than ten hours, the men were making progress on their efforts.

Mark finished bringing the Chairman of the Joint Chiefs of Staff up to date on their efforts to find and eliminate Sam Sturgis. General Howard Miles provided his assistance and they were able to get ex-Russian General Demitri Serakov assigned to their team for the duration.

They explained what they wanted to do by phone to Demitri as he was traveling to Denver from Washington.

He listened to the requirements and the locations involved. Then he responded, "I think I have an idea how we can not only get in undetected, but get out alive after dispatching this person. I will explain it to you when I see you."

After they hung up Jack told Mark, "Good old Demitri, straight to the point."

Mark laughed and shook his head, "If it were only that simple."

CHAPTER TWENTY-ONE

As the seven Crossfire Team women sat on the 767 airliner on their way to Virginia to meet up with their tour mates they chatted and acted like normal people. One pair at a time read up on the literature on Serov and the wine cavern they were to visit and tour and quizzed each other as to the details. Laura reminded the team that the women they were going to partner with may not be Christians and have different morals and mores than the people in the team were used to.

Sarah thought back to her farewell from Mark and it saddened her to realize they wouldn't be together on this mission. Relaxing into silent prayer she sub vocalized her love for the Son and the Father and felt peace flow through her mind and body. She knew they would always be together, in heaven if not here on earth. She recalled the look of knowledge in his eyes that he was thinking the same things she was about their splitting up for the assignment. He had hugged her gently and told her that he would see her in a couple of weeks, if not sooner. She hadn't gotten any details out of him as to what they were going to do because he didn't want her to have to try and act like she was innocent of his doings, she would be innocent.

Laura was also in silent prayer asking Yahveh to cover each and every one of the men and women assigned to this mission. She asked for a special cadre of angels to protect Jack and to help her in her spiritual combat with the demons involved with Sam Sturgis.

In the heavenly realm Rose looked at Caleb with determination and concern for the welfare of the humans in their care.

As the sun climbed into the sky, the big airliner landed at Washington Dulles International Airport located in Chantilly, Virginia. The airport was about twenty six miles from downtown Washington, DC.

The other eight women had taken a shuttle from Roanoke, Virginia to the airport. When the team members exited the walkway from their flight it wasn't hard to spot the other half of the tour. Roseanne was holding up a big sign saying "Serov - This Way!" in bright pink letters on a blue background.

The two groups came together and exchanged hugs. In the milling crowds on the main concourse they introduced the members to each other. Sarah introduced herself, Laura, Alexis, Linda Wu, Su Li, and Debbie as avid travelers who were interested in touring a part of the world most people don't even know exists.

Roseanne introduced herself and her group of eight. Su Li was intrigued by the nonchalant way these women were planning to go traipsing into a relatively hostile nation for a sightseeing trip. She sized up the women as they were introduced. Roseanne was of average height, a little overweight but pretty. She said that she was an account executive in an accounting firm in Washington. Su Li knew from her file she was a solid worker and still moving up in her company. The entire group was Caucasian except for the second lady introduced, Mary Burrows. Ms Burrows was African American and a very sweet person. The others were introduced and became a blur for Su Li. One thing she was sure of was that none of these women had ever had to fight for their lives, at least not yet.

Roseanne looked over the new additions to the tour and noted that each of the women were physically fit with no extra pounds and a grit and determination in their eyes which belied their chatter and quietness. It caught her attention that the two Oriental women didn't form a separate little part of the group but were integrated totally with the others. Even the smaller woman, Debbie, had an aura of power or hardness that spoke volumes to Roseanne about her being in command of her part of life.

The entire gaggle of females moved to the boarding ramp which was only three doors down from where the Denver flight arrived so that no one had to go through security again.

As they presented themselves to the airline staff at the podium, Roseanne quietly said to Sarah, "I'm afraid that it will be a long trip because we have to travel in coach and these days the airlines are squeezing the seats and luggage space as tight as they can. We just try to endure the flight by playing games and switching seats so we can all talk to different people on the flight."

Sarah smiled and displayed a naturally casual command of the situation, "Well then, I've got some good news for you and the rest of the ladies. Su Li is a pilot and she pulled some strings for us. We're all flying business class both ways!"

Roseanne stared at her in unbelief. "Those tickets have got to cost seven thousand dollars each!"

Sarah laughed, "No, actually it's closer to nine thousand but we get Thank You points on all the tickets. Anyway, it's my husband's money and he makes enough to let us treat you because you were nice enough to let us join your tour." Roseanne blinked several times as her financial mind ran tallies of the costs. The she smiled and turned to tell her group the good news. There was a group yell of "YES!".

The ticket agent at the podium handed out the business class tickets to all of the members and led them past the other passengers to the boarding ramp. He turned to them and smiled. "Your group will be the first to board today, Have a pleasant trip and if there is anything you need just ask the flight attendants and they will do their best to take care of you." He stood aside and let the women pass into the loading tube. He then went back and announced the normal business class boarding call.

After they had boarded and gotten to their luxurious seats, Mary Burrows came up to Sarah and smiled somewhat timidly. "Ms. Miller, I don't feel right taking this expensive seat and costing you all that money."

Sarah had become very experienced in handling personal interactions in her varied careers and she was touched by the humble woman's words. She took the older lady's hands and turned her around and invited her to sit down in her seat. Once she was seated, Sarah sat down next to her and looked into her eyes. "Ms. Burrows, I have seen a lot of people in my time that don't deserve to ride in business class and you are not one of them. Your Father in heaven loves you. This is an opportunity for us to bless you as we have been blessed by the Lord." Sarah took Mary's hands in hers and softly, with passion, she told the smaller woman, "You ARE an adult daughter of the Most High therefore you deserve all the blessings of a King's daughter. That includes having a first class seat. Its way past time you got the chance to enjoy it. You know who you are, don't let other people's attitudes keep you from being who you are, okay?"

Mary Burrows was surprised, comforted, and built up in her estimation of herself. She felt something special in her heart and somehow knew that Sarah was speaking the true love of God. Mary sensed something special about this woman which didn't have anything to do with the money. This woman was special and Mary wanted to know her better. She would stay close to her during the trip. Mary smiled at the dark skinned Caucasian and said, "You obviously have had some of those attitudes in your face and I'll bet my last dollar you came out on top every time."

Sarah smiled a little ruefully and winked at Mary, "Well, maybe not every time but a lot of the time." She patted the smaller woman's hand and got up to go to her seat as the flight attendants asked everyone to sit down and put on their seat belts.

Mary Burrows buckled her seat belt on and reclined into her very plush seat. She thought about what that nice Ms. Miller told her and realized that she had forgotten who she was in Christ. She saw Roseanne looking back and grinning at her from the row in front of her and to her right. She grinned back and gave her the thumbs up sign.

The huge 747 rose majestically into the air and came around to the east towards Europe and begin to climb and accelerate.

CHAPTER TWENTY-TWO

After seeing the women off to the airport, the men hung around for an hour and met Demitri Serakov as he deplaned from his flight from Washington.

Demitri looked Slavic, even distinctly Russian. He was about six foot one inch in height and probably weighed about two hundred and ten pounds. He was a bear of a man with a large chest and bulked out arms and legs. You just knew he could run through walls and not stop.

He came up to the team and gave each of them a bear hug. "It is good to see you again my friends. So we go in the way of danger together again?"

Mark smiled, "Demitri, when it comes to Russia I don't know anyone else I'd rather have with us than you."

The Russian laughed, "That's because I know where all the good bargains are, right?"

Jack laughed, "Sure, that's it."

They got Demetri's bag and took him back to the Fortress in one of the Cadillac Escalades. It was a good thing they brought two of the larger SUVs because the ex-General wouldn't fit in a much smaller vehicle.

Demitri was more than impressed by the Fortress, he was awed. "I have never, ever, seen such a magnificent dwelling. The Tsars palaces were rubble compared to this place. I am honored to be here."

Stan Hargrove laughed. "It is nice, isn't it? I am becoming attached to this place myself."

David Zahavy shook his head. "Guys. We need to get to work planning this operation or we will miss the grand finale for Sam Sturgis."

The whole team fell to discussing the various aspects of the mission. After forty minutes of listening to all the different views, Demitri held up his paw of a hand. "Enough! We can do this and I will now tell you how."

He stood up and put his hands behind him and stood at ease in front of the rest of the team. "As I see it, there is only one way we can pull this off on my old comrades and hope to live to tell the tale." He waved one hand in front of himself. "Concerning the military, the radar, the guards, pffft –they are nothing! We can get by them without a hitch. It's the criminal element we could have a problem with. They are stupid, rich, armed to the teeth, and aggressive as a wolf that hasn't eaten in ten days. They are highly unpredictable and given to excesses when they feel like it. But, I think we can cow them too."

Mark smiled, "Pray thee, tell us how."

Demitri smiled back. "By becoming part of the Russian Army! That's how!" He resumed his at ease pose and continued, "Let me tell you how that can be done by us. I have many contacts in my homeland and I haven't been gone long enough for them to have all died or been captured. I will arrange for us all to have the appropriate papers and be smuggled into the country. We will then meet with some of my contacts and acquire some clothes and weapons and suddenly, we will be a Spetznaz Commando Strike Team."

He grinned at the concerned looks. "Don't worry, we will acquire the proper papers and code words and transportation. What I see is that this Strike Team will have orders to arrest this Sam Sturgis for crimes against the state. The criminals will argue but who cares? If they give us any resistance we will shoot them. If they escalate, then I will call in more, real Russian Strike Teams and the criminals will lose. While they are sorting out all of the players we will take our prisoner and fade out of sight. Never to be heard of again as a Spetznaz Strike Team."

He looked at the collective faces in front of him. "You like?"

Working out the details actually only took six hours and the entire team was on a military MATS flight to Germany immediately after that.

While the military air transport service aircraft was winging its way across the Atlantic Ocean, Jack was talking to Mark. "Do you think this operation will go as smoothly as Demitri thinks it will?"

Mark shook his head. "No, that's why the Americans are way ahead of the Russians at innovative warfare. The concept is solid but the secrecy sucks. Anyone of his "contacts" could sell us out and probably will. But, Yahveh says go with it and go we will."

Jack looked at the assembled team asleep or resting in the cargo netting seats on the MATS plane. Besides Demitri, Mark, and himself, there was David Zahavy, Charlie Wu, Stan Hargrove, and John Harris, Mike Coffer, and Willie Peterson. The last three were Crossfire SOG warriors who volunteered for the mission. All three of them looked like soldiers in top shape. Demitri had insisted that there be eight "Spetznaz" soldiers to make a normal squad. With him as the officer and his eight troopers he felt they could pull off the mission and get out alive. Mark wasn't so sure. He held his silence because Yahveh wanted him to go along with the gig. But he was sure going to keep his eyes open.

The plane landed in Germany and the crew was ferried through what used to be East Germany, Poland, and finally to a dark little basement near the Russian border.

The rat-faced man who stood in the basement would only deal with Demitri. He took the American dollars the General had been given and produced a leather bag with official papers in it. Demitri handed out the papers to each of the crew and everyone examined them.

Fortunately, besides Demitri; Mark, David, John Harris, and Willie Peterson were also literate in spoken and written Russian. Mark was impressed by the quality and used look of the identification papers, passports, and orders he had. The pictures of him were current and the one showing him in his Spetznaz uniform and helmet had probably been photo shopped but you couldn't tell it. He took out another thousand dollars and gave it to Demitri to give to the man to insure his silence and to also thank him for the impressive work in such a short time.

The man looked at the extra money and blinked. He walked over and shook Mark's hand and told him that if he needed anything else just ask for Isak.

Mark replied in Russian that he would.

Outside they walked over to a large canvas covered vehicle which turned out to be a Russian BTR-60. Demitri explained about the vehicle. "The replacement for the

BTR-152, the eight-wheeled BTR-60 evolved the Russian APC design from the "truck overloaded with armor" setup to the more advanced boat-shaped hull layout. This allowed the BTR-60 to gain full amphibious availability, a foreboding profile and significant protection from small-arms fire and shrapnel. This vehicle is able to transport 14 fully-armed troops across rough waters and rough terrain, the addition of a heavy machine gun with a turret similar in design to the BDRM-2. This feature enhanced the offensive ability of this fierce transport. Though no longer used extensively as an APC, the BTR-60 still sees use as a combat operations support vehicle. It is a suitable transport for our uses and will not incur attention."

He turned to Isak, "Is it fully armed and equipped?"

Isak smiled, "Only the best for you and your American dollars."

They entered the vehicle and Demitri let Mike Coffer do the driving. Mike had experience in this type of vehicle when he was an "Aggressor" in the war games of last year.

Following Demitri's orders everyone else sat down and became Russian soldiers. The BTR-60 growled out of the barnyard and onto the dark, wet road. In less than twenty minutes they came to a checkpoint. There was a bar across the road, the small shack and the bored sentries. Their orders and papers were inspected and they were passed through routinely.

After about two more hours Demitri had the BTR-60 driven onto a dirt road and into the country towards a single prominent mountain. The road wove around the mountain. As the beast crawled along the Russian pointed to a large cave in the side of the mountain and had the vehicle driven into the cave. He had Mike Coffer drive the vehicle all the way to the back of the cave. In the gloom he had everyone get out.

Mark studied the General for a few seconds. "A double blind, right?"

Demitri nodded his head. "Da, it is good, no?"

Mark reserved judgment for later. Demitri had them open the engine compartment while he dug out some tools from a small compartment. He almost climbed into the engine compartment and proceeded to disconnect a device about the size of a toaster.

Holding it up he pointed at it. "A masterpiece of Russian miniaturization. No?"

Jack asked, "What is it?"

Demitri laughed, "It is a GPS tracking device. We've been tracked all the time we've been in Russia. Now is the time to change the rules and throw the dogs off of the track. He explained what he wanted to do and everyone got to work doing it. They prepared by packing everything they needed in three backpacks. Demitri told them, "Isak is double-crossing the double-crossers. He got paid by us, he will get paid for his part by Russian Intelligence, and he will get paid again by the criminals. We, on the other hand are going to disappear off of their radar."

Mark said, "We will disappear and it won't be his fault?"

Demitri shook his head. "No, no. He will have given the two groups the correct GPS signal and told them how many people but nothing more. I expect nothing less from him. Neither do the others. They are just checking every unknown group moving around in Mother Russia. A very tall order and we may not even warrant the extra effort."

He took one of the batteries from a sighting system and jerry-rigged the GPS system except for the final wire. Going over to the other wall of the cave he found a small wooden box. Placing the GPS device in the box he exited the cave with his hood up, just in case there was a satellite watching him. He put the box in a fast running stream and connected the last wire. Releasing the box he turned and re-entered the cave.

Poking his left thumb over his shoulder he said, "That should travel twenty to thirty kilometers before it gets stuck. If they are tracking it, they'd better have helicopters because the terrain is very bad where that stream goes, lots of canyons and wadis. Now, we need to be somewhere else before they track the GPS unit back to this cave.

Demitri wired a box of Sematex to a trigger and shooed everyone out of the cave under a tarp to hide their numbers and faces. He wired the entrance with a retro reflector switch and connected it to the trigger. He then set a timer and wired it into the switch.

Charlie watched him set the dual triggers and asked him why. Demitri looked over his handiwork and smiled at the computer genius. The timer is to blow everything up and hide our evidence. The optical switch is in case the timer doesn't work. That way I don't kill my countrymen unless they are just too close. Then it will be their fault for being so efficient."

Charlie nodded as he saw the logic to the arrangement.

After reaching the cover of the trees and ditching the tarp they started running. Demitri set a fast pace because they needed to be ten miles away in just over two hours. Everyone was in good shape and used to hoofing it but the extra weight of the weapons, ammunition, and the back packs made it rough work. Everybody, including Demitri shared the load.

After two hours of running they came to a railroad track. Demitri scoured around until he found a suitably large tree that had fallen. With the help of the others he pulled it to the track and laid it across the track. He motioned everyone into the trees on the west side of the track and waited.

Demitri called everyone to him and explained. "We are going to get on this train when it stops to remove the tree. It is essential that we are on the roof of the last car of the train before it stops so the guards won't see us when they get off."

Demitri continued, "There are normally five or six private cars at the end of these trains. We are going to commandeer the last car and use it to get to Serov. We will be going through Moscow but it is a casual check as the train was checked thoroughly by the military when it loaded and started on its trip."

CHAPTER TWENTY-THREE

The Virginia Women's Tour was being bused to Serov by luxury coach. It was easily comparable to the first-class air accommodations and made the long trip a fun exploration of the countryside and towns as they quietly sped along through the Russian landscape. The occasional roadblock with soldiers with machine guns seemed quaint and not threatening to the non-team members.

Laura looked out the window and wondered where Jack was and if he was safe. She gave her love to the loving hands of their heavenly Father and turned back to Roseanne to answer her question about Laura's normal life when she wasn't touring. Laura decided to consider the Crossfire Team's activities as touring and told Roseanne about her earlier life as a vice president in a Denver accounting office, similar to the one Roseanne worked for in Washington, DC.

The bus smoothly transitioned across a railway crossing and accelerated on down the road. Ten minutes later a loud blast of the air horns announced the arrival of an express train crossing the same path.

In the last car of the train, Demitri was looking through the mail to see if he could find anything useful. The mail car attendant was lying back in the forest southeast of Moscow with a broken neck and not a care in the world.

Jack recalled the assault on the mail car after the train started up again when the log was removed from the track. He and Mark had opened the door in the front of the car to find that the last car was a mail car and full of sacks of letters and packages. A skinny, medium height, young man with the facial results of a terrible case of acne when he was young, looked up from sorting mail and asked what they wanted. He wasn't aggressive because of the uniforms and the rifles they had at the ready.

Mark told him to mind his own business. They proceeded to search the car for other people and were involved in the search when they heard a "snap-crunch" and turned around to find the mailman dead in the very large arms of Demitri. He reached down and pulled the automatic pistol out of the dead man's grasp. Demitri had entered from the back of the car in time to catch the mailman before he could shoot both Jack and Mark in the back.

Demitri reopened the back door of the car and looked around the corner toward the front of the train. When the train went around a left hand bend he tossed the body away from the train into the brush on the side of the tracks. He then climbed the ladder and signaled the others on the roof to join them on the inside of the car.

Jack prayed for the lost soul of the mailman and sat down on a bag of mail. At the rate the train was moving this could be a long trip.

Actually, in a Moscow suburb, the cross country engine was switched for an express engine and the trip became much shorter, only about twenty hours.

When the train reached the station at Serov, Demitri marched his elite Spetznaz team off the train and into the town. No one interfered with them or even looked at them so as to not attract their attention.

Having spent two miserable days in Serov in his recent career Demitri knew where the military barracks was and marched his troops through the frigid Russian October evening and arrived there in less than ten minutes.

He put them at ease while he talked to the post commander. He showed his phony orders to the man and insisted on secrecy to prevent the traitor they were after from learning of their presence. The post commander was only a first year officer and was both impressed with Demitri and at the same time terrified of the presence of such an elite unit on his poor post. He gave them the best accommodations he had and cautioned his men to not notice the newcomers, they would be gone soon, hopefully.

For Charlie, Jack, and Stan, the conditions were military and rough. For Mark and the three SOG warriors the whole scam reminded them of their years in the service and they easily fell back into the routine of hurry up and wait. Jack realized it was new to him but he was a quick study and he emulated the actions of the others so that he fit in. At least the barracks were heated and didn't stink too bad.

Demitri changed into civilian clothes and told Mark to keep the troops from getting restless while he went out and scoped out the villa that Sam was supposed to be in and the layout of the villa if possible. He left on the note that "everything is available for hard currency in the criminal world."

Mark and John Harris went out and came back with a couple of bottles of Vodka and some tasty bread. Even this late at night there were vendors on the street and like Demitri said, "everything was available."

Jack wrinkled his nose at the smell of the Vodka and looked at Mark. "Do you think it's smart to drink before we go after Sturgis?"

Mark made a lop-sided grin. "No, but we would be way out of character if we hadn't searched for Vodka and vittles while the boss is away. That little non-standard action could cause someone to think we're not who we want them to think we are."

Jack could agree with that but he and the others refrained from drinking the stuff that smelled a lot like jet fuel.

Two hours later Demitri came back in and made a lot of noise about the booze for the entertainment of the other troops.

Then he unfolded some drawings of the villa that Sam Sturgis was in and the grounds around it. He also had some good intel on the rotation of the "criminal" guards that protected the terrorist.

After considering the time clicking away on their discovery clock they decided to take the villa tonight since Sam was supposed to be there according to semi-possibly-reliable sources. Actually they decided on three o'clock in the morning, local time as the best attack time. That's when the guards circadian rhythms were at their lowest and they would be the least wary. This was true anywhere around the world. After a long, uneventful watch which would be over in two to three hours a person was just not at the top of their game.

CHAPTER TWENTY-FOUR

Earlier that morning the women's tour had unloaded from their bus and moved into their four-star hotel rooms. Most of the Virginia girls decided to get in a nap before exploring the city. The six women from the team were in much better shape and asked for a guide to show them the city.

Alexis and Sarah were conversant in Russian and got a reasonable guide for the group and while they took digital pictures of everything and stopped to shop in some of the stores they kept their eyes open and spotted the members of the Russian Mafia without a lot of effort. When the guide was about to direct them to another group of vendors, Alexis asked him to show them the flashy villas set into a gated community on the edge of town.

The guide demurred and strongly suggested that they not get involved with those buildings as they were off limits. A little prodding produced the fact that they were maintained for special guests and there were armed guards.

While they were discussing the options the smaller gate swung open and three men walked out. They walked past the gaggle of tourists without looking at them. Sarah's blood grew icy as she recognized Sam Sturgis as the lead man in the pack. She really wished she had a pistol right then.

Sam's guardian spirit recoiled from the bright light of the spirits of the tourists and tried to make Sam turn away or bettered yet, run. Sam ignored the urgings. He was professional enough not to show even a flicker of his internal strife. He had noticed this reaction around other people and just felt that the spirit riding him was a coward. Sam was not about to let a wimpy ghost direct his mind or activities. He didn't look to see what the people around him looked like because he had a lot on his mind right then.

Sturgis and his guards disappeared into a store and the guide insisted that they move along. They continued the tour for another half hour and then went back to the hotel. Once in their rooms Laura stared at Sarah. "Do you think he recognized any of us? He had to have some kind of picture of you and Su Li from the action at the airport hanger battle in Denver."

Being used to working undercover, Sarah shook her head. "No, he didn't even bother to look at us. We were just another bunch of silly tourists."

Alexis frowned, "We need to reconnoiter that villa area tonight and see if we can't pinpoint Sturgis' den of iniquity. Then we can plan an attack. How do we find a rifle for Debbie?"

Sarah had been thinking about that. "Tonight we need to find some drunk soldiers from that military post on the north side of town and get the rifle we want. Who's up to rolling drunks?"

They all agreed that they should do both activities at once to reduce the possibility that Sturgis could get wise or leave and the trip would have been in vain. After spending the afternoon with the tour group, Sarah and Laura would look around the villas while Alexis, Linda Wu, and Debbie would get a sniper rifle from the military base. Su Li got the short straw and would stay at the hotel to remove any suspicions in the event one of the other ladies wondered where they had gone.

It was an interesting evening which involved a significant amount of wine tasting and just flat drinking. By the early evening hours the Virginia girls felt the need to get some real sleep because things were getting fuzzy and quite tiring. The team members played along and looked like they were getting tipsy also. In reality everyone had nursed a single drink all afternoon and didn't drink it until it was so diluted by ice cubes it was mainly a flavor.

After wishing everybody a good evening and arranging to meet in the morning to tour the wine cavern they had heard so much about, the women parted ways and went to their rooms for the night. It was about three a.m. local time.

Laura and Sarah dressed in black slacks and pullovers and took black gloves and ski masks with them. Slipping out the back entrance where they wouldn't be noticed leaving at that late hour, they made a beeline for the nearest bar just in case there were watchers.

A few minutes later they left the bar and headed for another one. When Sarah was sure they weren't being watched or followed she led Laura to the gate to the villas. There was an keypad for the smaller personnel gate and Sarah pulled out a small spray bottle. Carefully spraying the keys she saw which ones were the most used. Trying different combinations resulted in the door swinging open. The two women walked in and then walked carefully down the street checking out the villas.

Laura spotted the guard first and touched Sarah's arm. They melted into the shrubbery near the entrance to the next villa and studied the setup. Sarah whispered in Laura's ear, "There's only one guard here. There may be another one in the back or even a roving guard. Let's see if we can use this villa's fence to circumnavigate the guard's coverage."

They crept into the front area below the entry to the next door villa and ghosted back to the back area. Laura pulled her black ski mask down so that only her eyes showed and her blonde hair was hidden. She slowly pulled herself up on the connecting fence and studied the back of the target villa. Letting herself down she quietly told Sarah, "There doesn't seem to be a roving nor a back door guard. Is that suspicious?"

Sarah shook her head. "I really don't know what the normal setup is. We'll have to risk it to check out the place. Remember, we don't want them to know we were here if possible."

Laura took a minute to pray about what they were doing and ask Yahveh for his mighty protection for each of them and the others that were doing His business this evening so far away from home.

Sarah put her ski mask on and together they climbed the fence and quietly dropped into the back yard area of the target villa. Sarah noticed that there were lights shining on the second story of the villa. She checked for IR detectors, video cameras, or other sensors but didn't find anything. She tried the back door knob but it was locked.

Laura was looking the rest of the building over and found an access to the basement. Signaling Sarah to join her she waited quietly. When Sarah was ready they carefully lifted the door that covered the entrance. Leaving it open they crept down the stairs. Down there, they brought out small flashlights and looked around. Mainly storage and supply bins and cabinets. Sarah went back and carefully closed the door to the outside so if the guard did walk by he wouldn't see the open door.

Halfway down the basement they found stairs that led upward. Checking the stairs for sensors and finding none the two women crept to the top of the staircase and listened at the door. Everything was quiet. Laura tried the door knob to the first floor only to find it locked, She looked at Sarah and whispered quietly, "What? Doesn't this guy trust his neighbors?"

Just then Sarah heard footsteps headed towards the door from the other side. Leading the way back down the stairs she slid down the handrails and landed lightly on the cement floor. Laura was right behind her. They went two different directions and found cabinets or crates to hide behind and turned off their lights.

With a click and clack the upstairs door was unlocked and light beamed into the basement from the open door. Someone stepped onto the first step and flicked a switch. The basement was suddenly lit by a dozen light bulbs. Both women crouched lower so as not to be seen.

Someone came down the stairs slowly and stopped at the bottom of the stairs. After a few seconds a man's voice rang out in Russian, "Whoever you are, you'd bettered come out and let me see you or it will go badly for you."

Knowing that they had been detected somehow Laura decided to try to bluff her way out and keep Sarah as a backup. She pulled the gloves and the ski mask off and stood up. She saw a heavy set man in a bad suit holding a large pistol. She walked out into the main walkway and said, in English, "I'm terribly sorry, I must have gotten the wrong basement."

The man stared at her for a second and then asked in broken English, "How ded you past guard at front door?"

Laura was about to give him a story when he lowered his pistol at her and told her "Take off clothes, now!"

Laura looked at the man and said, "I will not!"

The man said, "Then I shoot you." He cocked the pistol as a chair smashed into the back of his head. Sarah had swung the chair with a lot of energy but it bounced off the man's head and he simply backhanded her with his left hand and knocked her to the ground. The man yelled something in some incomprehensible language and got a reply from upstairs.

Laura began to pray and her armor and sword appeared suddenly. She knew then that the "man" was actually a demon. She prayed the 23rd Psalm as she ran at him in holy anger. She brought her sword up to middle guard position in case he fired at her.

The demon realized his disguise had been seen through and the man shimmered into your standard, large, ugly as sin demon. As Laura neared him, the demon stepped behind a large crate and tipped it over on Laura.

Laura tried to stop but the falling crate caught her at the waist and knocked her to the floor. She kept her sword up but couldn't move the weight of the crate and get free. The Demon produced a large black sword and stepped out into the aisle and walked towards Laura struggling under the crate.

He would be able to strike her without exposing himself to the deadly fire of her blade. He was grinning and grunting at the same time.

Sarah stumbled back to her feet and saw the situation in a glance but didn't know what to do because she couldn't seem to hurt the ugly thing. Her heart went out to Laura and it hurt her to realize that she was powerless to stop the brute. But, she knew someone who wasn't powerless. She prayed that Yahshua would give her the means to keep the demon from killing her fellow warrior and best friend in the world.

There was another bellow and a second demon was thundering down the stairs. His weight was so much that the stairs collapsed and the demon fell to the floor behind the remaining stairs. Roaring his anger he started to climb out of the trap he had created for himself.

Laura knew that if she died, so would Sarah and she plead with Yahveh to give her help. In her spirit she realized that the Father was touched by her concern for her friend rather than selfishly for herself.

CHAPTER TWENTY-FIVE

As the demon came around the side of the crate to get a clean swipe at her, Laura clearly heard the commanding tones of the angel Rose. "Laura! Throw your sword to Sarah, Now!"

Laura didn't think or doubt she yelled, "Sarah, catch and pray!" She threw the sword of the Spirit to Sarah, hilt first.

Sarah started praying from the old testament, Jeremiah 29 10-11, *"For I know the plans I have for you, says the Lord, plans for welfare and not for evil, to give you a future and a hope."* as she caught the flaming sword in her right hand. She had been taking sword lessons from Jack ever since the trip to China and knew how to hold it and use it. Her righteous anger at the ugly monster knew no bounds and she attacked it like a whirlwind.

The demon forgot about Laura and backpedaled as quickly as he could while parrying Sarah's attack. Seeing an opportunity he stopped backing up and swung his big black sword in a downward crosscut at Sarah.

When she had caught the sword Sarah had been so intent on driving the demon away from Laura she hadn't noticed that as she grasped the hilt that golden armor flowed from her hand, up her arm and spread out all over her body. Instinctively she raised her left arm to block the blow although she thought she would lose the arm to the black sword.

Instead, when the black blade hit the shield of faith it shattered into dozens of pieces. Sarah squatted down and drove the sword with the Esteem of Elohim flowing off of it all the way through the demon's body. He dissolved into an ugly cloud of red smoke out of which his buddy attacked Sarah from above by jumping up and coming down at her.

Laura yelled, "Look out!"

Sarah continued to let reflexes that Jack had drummed into each of them dictate her fighting technique. He always taught that when fighting multiple opponents you return to your basic position after a strike so that you are prepared for the next attacker.

That position was at midguard. The demon crashed down on Sarah and knocked her to the ground. His face was only inches away from hers but all he said was, "Arrgh, Oooh!" and then he repeated the red cloud evaporation. As he had driven her to the ground he had driven her sword through his chest.

Shaking her head from the pounding she had just gone through Sarah rolled to her knees and stopped to say thanks to a loving Father. As she did the sword and armor disappeared. She jumped to her feet and went to help Laura. Using her legs with her back against the crate she was able to lift it enough to free Laura's legs. Laura backed away and Sarah dropped the crate to the floor with a crash.

Laura bent her knees and got to her feet. She walked over to Sarah and laid her head on the shorter woman's shoulder as she hugged her fiercely. "I love you! You Israeli Amazon! You were magnificent! Thank you for saving me from that unspeakable filth."

Sarah hugged her back just as hard. "I couldn't bear the thought of losing you." She stepped back and looked a bit confused. Did I just do what I think I did?"

Laura was nodding her head. "Oh Yes you did. Did I tell you that you look good in gold?"

Sarah shook her head, "But, I thought the angel Rose gave that armor and sword to you alone."

Laura smiled, "Rose is the one that told me to throw the sword to you."

Sarah was about to reply when she heard the tramping of many feet on the floor above them. "We need to go, Now!"

They ran to the end of the basement and eased the door up carefully. Looking around and not seeing anyone they pushed it up and got outside. Laura closed the door and stepped away when a half dozen bullets smashed out of the door and flew into the sky.

Sarah and Laura ran to the fence and were about to climb over when a light sprang out from the rear porch of the villa and a shout was followed by gunfire.

Dodging down behind a bunch of shrubs Laura asked Sarah, "Did you by chance get the gun the demon was carrying?"

Sarah frowned at her. "No! I didn't want to touch anything of that creature."

Laura risked a quick glance around the bushes and saw a half dozen men headed their way and all of them were armed. "Then I think we're way outgunned here."

Sarah was determined not to go down without a fight and led Laura several bushes away. It wouldn't stop the men from finding them and killing them but it would take a few more seconds. She decided to sprint out and attack the men and try to give Laura a chance to get away.

Just as she started to move she heard an authoritarian voice in Russian tell everyone to drop their weapons and freeze or die.

Hearing the rattle of dropped arms she stood up and saw an even worse fate coming toward them. A Russian military unit stood with their rifles aimed at the men in the yard. Coincidently they were also aimed at the two of them at the same time. The men were obviously an elite Spetznaz unit with their faces covered with assault masks and goggles.

The Russian officer in charge told each man to come forward one at a time. One of the troops frisked each man and tied his hands behind him with plastic riot cuffs.

The officer then told Laura and Sarah to come forward with their hands in the air. There was no way out this time.

Sarah walked forward first determined to find an opening and do the most damage she could. The large soldier that came to her had given his weapon to the next man so she couldn't use that. Her mind spun at high speed looking for a opportunity.

The man quickly frisked her and didn't spend any time groping her as she thought he might. He pulled her hands behind her he tied her wrists. As he was doing that he whispered to her, "Try not to kill us Spy lady, we're just here to help you."

Hearing Mark's voice almost made her give the whole thing away. The change from dire circumstance to miracle reprieve was almost too much. But, she managed to contain herself and acted like she was trying to pull away from him. He roughly pulled her back while Jack did the same search and binding on Laura. Sarah saw the small smile on Laura's face and knew she was aware of the situation.

CHAPTER TWENTY-SIX

A sudden shot out of the dark hit Demitri in the back and punched him to the ground. The team ducked behind whatever was available and three of them searched for the shooter while the other three kept the captives from doing anything.

Mark snap aimed his AKS and fired several shots. He was rewarded with a fading scream. Then more shots came from the area of the front of the house. Leaving Stan to watch the captives, the women, and to tend to Demitri the others started leapfrogging towards the front of the house firing at any target of opportunity as they went.

A group of Russian Mafia soldiers had responded to the summons sent out by Sam Sturgis as he heard the battle in the back yard.

The battle quickly turned into a stalemate as neither force could advance on the other. Jack was about to attempt an end around to put the criminals in a crossfire when a big hand on his shoulder stopped him. He looked back and saw Demitri crouched next to him. "Welcome back big guy."

Demitri didn't laugh at that one. The pain in his back from the big bore handgun hitting a trauma plate had knocked the wind out of him and actually knocked him out for a minute. "Don't do anything heroic. I've already called in more troops from the real military base eight miles from here. They should be here," he looked at his watch "right about now."

There was a roar and suddenly the entire front area of the villa was lit up by high intensity lights on the bottom of a Mi-24 HIND helicopter. Anybody in their right mind would not mess with one of these war birds. They carried enough firepower to destroy an entire village by itself in less than twenty minutes.

Of course the hard men of the mafia had egos that knew no bounds and they turned and fired on the armored chopper. The response was instantaneous and highly effective. One right to left pass of the multiple barreled cannons on the aircraft eliminated all threats in the front yard, whether they had fired at the chopper or not.

The noise quickly died down after that. The HIND flew away as fresh troops arrived to mop up the rebellious criminals.

By the time the officer in charge reached the back yard there were only nine bound captives left to see. His troops were none to gentle as they dragged the captives to the brightly lit front yard and asked them who had taken them captive.

The only answer they got was soldiers like you. One man said Spetznaz! and the whole picture came clear to the officer. He'd heard that there was a special detachment here to arrest a terrorist the criminals were harboring. Well, he would take the credit and just not mention them.

Several blocks away a large garbage container was full of uniforms and rifles that had been spiked to prevent their use by anyone else.

Jack gently rubbed Laura's wrists as the morning sun started to edge over the horizon.

Mark was not very happy as he walked back to the hotel with Sarah. She looked at him and deduced the problem. "Sam Sturgis got away, didn't he?"

Mark frowned and nodded. "We were about to bust in and get him when all hell broke loose in the back yard. After we saw you and our priorities changed. We had to save you and that must of given him the chance to get away. I went through the whole place and he was gone." He looked at Sarah, "Don't get the idea I'm blaming you and Laura for his escape. He had a rabbit hole and would of escaped us anyway."

Sarah put her arm in his and pulled him close to her. "I think it was just the nicest thing I've ever heard when you whispered Spy lady to me. Don't worry; we'll get Sam sooner or later. At least we drove him out of his Russian hidey hole. Wait until I tell you something. You won't believe what happened to me in the basement of that villa!" Mark's interest was piqued.

Three miles away from the returning team members another battle was in progress. This one was against time and gravity.

Having secured their sniper rifle and ammo, Alexis, Linda, and Su Li were headed back for the hotel when the HIND flew over and they could hear gunfire in the direction of the villas. It was just before dawn and they didn't know if they should head for the villas or the hotel.

A scream alerted them and they shrank back into the doorway of a closed tavern. Across the street they saw a man running from their left to their right. His running had all the signs of someone fleeing from someone else as he kept looking over his shoulder.

Quite a few of the townspeople were already up and out getting ready for the day. They were cleaning carpets, sweeping the sidewalk, and opening shops and generally following their normal routines. The problem was that they were interfering with the running man's path since he wanted to stay close to the buildings and out of the sight of the helicopter.

As he ran he bumped into people who yelled abuse at him and told him to slow down. He started hitting the individuals closest to him.

As the three women watched helplessly the man slammed into a woman with a baby and he knocked them both into the street and kept running. The woman fell and turned so that she could cushion the fall for the baby. The cries of the baby told the world of how the fall scared it.

Infuriated, Debbie pulled the sniper rifle out of the rug they'd hidden it in and grabbed at the ammo Su Li was carrying. The man continued to run and turned a corner before she could get the gun loaded.

Linda Wu said, "That's Sam Sturgis! He's out of his lair and he's running away from something. Laura and Sarah must have missed him"

Debbie took off running after the man with both of the other women right at her heels. She rounded the corner at the edge of town and saw Sturgis on a motor scooter he apparently had stolen. He was buzzing out of town to the southeast. He rounded a bend and Debbie lost her line of sight for a shot.

Looking around she saw a large foothill just behind the last shops in the town. It was at least two hundred feet high. She looked at the sunlit terrain. "Lights right, elevation is good, it's closer to the road, okay". She took off at a fast clip for the hill. Linda looked at Su Li and they took off after the woman with the rifle. Su Li noticed that Debbie was not at all distressed with having to carry the sniper rifle and run uphill at the same time. In fact, she looked right at home doing it. Hmmmm.

As Debbie ran she got a leading or at least an unusual thought. She removed the magazine from the rifle and one-handedly popped the rounds out of the magazine. When she had them all out she prayed, "Father I ask You bless these bullets in Your mighty name so that they will do Your will against the enemies of all mankind and their minions. Make these bullets an extension of Your will and esteem. Guide them in Your will and bless the work they do against the enemy." Reloading them was more complicated but she managed to reload the magazine and reinsert it by the time she reached the top of the hill. She ran to the far side and dropped to her knees.

Using a convenient mound of rock she adjusted the fixed 10-power sniper scope and scanned the road where it came back uphill about a thousand feet from the hilltop. "Nothing". Using the bolt she loaded the first round in the chamber. She took a deep breath and patiently scanned the road again. All at once the motor scooter appeared heading away from the town.

Debbie took a medium breath and steadied her sights. She had already sighted the scope in for the maximum range. She prayed that the Father would bless the work of her hands. She took up the slack in the trigger, sighted on the back of Sam's head, led the target due to his speed, exhaled half her breath and squeezed the trigger. The powerful rifle bucked against her shoulder and she reflected that she had missed that feeling lately, and it felt good doing what she was very good at, especially for the Father.

She quickly cycled the bolt and repeated the operation but a little lower. She got off three shots before the first one got to the fleeing terrorist.

Sam was rankling under the goading of the demon that seemed to be a full-time part of his life anymore. The smug being was telling how he had failed for the last time. Sam's master would not be pleased and was coming to collect his due on Sam's contract. He was after all, nothing but a miserable human being that could never succeed at anything important.

Sam was thinking of various horrible things he'd like to do to this particular demon when he got a sinking feeling and suddenly he couldn't see anything, feel anything, or hear anything. He wanted to scream but he didn't have a voice. Then he heard something he didn't want to hear. That same voice that had made a contract with him was chuckling. "Sam Sturgis, your soul is forfeit to me. You failed me and you will now pay for that for the rest of eternity."

The first wave of excruciatingly painful burning heat felt like it roasted his skin off his body. And that was just the warm-up.

On the hillside, Debbie was praying her thanks to a Father she loved more than her own life. Her mind played over the two things that startled her this time. The first was that she could actually see the bullets in flight. They weren't lead or copper like normal; they were glaringly hot white with an incandescent center that had the same esteem rolling off of them she'd seen on Laura's sword. They were running true and straight towards her target when she half saw a demon try to deflect the rounds. The first round went right through the demon's hand and blew him up. That round impacted on the back of Sam Sturgis' head terminating his life, career, and incidentally, his body. The other two insurance rounds impacted on the headless body throwing it off the scooter and into the ditch where it belonged.

Being the professional she was she quickly wiped the rifle down and did the same to the unused rounds and the magazine. She picked up the fired shell casings and pocketed them. Holding the rifle in the handkerchief she threw the rifle down the hillside into the rubble and brush where it disappeared from sight.

Getting up and turning around she was surprised to see the other two women standing there with their mouths open simply staring at her. She tipped her head to one side and asked, "What's the matter?"

Su Li smiled and commented, "He was just a speck on the horizon and you hit him. That was some really remarkable shooting."

Debbie grinned, "I had help." She pointed upward.

Putting her arms around the waists of the two equally diminutive Oriental women she headed back to the hotel.

CHAPTER TWENTY-SEVEN

Su Li, Debbie, and Linda Wu were thrilled when they saw the men of the Crossfire Team sitting in the restaurant with Laura and Sarah. There were even some of the Crossfire SOG warriors there.

Joining the group they hugged everybody and found seats at the big double table. Sarah quietly brought everyone up to date on their excursion at the villas and Mark did the same for their parts. He ended with, "The only sad point is that Sam Sturgis got away, again.

Linda Wu laughed. She stood up and smiling at Mark she shook her head. "No he didn't." She held out her hand to Debbie. "This little package of dynamite blew him straight to hell at well over a thousand yards."

Jack narrowed his eyes in concentration. "Great shot! Are you sure it was him?"

Debbie nodded, "Oh yeah. It was him. I made a one-hundred percent visual identification as he passed us on the street, where he was indiscriminately hurting anyone in his way."

Mark smiled. "That sounds like Sturgis. We just drove him from his comfortable safe house and eliminated his criminal overseers with the help of the Russian military."

Jack asked for the location of the body because he wanted a DNA sample to confirm the kill and make sure this time it was really the assassin.

Debbie explained where the man fell and Jack pointed at Charlie Wu and two of the SOG soldiers. The four of them left the table and went to rent a car. Charlie stopped at his backpack and pulled out a DNA sample kit.

Everyone continued to talk about the mission until some of the Virginia girls showed up for breakfast. Sarah introduced Mark to Roseanne and the others as "Mr. Miller, my husband". The envious looks she got from the other women reinforced her feeling of having the right "guy". She went on to introduce Stan Hargrove, David

Zahavy, and John Harris the lone SOG member left at the table.

The rest of the women's tour ladies arrived and the introductions were repeated. Mary Burrow was impressed with Sarah's and Debbie's husbands and whispered to Sarah, "You have a gorgeous husband. It's too bad that Ms. Laura and Ms. Alexis don't have ones that nice."

Sarah was about to answer when Jack and Charlie came back into the room with the other two SOG members.

Laura introduced her husband as Mr. Davis to match her alias.

Jack realized things were getting out of hand with the fourteen women and eight men so he got everyone's attention and suggested they get a private room rather than taking up the entire restaurant's only tables.

Roseanne talked to the Concierge and they were allowed to move into one of the larger conference rooms away from the other people of the hotel.

After everyone was seated and had ordered breakfast, Laura stood up and attempted to clarify a lot of the unasked questions for the other women of the tour. None of them had any idea what had gone on during the night or any concept how tired the members of the Crossfire Team were right then.

"Ladies, I just wanted you to know that the men here couldn't live without us and came here just to be with us on this tour. The inclusion of four husbands and five single men will make this tour memorable I assure you."

She had Jack stand up. "My husband, Jack Davis, is the one who is financing our tour and will probably do a lot more before we have to head back home."

There was a loud round of applause for Jack and the suggestion that they tour the wine cavern and Jack buy the drinks.

Jack held up his hand until they quieted down. "I will be pleased to foot the bill and want to thank you all for allowing us to join your tour."

There were a chorus of "Yeas and thank you's" from the assembled group.

Jack smiled and pointed out their host, Demitri, and the three SOG members as unmarried and potential escorts for the unmarried women. None of them declined but Willie Peterson whispered to Mark who was sitting next to him. "Do we get hazardous duty pay for this?"

Mark looked at the handsome young man and smiled, "Sure, I'll bet these ladies might give you a tip if you're nice."

Willie made a face and slowly shook his head grinning. "The things we do to protect our country."

The next two days of the tour was a lot of fun and relaxation for everyone. The tour of the wine cavern was interesting and it turned out the wine was free, but the entrance fee for twenty three people was a bit pricy. Jack rented another bus and took everyone up to a large spa thirty miles from Serov and everyone enjoyed the bubbling hot springs and all the amenities an exclusive spa could provide.

While they were relaxing in a hot spring outside the spa, Mark leaned over and told Jack, "This is the perfect cover for us. I'll bet the Russian Mafia and the military have locked down everything travelling anywhere while they look for whoever held a shooting riot in a mob neighborhood and killed Sam Sturgis. Since we are not going anywhere at all but actually staying at a mob establishment and using their bars and spas makes us look like we're nothing but some rich American tourists. Very good, I also see that Ms. Burrows has attached herself to Demitri which is a great cover for him."

Jack agreed with his friend. "Have you figured out how we are going to get out of the country since we never formally got into the country?"

Mark leaned back and let the heat of the pool soothe his muscles. "Yeah, Demitri has already got our paperwork, from a different source than Isak that shows we flew in on a commercial flight to join our wives and we have a flight out the same day the tour leaves. There were no open seats on their aircraft so we got one that leaves slightly later than theirs but gets to Germany ahead of them." He looked around and asked quietly. "Did the DNA on Sam work out?"

Jack nodded his head. "It was him this time. There were additional indicators that back up the DNA. His left arm and shoulder were withered and the scar from your

.50 BMG round is still fairly new. Sorry, I didn't bring any of the pictures we took. They weren't very good because Sam no longer has a head for photography."

Mark reached over to his shorts on the ground above the pool and picked up his satellite cell phone and sent a message to the JCS Chairman, General Miles. "Found SS, problem eliminated triple verification complete and accurate this time. - Mark"

CHAPTER TWENTY-EIGHT

On the third day after Sam Sturgis' termination dark clouds began to gather over their vacation. First, Jack got a call from Carol with the warning that the indications in the heavenlies were for a major push against the Crossfire Team through human agents.

Then Charlie got a call from Al Trotter who was overseeing the computer center at the Fortress while Charlie and Linda Wu were absent. He hung up and ran to find the leaders. He opened his door and found both Jack and Mark as they were walking down the hotel hall. He pulled them into his room. "We got some serious problems coming our way and fast!"

Mark frowned, "What problems?"

Charlie held up his cell phone. "I just heard from Al at the Fortress. Crayton has tied together several Russian phone calls with the keywords Crossfire and two CIA-intercepted wires from Moscow to the military base outside Serov. These communications included all our descriptions and pictures on it. It is presumed that they've made the connection to Sam Sturgis and the newly discovered presence of members of the Crossfire Team in the area".

"The assumption is that there has been a leak of major proportions concerning us since the pictures are the same as the ones on our Russian passports that Isak gave us. There is a full court press to find and arrest all of us, and that includes the women from Virginia."

Mark asked, "How long before they get here?"

Charlie didn't break his eye contact with Mark. "Within ninety minutes on the outside."

Mark used his cell phone to get Demitri up to Charlie's room. Mark explained the problem in very terse terms to the Russian.

Demitri thought for a few seconds. "Okay, get everybody together as if for a tour of something. Grab only what you can carry easily. Be at the front door ready to leave in ten minutes. Move now!"

Everybody headed for their rooms and the rooms of the other members.

Dashing into his room Mark started loading a backpack while he explained the situation to Sarah. She bent over and picked up a packed backpack and said she'd round up the Virginia girls and have them at the front door in less than eight minutes. Mark stared at her back with the prepared backpack and was still amazed at her forethought in the field of spy craft.

The word was passed to everyone and fifteen minutes later they assembled in the lobby all dressed for a mountain hike and sporting a lot of backpacks. Demitri said quietly to Mark, "This is good, I would have thought it would have taken more time to organize the civilians."

Sarah overheard the comment and leaned over to Demitri, "They've been in lots of places that are unstable and are usually ready to run at a moment's notice."

Loud enough for the hotel staff to hear, Mark told everyone that they were going to visit the old wine cavern, again. The cavern was about eight miles away to the south. They formed up in two lines and were chatting and giggling like it was a real tour.

After they left the hotel they headed to the south until they passed beyond the town. Charlie and David lagged behind to make sure no one was following them. Their backtrack was clear and they raced up to the front of the lines. David told Mark, "Don't see any hanger ons."

Demitri led them to the right off of the beaten path and uphill behind a large foothill. Sarah and Mark went back and removed any sign of their passage for the three hundred feet back to the pavement.

The sun was reaching the Zenith when they descended into the next valley and Demitri had them all sit down underneath trees in the event there were helicopters involved in the chase. By himself he walked over to a single-lane road and waited. Five minutes later a large truck with a canvas-covered cargo area pulled up and the driver got out and talked to Demitri for several minutes. Demitri gave him a roll of money and signaled the rest of the tour to join him.

He explained the on-going action. "I have much better travel accommodations not too far from here. The need now is for speed so that we are not in the area anywhere when the troops come to look for us. Please be so kind as to climb into the back and sit down with the canvas cover closed."

Roseanne and her group were confused as to the change in plans and the references to "troops" searching for them. But they complied without complaining.

The men helped the ladies into the bed of the truck and then climbed up to join them. The truck rumbled off. The ride was bumpy and noisy and stinky as the exhaust on the truck wasn't the best.

The truck turned to the right in a few minutes and after some really bouncy driving it pulled onto a paved road and picked up speed. Thirty minutes later it pulled into a large building. Quite a few men were present when Demitri and the truck driver lifted the canvas flaps covering the back of the truck. The men of the team jumped out and helped the women down to the straw-covered floor.

Mark looked around and realized that they were in a building that had at one time been some kind of manufacturing facility. Abandoned years before it had apparently become home to a group that smuggled contraband into and out of Russia.

Demitri spoke to Jack for a few seconds and then they both walked over to the leader of the group. The man was aware of their situation and was willing to help them if they could meet his price. He was risking his life and operation to help them get away from the police and wanted a high price. Jack had been praying and already knew what to do.

Bela, the leader could speak English. He told Jack, "I can give you a way out of Russia and keep you hidden from the intelligence operatives who are seeking you. But, to do it I will need three million dollars."

Jack thought for a second, "Okay, but there is a rider on the deal."

Bela frowned, "What is rider?"

Jack's eyes frosted over and he locked eyes with Bela. "If anyone from this group talks or turns us over. I will make it the number one priority of my organization to deal with you. Can you keep your men that know about us from making an extra buck by talking to the police?"

Bela knew men and gauged Jack's statement. It was obvious that he meant exactly what he said and had the means to accomplish it. "I will accept your rider. Do you have the money?"

Jack pulled out a credit card and handed it to Bela. Bela turned around and opened his desktop. Running the credit card took only three minutes and the transaction was complete. He closed his desk and gave Jack back the credit card. He then led the entire group through a door into a large area that had many late-model European sedans. By twos or threes the team and the lady's tour members climbed into the cars. Bela handed Jack maps and paperwork for the cars. "Follow the maps and break into groups of no more than two or three cars so as to not arouse suspicion. When you come to the final spot on the maps there will be a luxury bus waiting for you. Leave the cars in the building at the end of the map. We will pick them up and return them to their rightful owners who won't be back in the country for three weeks or more. Have a good trip."

Bela opened a door and one by one the sedans left the building and drove south.

Jack called Demitri on his secure cell phone. "Do you think we can trust Bela and his men?"

Demitri smiled, "Oh yes, he has much more to lose than gain by telling the authorities where we are or where we are going." After Jack's threat, Demitri was fairly certain that any of Bela's men who knew what was done at the garage would not live to tell anything to anybody. In fact they were probably already dead. He continued, "Still it would be prudent to have a backup plan. What do you suggest?"

Jack talked to Mark about the situation and then told Demitri, "It looks like we're driving as separated groups to Odesskye and will leave the cars there. If the authorities get wind of this deal that's where they would be waiting. We will make other arrangements to prevent that. Talk to you later."

Switching drivers and driving all night cut down the seven hundred miles. Short stops at the infrequent rest areas and gas stations brought them to Odesskye three hours before they would be expected. They parked all the cars in the street in front of the building that would be opened soon.

Everyone split up and met again at the western edge of the town near Odesskye's main marketplace. In the cold October air the vast sky seemed endless as they started trekking south west until they reached a large open plain where Mark made his latest satellite phone call.

CHAPTER TWENTY-NINE

Everyone sat down and rested, ate power bars, and drank the water they had brought with them. They had left Odesskye at seven in the morning, local time and now it was almost five in the afternoon and everyone was tired from walking. Roseanne cleaned up her rations and got up. She walked over to where Sarah and Mark were talking and sat down. She stared at Sarah for a minute and then asked, "Okay, what is going on?"

Sarah looked at Mark and then turned to Roseanne. "It is somewhat of a complicated situation but I'll try to give you the short version. All six of the women, including myself, who joined your group work for an American antiterrorist organization known as the Crossfire Team."

Roseanne's eyes widened. "I know about your team. I saw the confrontation in Zyngola on TV. Was that you in the wired in area?"

Sarah nodded, "That was Mark, myself, Laura, and Jack."

Roseanne suddenly grinned and got up. "Don't tell me anything else." Then she thought for a second and sat down again next to Mark, "No. Do tell me that we're going to be all right."

Mark smiled, "Yes Roseanne, we're going to be all right."

She smiled and got up brushing off her pants and hurrying back to the other members of the tour to give them the news.

Sarah looked sternly at Mark. "Honey, you forgot to tell her about the possibility of our being captured, tried, and sent to the Gulag for the rest of our miserably short lives. Bettered yet, the possibility of being killed outright because we are now labeled as enemies of the state. And, you left out the part about abuse, rape, torture, and really bad accommodations and water."

Mark laughed, "Yeah, there are those little things. But I don't think we need to tell her about them because they're not going to happen."

Mark looked to his left as the large rotors lifted above the grass line and two MI-24 HIND armored helicopters appeared and rapidly flew toward them with all the guns and missile racks aimed in their direction.

Sarah snorted and looked back from the helicopters to Mark. "You were saying?"

Mark smiled at his wife, "Trust me." He stood up and walked towards the choppers as they settled to the ground a hundred feet away from the group. The door opened on the first chopper and the Russian officer waved them all over to the craft.

Mark also waved them over so everyone picked up their stuff and ran to the helicopter. The officer jumped out and took off his red star cap and shook Mark's hand. Turning to the others he said, "I'm Captain Ron Amherst of the USAF's 64th Aggressor Squadron and we're here to give you all a ride home. Please split into two groups and hop on board, we need to move along."

After the twenty three people had split into two groups and were on board the helicopters lifted off and flew nap-of-the earth to the south until they were out of Mother Russia and into Kazakhstan. Because they were obviously Russian war birds nobody bothered them as they flew toward the city of Astana in northern Kazakhstan. On a dry and arid plain the choppers settled down near a large mound.

Everyone climbed off and waved to the helicopters as they lifted off and flew away to the west.

Several men walked out of the mound and came over to the tour group. The leader introduced himself as Major Gene Cowland, commander and pilot of a C5A Starlifter. His fifteen man crew began pulling the camouflage off of the aircraft. When the camo was stored in the back of the plane everyone climbed onboard and found comfortable seats in the front crew area. One of the ladies was taking pictures of the plane when Major Cowland asked her for the camera and proceeded to erase all pictures of the helicopters or the C5A. He handed back the camera and explained that neither the helicopters nor his plane were ever here and he couldn't allow proof that showed otherwise.

Jane Pulman understood and stuck her camera back in her bag and shook the Major's hand.

While the plane was being preflighted and warmed up, Sarah called everyone together and explained about the aborted tour of Serov. "I'm terribly sorry that we interrupted the tour. Jack and Mark have promised to make it up to us on our return to the western world."

She looked at all the ladies from Virginia and grinned broadly. "I want to congratulate you all for being so capable when we had to escape from Russia. I hope you didn't have to leave any valuables or special clothing at the hotel and I know you feel I cheated you by using your tour to accomplish our mission but I assure you that it is worth any bad feelings you might have so we were able to remove a evil cancer from the world. Without your, albeit unknowing, help, we could not have accomplished the task. Unfortunately, as James Bond characters, you have to understand that the actual facts of the case cannot be revealed for many years due to the sensitive nature of the American-Russian relationship. I can tell you that you did a great service for your country and will receive commendations for your part in the action that no one can know ever happened. I want to thank you for being good friends and one heck of a party group."

That got a round of applause from the Virginia ladies. Roseanne stepped up and faced the group. "Sarah, first I want you to know that this wasn't our first rodeo or quick escape either. We all keep the important things in our "go bags" and the other stuff is replaceable. We want to thank you for saving us from whatever happened back there. Yes, we were unknowing and unwilling victims of the action involved and can probably never go to Russian again without being arrested. But, I for one want to thank you from the bottom of my heart for one of the best and most exciting tours we've ever been on! Isn't that right, ladies?"

This time the Virginia women mobbed the two female leaders and there were tears and hugs and smiles and an overall congratulation to the Crossfire Team for their faithfulness when they could have escaped and left the tour to fend for themselves, which had happened to them earlier.

Alexis stood up and had to grab for a handhold as the C5A began its ground roll for takeoff. "I've had a chance to get to know each and every one of you "civilian", ladies. I can honestly say that you present the best that America has to offer in grit, determination, heroism and smart dress. Thank you for the opportunity to get to know you and see you all in action. "

The whole group yelled or whistled at that point. Everyone sought a seat as the giant plane lifted off of the plain and swung around on a heading that would take it out of Kazakhstan and all the way to Israel.

CHAPTER THIRTY

After landing, the C5A was carefully hidden in a large hanger on Ben Gurion airport. The crew was released to enjoy themselves while the plane was refitted and prepared for a trans-Atlantic flight in three days.

David took over as the master of ceremonies and took everyone down to a five-star hotel in Tel Aviv and treated everyone to a fantastic dinner and dancing evening. The next day he got everyone out to one of the Israeli beaches and the Virginia girls grinned at all the handsome, unattached men at the beach. Only David and some of the Crossfire Team knew that many of the people on that particular beach were members of the military or the Mossad for the protection of the escapees. Israel isn't always a safe place regardless of appearances.

That evening there were many photos taken and after that no one kept track of what happened. Jack and Laura were leaving with David and Alexis when Mark and Sarah joined them. Sarah laughed, "We wanted to be a group again."

David grinned, "Wait until you see what I have in store for us."

He got them in a limousine and they stopped at a quiet but very exclusive restaurant in an upscale neighborhood. The late-night snack food was excellent and the entertainment was cultured and refined.

After the show they decided to walk to the beach near Dizengoff Square. They walked out on the sand and breathed the rich night air which was cool and hinted of coming rain. They could sense the great expanse of quiet water in front of them. Laura asked quietly, "Why can't it always be peaceful like tonight?"

David answered her, "Because there are forces in the world that are bent on robbery, destruction, and death. These forces move men to criminal acts, to commit evil acts to others, and general mayhem. As long as there is a devil there won't be real peace in the world for very long.

Jack put his arm around his wife who realized that she was getting chilled and welcomed the warm embrace. "Are you getting tired of our adopted life style?"

Laura thought about that for a few minutes. "No, I still want to do Yahveh's will and that has proven to be a counter force to unbridled evil. Occasionally I get tired of the constant stress and danger. Then I pray and ask Yahveh if that this is what I should be doing. He never fails to tell me He loves me and that, yes, this is what He needs me to do. End of debate. He fills me with a peace that this world can't match."

The entire group agreed with Laura and stood there in silent prayer.

David jumped a little and then dug out his cell phone which had been on vibrate and answered it. He listened for a few minutes and then answered in Hebrew and closed the phone.

He shook his head and said, "Well, I certainly hope you've enjoyed your peace and quiet. The head of the Mossad is asking that all members of the Crossfire Team who are here to meet at Mossad headquarters in one hour. It seems President Bollen wants to talk to all of us."

An hour later the team was seated in a secure room at the Mossad headquarters. The large screen in front of them lit up and they greeted the President of the United States warmly.

He smiled at the crew and said, "Okay, let's see, I see Jack and Laura, Mark and Sarah, Charlie and Linda, Stan and Debbie, David, Alexis, Su Li, and three people I haven't met. Jack could you do the introductions?"

Jack said, "Certainly Mr. President. On our recent mission concerning Sam Sturgis in Russia we needed an eight man team per Demitri Serakov's requirements. So we included three of the SOG warriors who are, from your right to left, John Harris, Mike Coffer, and Willie Peterson. They provided us with great teamwork and a host of necessary skills as professional warriors."

The President nodded, "Good to meet all three of you gentlemen. My congratulations on being part of what I consider the top antiterrorist organization that I know of in this world and maybe the next one. God be with each and every one of you as you faithfully serve Yahveh and our country."

Looking back at Jack the President asked, "Do me a favor and invite Demitri into our conference. His unique insight and talents may be sorely needed for this discussion."

David looked at Jack and Mark for approval and used an intercom to have the staff bring Demitri Serakov to their meeting.

Demitri came in and told the President he was honored to be included and to meet him for the first time.

President Bollen returned the compliment and thanked the ex-Russian General for his help to the U.S. since leaving Russian service.

Then the President got down to business."I see from the CIA report that you accomplished your mission and were able, with our help, to extract not only your team but a group of American women also. Why was that?"

Sarah stood up. "Mr. President, I involved the Virginia Women's Tour group as a cover for getting our team into the town Sam Sturgis was located in at the time. They were not to be involved but due to a major demonic blow-up at the villa Sam was in, the Russian Military became involved and we learned that they were about to arrest all of us including the cover group. We extracted the hostile country with the cover group to prevent a hostage situation." She sat down.

President Bollen chuckled, "I'll bet they got a tour they weren't expecting, right?"

Sarah grinned back and nodded her head. "Oh, yes Sir, they did."

The President sobered up and picked up some papers from his desk. "Well, I'm glad you all got out of Russia with your skins. Now, I'm going to ask most of you to go back into Russia."

Mark shook his head, "That may not be a good idea, Sir. They have our pictures and biodata and are probably still seeking us as we speak. We wouldn't stand much of a chance even if we could get into the country unseen."

Demitri added, "We are all marked individuals at this point. And please to remember, Mr. President, Russians don't forget easily and they usually don't forgive at all."

The President heard them out and then smiled. "All good points but inconsequential in this matter. Actually, the Russians are the ones asking us to have you come back to help them. They assure you complete immunity for any crimes against the state or Russian citizens or private property. Let me explain how I came to be involved in this request."

The President took a sip of water and sat back in his seat. This was obviously not going to be a short statement. "After you dealt with the assassin Sam Sturgis the government of Russia became involved in the case due to the use of their military to squelch the "disturbance" in Serov. Investigations into the happenings there were complicated by the lack of witnesses, the criminal effort to cover things up, and your disappearance. But, in the process of determining all of the above they ran into some heavy demonic interference which is working in conjunction with the criminal element." President Bollen referred to a paper near his right hand. "Demonic interference that has resulted in the loss of over two hundred Russian military, police, and citizens."

President Bollen looked at each person to see if they were getting his message. Satisfied that they were, he continued. "This created a major flap in the government for two reasons. First, they don't believe in supernatural beings as per state edict. Second, they have no way to combat these obviously impossible forces. Now they tell me that they have heard from an unnamed source that your team was able to overcome the demonic element associated with Sam Sturgis and demolish his operation, again, with the help from the Russian military."

Demitri interrupted the President. "Sir, I called in the military because the criminal element was flooding the area with gunmen. All of this is against the law and they should have been taken under arrest. Something, I humbly remind you Sir, that we could not do ourselves."

President Bollen nodded, "Yes, Demitri, a valid point. Nonetheless, due to that event in the villa the Russians are being threatened by a situation that they don't understand and can't defeat with anything in their arsenal. Knowing that your team is effective at defeating these "non-existent" beings is why they are willing to forgive anything the Crossfire Team has done on Russian soil to secure your assistance."

Mark asked the President, "Sir, do you think this could be simply a ploy to get us back to where they can arrest us and put us away?"

The President didn't even stop to consider the question. "No Mark, because our foreign assets, especially the CIA, agree that they are running scared due to these demons. I understand that it's just a manifestation of Satan's urgency as the last days run out. He wants to destroy all mankind, which includes the Russians, so in his haste he is allowing his demons to take liberties that are not what God's law permits them to do. The other reason the Russian government is forced to beg for help is because the Russian "Brotherhood" has upped the ante by threatening wide-spread demonic events if the government doesn't give them what they want."

Jack asked, "What do they want, Mr. President?"

The President shook his head, "Not much, just complete protection from the police and the military, fifty-fifty control of internal affairs for the whole country, and your heads on a platter or the treasure you possess."

Mark snorted and stood up. "To summarize, we got free after dealing with Mr. Sturgis and are in no way beholding to the Russians. They've gone through you to ask us to come back and help them with their supernatural problems or face possible death at the hands of the criminals. Have we got it about right?"

President Bollen nodded. "There's little the free world could do if things got out of hand over there. You'd be on your own militarily. I don't know how much our stance or vocal protests would affect their decisions, but, I can surely tell you that if they have to give into the control of Russia by a combination of Satan's demons and the criminals the situation for the rest of the world and for your team will not get any better. The Mafia would use their new leverage to demand your extermination either by Russian hands or by forcing international pressure against you and anybody that protects you." The President looked at the papers in front of him. "There is one exception to their amnesty, and that would be "the traitor Demitri Serakov", sorry Demitri. We are not asking you to return."

Jack frowned, "I wonder where they got the idea of demanding other nations to round up people in their country?" Mark was referring to the President's own demands concerning the ASF several years ago.

Laura said, "Mr. President, we will pray about this and see what the Father and the Son want us to do. Our mandate is to do war with those demonic incursions that you mentioned. Let us see what is in Yahveh's plans."

Jack nodded, "Thank you, Mr. President; we'll call you back as soon as we can."

The connection was broken and the team retired to a secluded assembly area in the building and got down on their knees to ask Yahveh's direction concerning their involvement in the Russian spiritual problem.

Guarding the assembly from outside of the building two of the Mossad personnel stopped for a smoke break. One of them smirked and told the other, "Why in the name of God are we wasting our time coddling these Christians?"

The older guard regarded his counterpart for several seconds. "For two reasons. One, we were ordered to by our director, and two, have you ever watched the video from Zyngola? If you had, you wouldn't ask."

CHAPTER THIRTY-ONE

Before they prayed, Jack had called Carol back at the Fortress and told her what the situation was and asked her to see what she could learn from the heavenlies. She said that she would call them back as soon as she had anything she could report.

Jack suggested that each person pray as they were led, alone, or in groups. He got down on his knees with Laura and the group just naturally formed around them.

As they begin to pray in earnest from their hearts for the Father's direction Jack felt the presence of Yahveh's Spirit among them. This came as a pleasant heaviness that breathed peace into one's life and spirit. He relaxed into the feeling and felt himself being immersed in the river of life that flows from heaven. He listened carefully for Yahveh's voice and wasn't surprised when he heard the familiar voice of the angel Caleb. Jack knew that Caleb was one of the mighty messengers from Yahveh and had dealt with the angel many times in the past. He felt a camaraderie with the supernatural being that went beyond friendship, more like brotherhood.

Jack opened his eyes and saw Caleb in his warrior image. He was young, powerful and adorned for war. There was a fire in his eyes that normally he kept veiled. The angel looked at members of the team and raised his arms outward. A field of force like a white ring expanded from the angel and moved outward until it had included all of the team members where it was absorbed by each person.

Caleb looked at Jack and spoke. "Jack Malone, you have asked Yahveh for guidance concerning the team's response to the request from the Russians to return to their land and to help them battle Satan's demonic intrusions on the human plane. He has blessed me with the response to give to you all. "*Heed the words of Yahveh, Elohim of the universe. You and your team are being sent to Russia as My response to this forbidden union of the enemy's messengers and the morally debased in that country. You will stand as My warriors on your Earth against this enterprise. I will go before each battle and give the enemy into your hands as a sign that I am Elohim! There is no other like Me and My commands are not to be lightly disobeyed! All of you are to go as a consuming fire in My Name. This is not a war between men or their nations. This is a war against the disobedient and willfully lawless, both in the spiritual realm and in the human realm."*

Caleb looked at Laura and smiled. "You have been faithful to do battle against the enemy even when your spirit wasn't sure it was a battle you could win. You have trusted Yahveh and His strength and because of that you will be given more. The angel raised his right arm and a vortex of energy flowed from him to Laura.

He turned his penetrating vision on Sarah. "You, Sarah, have given your life and your heart to Yahveh and stood for His Word regardless of the threat to your being. You have placed yourself between the enemy's agents and your friends. There is no greater love one can express than to give their life for their friends. You will, from now on, be armored as your sister Laura to do battle in the spiritual realm as you pray. This is because the enemy is aware of Laura's capabilities and her level of combat is increasing. She could be overwhelmed without help. The two of you will be bound together with the Son and remember that a three-fold cord is not easily broken. But be wary, the enemy knows about your elevation and will attempt to use it against you. Remember to stay humble in your new power."

Turning to Mark he said, "Pray for guidance in all things and listen to Carol to find the team's way through the pitfalls and snares of the enemy. Mark, Yahveh loves you because your heart is pure in your efforts to walk in His will and He understands the great effort you have made to be His agent on Earth. He wants you to stand against the enemy in leading the Crossfire Team in combat. He is expanding your abilities and your strength to lead the team in wisdom. Be wary of pride! Be humble in the knowledge that you are being blessed because you have been humble not because of whom you are or what you have done. You have always been blessed by the

Lord to achieve and that will continue as long as you acknowledge Him as the source of those abilities."

The angel seemed to listen to something no one else could hear. He turned and looked at David Zahavy and Alexis Hutton. "David, you and Alexis will be important in the coming battles against the human enemy in the land of Russia. Stay in prayer and walk according to the word. Yahveh is proud of you both and your zeal to do His work. Each of you is a formidable force but together you will present a Kingdom force that the enemy will not be able to defeat or even understand."

Caleb seemed to grow brighter and he looked at the others in the group. "Su Li, you have already earned your wings in Yahveh's Air Force and His blessings will give you the strength to soar in your service to him as he directs the team. Listen to Michael White as you two join forces, he has much to teach you and the time is short."

"Stan and Debbie, Charlie and Linda, John Harris, Mike Coffer, and Willie Peterson, know that Yahveh is with you in Spirit and will stand with each of you in your battles as you strive for Him. John, Mike, and Willie will not be returning to Russia because Yahveh wants them to do His will back in the United States."

Caleb lastly looked at Demitri. "Demitri, your new faith is being strengthened so that you truly understand that the Lord's kingdom is eternal and that the gates of death cannot stand against his empire. While you are also not going back to Russia this time, your role in coming battles will be pivotal in bringing an important remnant in your country to true faith in Yahshua. Do not worry about your life or your position. Just remember your position in Yahveh's realm. That is the only important concern. Yahveh will be with you always."

Caleb included them all in his last comments. "Understand that by defeating this demonic union the Crossfire Team will strengthen the control of the country by the leaders who will eventually lead their people against Israeli in the future. This is how it has to be to fulfill the scriptures. Remember also, that we will be with you as you do Yahveh's will."

Caleb faded from sight and the room seemed darker with his going.

Jack looked around at the amazement on the faces around him. Especially on the faces of the three men of the SOG. This is the first time they had encountered an angelic messenger that addressed them directly.

Laura took a deep breath, thanked the Father for His message and turned to Jack. "I would say we got our answer and we need to tell the President what is about to happen."

David spoke up in awe. "Do you all realize the import of the angel's words? The Crossfire Team, as one of Yahveh's hands on Earth, is going to directly affect the world as described in Biblical prophecy. Our part will impact the entire future of everyone in the human race. Do you know how momentous that is? I can only truly stand in awe of the trust and responsibility Yahveh has placed on us."

Alexis nodded and added, "This is truly fantastic for all of us, especially me. My parents would be so proud to know what I am doing."

Laura smiled, "Don't worry about that Alexis, you'll get a chance to see them in heaven and trust me, they will know."

CHAPTER THIRTY-TWO

After contacting the President with their agreement for most of them to return to Russia, Jack asked for the particulars concerning their return.

The President did not seem surprised at their decision. It was simply a confirmation of the dream he had had the night before. "I personally want to thank each and every one of you for putting your lives on the line for, not only Yahveh, but for your country also. I have six scenarios in front of me from the alphabet agencies as to the probable future if the Russian criminal element gains control of Russia, its military might, and its foreign policy. The best is very dark and pessimistic. The worst is the stuff nightmares are made of with the entire world waging war and driving the remaining humans back to the Stone Age in less than six months."

President Bollen stared at each of the people facing him. "I will see that this country honors each of you and the Crossfire Team after the successful conclusion of this matter. I assure you that this time you will not be ignored or forgotten by this country."

Jack smiled, "You know you don't have to reward or honor us Mr. President. Our bill will be in the mail when we return." That was a running joke between the two men for the last few years. Besides, you don't know that we will be successful."

The President laughed. "Oh, but I do know. An angelic being told me that you would stand to battle and be victorious. If there is anything this country can do to help you, let me know. I'll be listening for your call."

The President moved some papers aside on his desk. "You are to present yourselves, armed as you want, to a General Lenoid Gennadiy at the Moscow Airport at a time of your choosing as long as it is not later than tomorrow at twelve noon, Moscow time. He will give you written bona fides ensuring your freedom from any previous actions and the actions to be taken in this matter. You will be given controlling rank in the Russian Army and can command their troops as needed to quell the criminal elements and their attempts to subvert the true authority of the leaders of the country."

The President smiled, "This demonic angle has them committed to support your team to the nth degree. Can you meet their timetable?"

Jack thought for a few seconds. "Yes Sir, we can meet their demands for being there. I just hope they plan to keep their word on our support."

The President looked narrowly at Jack. "What are you implying?"

Jack shook his head, "Yahveh has said that he will come against any criminal element in the human or spiritual realms. If the leaders of Russian go back on their word to us I don't think they will have a prayer of escaping hell."

The President thought over that statement. "Oh, I see. Well, I will wish you God's speed and will pray for your success. Keep in touch as you can."

After they concluded their business at the Mossad the team rounded up the Virginia Tour ladies and gave them into the hands of the three SOG forces and Demitri to get them home safely.

Demitri looked at Mark, "And who is going to see to our safety?" He was implying that the ladies might be more than they could handle.

The rest of the Crossfire Team headed back to the airport to find a flight to Moscow.

Once the trip was arranged everyone had dinner and waited for their departure. It was the only flight they could use to get to their appointed place on time. It would be a red-eye special out of Greece and would get them there two hours before noon Moscow time.

Jack thought back to what the President had passed along from the Russians, "armed as you want". There was no time to get specialized weapons and they had no authority to take them on a commercial airliner anyway. The Russian General would be surprised to find them unarmed at the airport. He looked over at Mark and Sarah who were talking like any other married couple. Jack got everyone's attention and the six of them were led to a table and sat down.

Jack grinned at the others at the table. "I don't think we've ever gone on such a major mission without a plan, without weapons, without any Intel as to anything about the enemy. The enemy, the spiritual enemy, is gearing up for us and the human enemy wants us dead yesterday. Yet," He looked at each of the others, "I feel that we are totally focused on doing Yahveh's will and that regardless of the personal outcomes in this matter, we win."

Sarah had been nodding through his whole spiel, "Jack, you are so right. This assignment is going to be a huge test to see if each of us will lean back into Yahveh's arms and walk out His will."

Mark shook his head while grinning. "I have to agree with both of you. Still, it would be nice if we had an idea of what we are going to do when we get there."

Laura listened carefully to her husband and her best friends as they were being stretched in their faith and belief. She held up her right hand. "We will do well. Just remember your confidence in the Savior and the Father and walk it out. I'm sure that the challenges will be enormous and will tax each of us beyond our previous personal bests, still, it is a wonderful opportunity to show the world your complete love and reliance on the Father of the universe." These were not just words of encouragement they were words of truth.

Alexis and David had been listening to the four core members of the team and were in awe of their reliance on Yahveh's provision and protection. David grinned a small grin at Alexis and tipped his head to give her the permission to speak before him.

Alexis stood up and said, "Excuse me a second. I realize I'm the newbie in this group, especially in matters supernatural, but doesn't it strike any of you a little harsh that you're going in blind, dumb, and uninformed?"

Laura laughed and got up. She walked over to Alexis and hugged her. "Girl, you'll catch on soon. The very fact that we're trusting Yahveh while going in blind, dumb, and uninformed is the core statement of the team's faith in Yahveh."

Laura leaned over so that she was on a level with the younger woman and looked in Alexis' eyes. "Don't you see? The fact that we're ill equipped for this trip tells us that Yahveh is completely in charge of everything we're going to do. It is no surprise to Yahveh that we have no knowledge of the enemy. He gave us the job to do and He will supply all our needs as they arise. You watch and see if I'm not right."

Alexis realized at that point that she had not given her whole life to Yahveh and Yahshua. She had been keeping back just a little part, just in case God let her down. "How silly of me." she thought. Taking a deep breath she prayed silently, "Father, again I sin the sin of pride in my abilities, training, and experiences. Please, please, forgive me my audacity in thinking I could never do better than You at anything. I know You are my provision and my protection. Help me to repent of my sin and turn away from it completely. I will trust You to run my life and use my talents and abilities as You want to."

She turned to Laura and smiled at her. "A hard lesson to learn when my whole life and training taught me to rely on myself."

David leaned over and put his hand on Alexis' arm. "That is a lesson we have all have had to learn." He smiled at her. "Try doing it when, as a dedicated Jew you've been killed and Yahshua heals you and tells you that it wasn't your time to die." David was referring to the time he had been shot saving Sarah and Laura in Israel before the poisoning."

Their dinner was served and afterward they relaxed at the table while each one of them was thinking about their near future involvement with Russia.

The announcement of the boarding for their flight caused them all to quickly get their things and get to the loading ramp. Jack silently thanked their connection to the Mossad which allowed them to ease through the famously strict Israeli El Al airline's security measures.

On the flight Debbie sat between Laura and Alexis. She looked at Laura's relaxed face and asked, "How can you be so relaxed when you don't have your cosmetics, toiletries, makeup, or even a washcloth?"

Laura almost laughed, "Debbie, between almost being fried in a nuclear explosion, poisoned to death, killed by demons in more nations than I knew existed four years ago, not to mention all the other people trying to destroy all of us, I have learned to do the best I can for my looks with whatever is available. Do you know that I used to wish that Jack would take me camping so that I could get out of the city? Hah!"

Debbie thought about that. "Maybe I have my priorities out of order. Okay, I think I'll see if sleep will make me more beautiful."

Alexis grinned at the girl talk. She closed her eyes and settled back in her couch seat as best as possible. Her dreams included massive deadly forces rushing at her and her trying to bat them away with an eyeliner brush.

CHAPTER THIRTY-THREE

The flight seemed endless compared to their flights on the Shrew or on other military aircraft. Eventually though, it landed at Sheremetyevo-2 and the team assembled at the customs area at 10:30 a.m. Moscow time. The outside temperature was a balmy five degrees F when they got off the plane.

The customs officials had not been informed as to their arrival and since none of them had passports with visas for their trip to Russia they were not granted entrance to the country. In fact the customs officials would not listen to their explanations of being there at the country's invitation. Several police officers watched them carefully, keeping their hands on their sidearms while the customs officials determined what to do with them.

Twenty five minutes later there was a commotion at the entrance door and a conflict erupted with the customs officials and the police attempting to restrain people from entering the customs area.

Suddenly a machine gun was fired at full auto rate and everyone scattered or dropped to the floor with the exception of the Crossfire Team who was so used to firefights they just watched curiously to see what would transpire since the bullets didn't seem to be directed at them.

The chief customs official was shoved back into the customs area so hard he fell to the floor and rolled over twice. Several armed military officers walked through the door to customs and looked at the team. The General in charge of the military was holding a smoking submachine gun. He made a short statement to the three dozen military troops which followed them into the customs area. Since five of the team spoke Russian it was clear the General wasn't happy. "If any of these customs flunkies or policemen so much as asks a question I want him, or her, shot. Failure to do so will result in your being shot, immediately. Am I perfectly clear on this matter?"

The troops snapped their heels together and saluted the General. They commenced locking and loading their weapons and pointing them at the various customs officials and police in the area.

The General handed the weapon to an aide and strode over to the Crossfire Team and bowed slightly. "I am General Lenoid Gennadiy. I apologize for Mother Russia for the mistake of these, well-intentioned, but paperbound officials. I also apologize for the communications mistakes that did not inform them of your impending arrival. Please forgive us."

He stuck out his right hand to Mark who took his hand and shook it with a slight smile on his face. "We accept your apologies General. I am Mark Connelly of the Crossfire Team. I have heard of you and your efforts to make the civilians as well as the military more efficient. How has the effort been going?"

The General's face lit up when he heard his name was recognized outside the country. "It is like teaching a pig to sing. But then, General Connelly, we are also aware of your well-known history. Many of my comrades speak highly of your efficiency and professionalism, even if you do work for a decadent government"

Mark thought, "If he only knew", and proceeded to introduce the rest of the team. He then suggested to General Gennadiy that it would be more efficient if they got the paperwork completed so that they could enter into the country before the entire city of Moscow showed up to see what was going on at the airport.

The General appointed one of his troops to acquire the necessary documents. Then the General and two squads of his troops escorted the team out of the customs area and through the airport to waiting vehicles. The three cars were modern Mercedes Benz S550 Limousines which said a lot about how much the military would spend to impress them considering the crippled Russian economy.

Jack, Laura, Mark, Sarah, and David got into the first limo with General Gennadiy. The rest of the team split into two groups and climbed into the other two vehicles. There was little talking on the trip and the three vehicles eventually pulled into a garage. Jack noticed that there were numerous military vehicles that had been pacing them. These vehicles and the majority of the troops remained outside the building and formed a defensive ring around it.

After exiting the limos the team walked over to a large conference table that was set up in the empty part of the garage. It was professionally lit from above with suspended lights and was well set up with communications equipment at every seat including computer monitors and large screens suspended beyond the ends of the table. The chairs were comfortable and ergonomically designed for support.

After everyone was seated the General looked at the team and summed up the operation from his view. "This will serve as a general headquarters for the operation of your team. It was selected at random to prevent any spying on your activities and to give you security from the scum that are terrorizing our city. I have assigned troops and drivers for a dozen different parallel operations. As you need to confront this "unusual" enemy you will contact me and I will authorize detachments of troops and vehicles to respond to the events. We will be monitoring the country and will advise you when your services are needed. Are we clear on how we are to operate?"

Jack looked at the other team members and spoke to the General. "We want to thank you for the efforts you have expended on our behalf General. The original terms that were communicated to our President indicated that we would be free to operate as we needed to, when we needed to, and did not include clearing everything through you. We are here to assist your country in your battles, especially with these, "unusual" entities. But, we need to do it on our terms if we are to be successful. In anticipation of your next question which will be "why?" I will offer you one significant factor."

Jack waved his hand to indicate the entire Russian countryside. "While the mandated lack of religion in your country is causing you to deny what you actually see happening, it is real. The power behind these "beings" is antithetical to human life and has had thousands of years to perfect their ability to control people who are not protected by the God you say doesn't exist. We have the ability to resist these "urges" and "suggestions" that are normally spoken in a voice the person has heard for their entire life. This makes one think that it is their thoughts telling them what to do. We have to have autonomous control to combat these forces. If that is not acceptable to you then we might as well head back to the airport and go home." Jack sat down and waited for the General's response. It should be a doozy considering the darkening color to the General's face as he listened to Jack.

The General shook his head. "I cannot allow you to run around Russia without oversight. It would be…"The ringing of a cell phone interrupted the General's comments. He stopped talking and fumbled the phone out of his tunic pocket. He flipped it open and put it to his ear. "Da!"

The General listened to the loud voice on the other end of the phone. He slowly rose from his chair and stood at attention. After several minutes he said, "Mr. Secretary, I must submit my resignation before I can obey those orders. You can surely find another…"

Again the voice came over the other end of the conversation. The General blanched and almost turned white. He frowned and then sighed loudly. "Yes Mr. Secretary. I will do as you have ordered." He shut the phone and sat down slowly.

After a minute of reflection he looked up at Jack. "it seems I have no choice but to do as you have asked me to do. I will help you in any way I can." His voice was hollow and devoid of emotion. It almost sounded like a dead man's voice.

Sarah had a revelation and went over to the chair next to the General. She sat down and looked the man in the eyes. "General, God has told me the threat that the Secretary has made against you to have you do this thing our way."

The General looked at her and then at his phone like it was a snake.

Sarah put her hand over the phone in his hand. "Don't worry; we haven't compromised your communications. I know it is hard for a life-long atheist to understand but God really does know everything. He told me He will protect you and your family because you are working with us in His name to defeat the enemy of mankind. Also, don't worry about negative reports from us because there won't be any. We are here on a common mission and we will succeed."

The General looked at the intense young woman in front of him and realized he trusted her. He nodded and told her, "Thank you. I owe you my life and those of my family. I will not let you down."He looked at Jack and asked what the team needed to do their mission.

Jack deferred to Mark who started telling the General what they needed in the way of Intel feeds and gave him a website to contact.

The General told one of the technicians to set the website up and project it on the large screen at the south end of the table. In a few seconds the screen lit up with six windows. A large window showed the entire Russian state while the other screens were blank. A pattern appeared on the large screen with bars on the sides and top and bottom.

Charlie Wu, who spoke passable Russian, explained to the General and his aides that this projection was a composite of satellite images from all birds covering Russia at the present time. He indicated that any demonic activity would be spotted and indicated by the big screen. As each one occurred it would be split off into one of the smaller screens at greater definition.

Suddenly there was a bright flare of a red light on the map of Russia and one of the smaller screens showed a portion of Moscow with a square indicating one specific building.

Mark identified the building as the garage they were in right then. He looked at Sarah and yelled, "Heads up, we've got company!"

CHAPTER THIRTY-FOUR

While Sarah had been talking to the Russian General, Laura had been praying for Yahveh's protection for the site they were at and to make all the local demons blind and deaf to the team's operations.

Laura got the distinct impression that her prayer was not appreciated very well by the enemy. There was an ugly cracking, creaking, and groaning that blasted the entire audible spectrum making everyone put their hands over their ears. Laura watched as three demons stepped out of the spiritual plane and into the human plane inside the garage. The lead demon was probably as ugly as any of the team had seen so far. Its head that would have made an alligator look friendly. It had a long snout with a fang-filled mouth and a lizard's tongue flickering in and out. The deeply inset eyes were malevolent with a hatred burning in them. It had an armored body and a black sword and balanced on legs as thick as tree trunks. The other two were just normally large and ugly demons with swords

Two of the Russian troops closest to the demons leveled their weapons but were hacked to death before they could fire. The demons were very fast with their swords. The three demons started running towards the table with the Crossfire Team around it. As the Russian troops tried to stop the trio they were thrown to the side or hacked to death.

Laura and Sarah began praying in earnest and headed towards the demons. General Gennadiy may not of understood what was coming at him but he was not a coward. He attempted to step between Sarah and the demons. Sarah put her hand on his chest and stopped the man in his tracks. She smiled at him and stepped towards the demons that were almost at the table. The General would always remember that smile. It wasn't a friendly smile but a confirmation that she would deal with the demon. The General was suddenly very glad she wasn't coming for him.

As Laura and Sarah paced toward the demons and continued to pray their golden armor, shields, and the swords of the Word appeared in an explosion of color and brilliance that lit up the garage. Both women went on the offensive and stepped between the demons and the table with their swords at high guard. The two side demons that were much more massive than the women attacked with their swords. Both Laura and Sarah easily parried the larger black blades with their brilliant blades streaming the Esteem of Yahveh.

As the women battled the two demons, the lead demon continued to advance on the team at the table. Mark stepped over and pulled the handgun out of the General's holster and fired three rounds into the demon. There was no noticeable effect and the demon raised his sword to swing at the two men. Mark and the General danced away from the demon's sword as he swung it in a viscous arc.

In her battle with one of the demons Laura relaxed into the combat knowing that Yahveh was her power and her protection. The demon knocked Laura's sword to the side and grabbed at the golden pest in front of him.

Laura's righteous anger grew beyond anything she had ever felt. She let out a combat scream that raised the hair on everyone in the room. The sheer power filling her was off the scale and she let the demon know she wasn't happy. As the demon knocked her sword to her right she did something she never thought she'd do. She rocketed her left fist into the face of the demon with the feeling it was steam piston. Her fist hit the demon so hard his face crumbled around the fist and he was thrown ten feet away to land in an unconscious heap.

Her anger still rising Laura walked over to the helpless beast and swung her sword so hard it decapitated the demon and sank eight inches into the concrete of the floor. She jerked it out as the demon evaporated into a nasty red smoke. Laura knew the battle wasn't over yet because she was getting more angry and if looks could kill the lead demon would have died right then and there. She ran at the back of the evil being that was destroying the table and chairs in an effort to get to Mark.

Jack stepped up and side kicked the demon hard enough to distract him from Mark and the General. The demon swung his sword in a nasty backhand that almost caught Jack who had jumped back away from the creature. Mark emptied the pistol into the demon which obviously only made it madder.

Sarah had blocked the black blade her demon swung at her and backhanded her blade at the neck of the demon. The demon leaned backwards and avoided the glowing blade. The righteous anger of Yahveh suddenly filled Sarah and she waded into the beast with her blade flashing in circles and slashes so rapid that the demon couldn't block all of them.

The demon attempted to kick Sarah with his right leg which left him with only one leg after she had cut the first one off with one swipe of her sword. The next three swings left the one-legged demon evaporating into red smoke without arms or head.

Sarah didn't say a word but ran at the demon at the table who was attempting to kill her husband. Both women came to the demon at the same time. It sensed the danger and swung around to battle them. There was something in the faces of the women that drove fear into the demon even though he had killed hundreds of angels and humans in his time. The combination attack of the two women overwhelmed his defense and ended quickly with both glowing swords skewering the alligator faced demon who died hissing and banging his feet on the floor.

Laura and Sarah were still attempting to work off the anger that filled them. Laura slammed her sword into the concrete hard enough to shake the vehicles in the garage. She raised her arms and beseeched Yahveh in heaven to place a hedge of protection around the team and the garage that the enemy could not penetrate. Sarah stood next to Laura scanning the garage for more demons to kill. Mark noted the look on her face and decided he wouldn't draw her attention at this particular time.

Both of the women's armor faded from view along with their swords and shields. They came together and hugged. Laura said, "You are very good with a blade for a newbie."

Sarah grinned and pointed upward, "I was just following His lead."

As they walked back to the table several things fell to the floor and bounced around. Laura eyed them and realized they were pieces of concrete she had carved out of the floor. She looked at Jack, shrugged her shoulders and sat down.

Mark handed the smoking pistol back to the General who just stood there in shock. What he had just seen couldn't possibly have happened, yet it did happen. He dropped into his seat and shook his head to clear the fog threatening to overwhelm him. He asked Mark, "Can they just appear wherever they want to?"

Laura shook her head and answered for Mark. "They have to obey certain rules and we can pray for protection against that type of attack. I was in the process of doing just that when they decided to try and stop me."

One of the troops in the garage stepped up to the General and saluted him. "Sir, could you please explain to the men what just happened here?"

The General looked lost and held out his hand to the team. Mark smiled; it was his turn to talk to the troops.

CHAPTER THIRTY-FIVE

Using four of the chairs, Mark and Jack constructed a set of temporary legs for the end of the table the demon had smashed with his sword. It was a bit shaky but it held for the time being.

The troops had removed the bodies of their comrades who had been killed by the demons and cleaned up the area. Five men had been killed and three injured badly enough to require hospitalization. The remaining troops gathered to one side of the table to listen to Mark as he attempted to explain what they had just experienced.

Mark walked over to the side the troops were on and told them in Russian to sit on the floor in a semicircle. He told them not to worry about staying on guard because this was a different enemy that did not fight in the normal way. Standing on guard was not a usable tactic in this type of battle. This was something that they couldn't guard against.

While the men were getting seated Mark prayed that Yahveh would give him the right words to say to them to encourage them and make it clear what they were up against. He also prayed that Yahveh would make his Russian acceptable enough to convey His words to the troops.

Mark looked at the men arrayed in front of him. Mostly conscripts but men who had shown a great deal of bravery. "Men, I want you to know that I am proud of you for standing against something you could not understand. To fight this enemy you need to think in a new way. I do not wish to speak against the atheism that your heritage, your parents, your leaders, and your training have instilled in you. But, I must. You cannot fight creatures like the ones you saw in this garage today by denying they exist. You will die as will those you are protecting if you ignore this enemy."

Mark raised his arms. "Soldiers of Russia! Your duty to protect your motherland is at stake here. You must learn to combat these demons that cannot be killed by weapons. To start learning about them you need to admit they exist. By extension, if these evil, satanic beings exist, then their master, Satan exists. If Satan exists then so does God and the angels who are God's messengers and warriors."

Mark lowered his arms and gestured upward with his right hand. God has an army just like Russia and the other countries of the world. He battles with Satan for the souls of all men, women, and children."

At that point Mark could see some confusion in their eyes. "Let me tell you about the spiritual world so that you can understand better. In the beginning, before time, there was God. He created the world and the heavens and he also created our ancestors. God wants a relationship with his children, which includes each one of you. This is an ultimately powerful being that loves each and every one of you."

One of the men asked, "If this God is so powerful why doesn't he just kill Satan and have peace on the Earth?"

Mark smiled at the man. "Because He is also a powerful judge who made rules for everything and everyone. He cannot break His own rules to remove Satan because He would not be a just God. He set rules for every man to obey and if He broke His own rules then He would not be God."

Another man asked, "Who is this Satan and where do these demons come from?"

Mark nodded at the questioner. "Good question. Satan was the highest of God's angels until his pride caused him to rebel against God in an attempt to take over heaven and rule in God's place. He got one third of the angels in heaven to go against God with him. In the battle that determined the control of heaven, God and his faithful angels prevailed and Satan and the angels that had rebelled against God were thrown down to earth until the day of judgment. Over time, Satan's evil infested the fallen angels until they became the demons they are now. You see, they didn't have God's love and presence to keep them from falling into evil. Satan hated the man and woman that God created to tend his world because God made men and women, like you and us, lower than the angels on this earth but higher than the angels after the humans are in heaven. Satan's ego couldn't accept anybody higher than himself so he acted as a serpent in the Garden of Eden to make them sin against God. Satan stole the control of the world from them and alienated all men from God."

The man asked, "How then do you get to God?"

Mark smiled, "God is a lot smarter than Satan. He had lost the world to Satan by man's sin and God needed a sinless man to get it back. Not finding a single man on the Earth who was sinless, He created that man who never sinned during his thirty-three years on earth and Satan had that man killed. When Satan killed an innocent man he broke a major law. God restored the life to the sinless man that Satan had killed and the man regained the control of the earth and restored man's access to God so that they could be together again. That sinless man is known as Jesus Christ and as the Son of God He rules the earth for God.

The first questioner asked, "How can we fight these fallen angels?"

Mark took a deep breath, this was the crucial answer. "You cannot fight them in your strength or with your weapons. Only God has the power to defeat the lowliest of demons. To do combat with these beings you have to partner with God and be working with Him here on Earth. That's not as complicated as it sounds. You will have to believe in your heart that He is God and that He and His Son exist. Then you need to ask His Son for His help in defeating these beings. Then, you need to do what He tells you to do. The Father and the Son love you and want the best for you. But God needs soldiers who are intelligent and willing to stand against the enemy as His agents on Earth."

Another of the troops asked, "What if my commander tells me to do one thing but God tells me to do another?"

Mark smiled, "If you are working for God you'll know the answer to that question if it comes up. Remember, God is in charge of all things on this earth and he gave your commanders their position to help you succeed. Not all commanders are great leaders of men." That got a chuckle and quite a few comments between the men.

Mark gauged the mindset the men were in and decided to step out boldly. "I need you to understand something about spiritual combat. You can be working for God and His Son Jesus and doing what they say, and your body can still die doing your duty. But, your spirit is immortal and will live forever. If you die for God, He will keep your spirit with him for the rest of time in a place called heaven. If you don't have a relationship with His son Jesus, then your spirit will be cast out into the darkness where there is terror, horror, and no hope forever."

Mark waved his hand to indicate the Crossfire Team behind him. "All of these people have given their lives to God and we are on the front lines of God's war against the enemy of all mankind, Satan. You saw the weapons the Father gave to Laura and Sarah. We could use you on our side if you really want to fight for Russia and all Russians against the criminal element and their new friends, the demons, any questions?" Every hand in the audience went up immediately.

Mark got David, Sarah, Charlie, Alexis, and Linda to work with him giving the troops answers to their questions since they all spoke Russian.

After the troops ran out of questions Mark turned to the General. "General, what I have spoken to your troops is the truth. I believe in Russia it is against the law to believe in Jesus or God. What would you have them do?"

The General had been thinking about the same things. He stood up and faced his men. "Men, I have been given wide-ranging powers by the President and the Secretary to deal with these "unusual" enemies and their infestation in our land. I hereby suspend any and all proscriptions against religion or Christianity for each and every one of you during the duration of these battles. I will have that in writing to each of you before the night is done. Afterwards, you will have to deal with whatever the law is then."

One of the men asked the General, "What about my parents or a man's wife and children. If we can join with God, why can't they?"

The General smiled at the man. "I didn't hear anything so I have nothing to report. You will have to do as this God says, not me."

That afternoon, forty-seven of the fifty-five support troops had accepted Jesus and given their love and lives to Him. The General had questioned if God would take him because of his previous life. Sarah had convinced him that God still loved him regardless of his earlier life and that his earlier sins would be forgiven if his confession was from his heart and he really meant it. Crying, from happiness as many of his men were also doing, he joined his troops in serving the Father and the Son.

Jack and Mark detailed the Russian speaking members of the team to help teach the troops the quick version of how to pray, be baptized, and to walk with and for God. They got the General to help them determine where and how they would spread the troops along with at least one team member across Russia to deal with the enemy and the demons. Their special emphasis was on defeating the demons. Therefore, they would wait until the Cray computers in Colorado pinpointed spiritual activity and then attempt to get to that point.

The problem was simply volume. There were too many places in Russia that could become hot spots to be covered by the few teams of soldiers and team members. By the time they got there, whatever the event was it would probably be over.

Laura reminded them that the Father sent them here to combat the demonic element and he wouldn't have done that when they couldn't do it due to the distances.

Jack got a call on his cell phone from Colorado. Carol said, "I've seen the resolution to your problem in the heavenlies Jack."

This was a revelation in itself because he hadn't communicated the problem to Colorado.

Carol laughed. "Don't be so surprised Jack. The problem is obvious. But Yahveh has leveled the playing field. He has limited demonic intrusions to Moscow alone by declaring that If demons break out anywhere else in Russia, He will handle the disobedience personally, before anyone knows it's happening. Just take care of Moscow and Yahveh will take care of the rest of Russia."

When Jack announced this to the others it gave them hope that they could combat the intrusions. Of course,

Moscow was a huge city in its own right with a population of over eleven million people.

CHAPTER THIRTY-SIX

It was a long three days before the first alert was detected by the Fortress. A popular eatery on Mokhovaya was a Georgian restaurant that had a long history of serving good wholesome food in Moscow. It was one of the best with one half of the restaurant slightly kitsch, with mock caves and rough wooden furniture and a terrace. The other half was more modern with multicolored furniture. The menu was very traditional: featuring items like kharcho (stewed beef in a walnut sauce), chikmirta (citrus chicken and coriander soup) and khinkali (spiced dumplings) which were all Georgian classics. This restaurant had some live and often loud folk music as the evening's entertainment and even some dancing.

The one thing that stood out in the police files about this restaurant was that it resisted the strong-arm tactics of the criminal element. It was a 'democratichny' to keep out hooligans. Apparently they were to be made an example of with this first demonic attack.

The combined American and Russian assembly had been separated into defensive teams stationed at strategic places around the city. As the closest "flying team" to the restaurant, Jack and Laura were dispatched as soon as a potential disturbance was detected.

The special combination of military and police escort got them to their target in less than six minutes and the team jumped out of the military truck and ran to the restaurant's front door. They were met there by the door guards who were going to deny them entrance until the police captain with them showed them his badge and credentials. They walked in quietly and looked around the somewhat noisy restaurant. They exited the old part of the business and entered the newer part.

Laura looked at Jack, "You think maybe we've got the wrong place?"

Jack shook his head and reached for his cell phone.

Just then there was a scream from the back of the new area and people started running for the exits. Jack's eyes turned icy. "Nope, we were just early for the party."

The team spread out with the owner rushing up behind them thinking they were causing the problem. He changed his mind when four of the local Mafia came walking towards them with a demon behind them. The demon was black, large, and had a bad disposition. Couple that with the big club he was carrying and nobody wanted to stay around.

As the last of the patrons exited the area, the police Captain called on the criminals to put down their weapons and surrender. The leader of the group shook his head and told the Captain to leave now while he had a chance.

The military members of the squad brought their rifles up and as they advanced on the criminals the demon pushed his way forward to deal with them.

Laura started to pray the 23rd Psalm and her armor and sword appeared with a sudden flash. She walked forward in her golden armor at the demon who suddenly didn't want to be there. The criminals urged the demon to destroy the woman and raised their guns to fire at her.

The Captain ordered the men to open fire on the criminals just as Laura made up the demon's mind by running at him with her sword at high guard. The esteem of Yahveh was streaming off of the blade and made a heavenly sound as it flew through the air.

The demon wasn't going to go down easy as the criminals were obliterated by the military rifle fire. He stepped up and tried to smash Laura to the ground with his huge club. Laura parried the blow and cut the club in half with a circular slash of her sword. The demon started backpedaling to get away from the sword but ran into one of the bodies of the criminals who had been shot. He almost tripped on the body and risked a quick look behind him to see how much room he had left. When he looked back all he saw was the gleaming blade as it swung from his right to his left and cleaved his body in two at the waist. He wanted to scream his anger but only managed a grunt as he faded into an ugly black cloud of oily smoke.

Laura kept praying until she was sure there were no demonic backups and then lowered her sword. Her armor disappeared along with the shield and sword. The restaurant had become quiet now. The owner stared at the black smoke and the bodies on the floor. He turned to the Captain and thanked him profusely. He then offered free food for any of the team whenever they came to his restaurant.

The police tagged the bodies and called for a disposal team to clean up the restaurant.

As the group reassembled outside the eatery, the Captain turned to Laura and bowed from the waist. In broken English he thanked her for her heroic effort on the part of Mother Russia. Laura smiled and shook his hand.

Jack called Mark and told him what had happened. At the end of the description he added, "I think they have to set up a portal for the demon or demons to come through and this is something we can detect early enough to get to the location in time. But, if I were doing their part I would figure this out soon and set up phony locations to have us running all over the place and not know which ones were real."

Mark thought about it and asked Jack to call Carol and see if she could detect which ones were real in the heavenlies before they happened. Jack thought that was a fantastic idea and rang off to call the Fortress.

The entire team got together twenty-four hours later by cell phone and recapped the action. Nine actual attacks with demons, all were countered either by gunfire, Laura, or Sarah. It turned out that the demons apparently had the right to step into the human plane but if the criminals with it were killed it faded back out of our dimension. At least so far that had been the result.

The next morning, Mark traveled over to where Jack and Laura were waiting for a new attack after resting. He greeted them and the Russians with them and then had a sit down with Jack, Laura, and the Moscow Police Captain on their team.

Mark started with, "Guys, we're batting one hundred percent right now but I have some concerns. First, the enemy is going to change their tactics now that they see they're being stopped by us. Second, Why this random series of attacks? Are they just distractions while something bigger is being planned? Hopefully Carol can find out what it might be if that is the case. But, the main point is, why? I have a gut feeling that this is not the main thing they are going to do and I think we have to pray about our efforts against this demonic effort."

Jack and Laura agreed while the Captain just watched this strange American group he had grudgingly come to appreciate.

CHAPTER THIRTY-SEVEN

As they got ready to pray, Jack's cell phone chimed. He looked at it and then answered it, "Yes Carol".

Carol's voice came clearly over the phone. She was upset, and reminded Jack of the first time they had seen her in the attack on her building. "Jack!, I am so worried for Mark, and you, and Laura, and all the rest of you guys over there. You have done nothing but the right things! How are you going to face what is coming? I didn't know in this case that there was much more than met the eye."

Jack frowned, "Okay Carol, it will be all right, but what can you tell us about this new revelation?"

Carol sighed, "Nothing, as yet. I'm being restrained because Yahveh wants you to hear this first hand. I'll be waiting for you to call after you talk to Him."

Jack hung up and tipped his head at Mark. "Seems you were right about this being a diversion. Carol says we need to pray and expect to talk to Yahveh."

The Captain and the troops near them watched them as they knelt and prayed.

This time was very different than most prayer times. As soon as they worshiped in the name of the Son and that of the Father they were transported, in the spirit, to a heavenly setting. Jack felt the peace of Yahveh in everything around him.

Looking around Jack saw a beautiful landscape and a sourceless light that illuminated everything with a clear light. Because the light was everywhere there were no shadows. There was a wonderful feeling of unlimited potential and an upwelling in his spirit that brought tears to his eyes.

There was a sweet quiet to the place that belied the serious matters they were there to understand. Still, Jack enjoyed the temporary peace and he sat down in the grass of the meadow in which they had found themselves.

Two people were walking towards them from the distance and Jack's excellent vision picked out both the angel Rose and the angel Caleb long before they drew close. Jack began to realize they weren't walking but sort of floating along at an unhurried pace toward them.

When they were near the angel Caleb held up his right hand in a greeting to the three warriors. He spoke quietly yet they could hear him clearly.

"Jack, Laura, Mark, it is grave tidings we bring to you this time.'

Mark answered for the three of them. "Our lives go as Yahveh wills them to go. We have countered their moves so far but I fear it is simply a distraction or a holding action while something worse is being accomplished."

Caleb glanced at Rose who looked at Mark closely. "Mark, who told you this?"

Mark shook his head, "I don't believe anyone told me, I've just seen similar tactics used by Earthly forces. I also believe that there could easily be many attacks at one time instead one at a time. It doesn't ring true from a group that once threw hundreds of demons at us at one time."

Caleb nodded, "You are wise in the ways of combat. And, you're right in your assumption that it is a distraction rather than the brunt of their attack. That is about to come at you."

Jack asked, "Caleb, how are the few of us going to hold off the hordes?"

Caleb stared directly at Jack and spoke. "I am but a humble servant of the Almighty Yahveh and cannot transport your minds as was done before to see the heavenly answer to your question. I can, however, give you Yahveh's answer to your question in four dimensions. You will have to rely on Carol to interpret the answer."

He seemed to take on a greater power, "Now hear the word of Yahveh, creator of the universe and this world. *The Crossfire Team will confront the forces of Qixalpaq himself. You will have to give everything to prevent a monstrous evil about to be laid on the unexpecting people of the earth before the man of perdition arrives. I will be with each of you and I will not abandon you but it is important that each member of the team stands against the enemy until you can no longer stand. And then to stand again.*

Laura prayed and asked Yahveh, "Is this the end for the Crossfire Team?"

Caleb fell silent as the roaring wind voice of Yahveh spoke directly to the three humans. *"Laura my child, there are many endings and beginnings for each of you. I cannot tell you what is to transpire because it has not been set in time yet. All I can do at this time is to depend on you and all of your team to face this enemy as best you can."*

In her mind Laura heard Yahveh say, *"Laura, the enemy is being allowed to listen to us right now to embolden them. Understand that you must play your part for history to be correct and righteousness to be fulfilled."*

Laura nodded slowly with a great foreboding in her mind.

Caleb looked hurt as he said, "Dear friends, we cannot be with you in the coming battle and for that I am very sad." He faded out and Rose's color changed from the golden hue to the violently white, power color. "Do not fear, do not doubt what every you see or hear. Fight for heaven and fight for Yahveh!"

After Rose faded out the team decided to return to the command center in Russia. Jack stood up and helped Laura up. He enfolded her in his arms and held her. He felt the tears on his face and buried his face on her shoulder. Laura patted his arm and kissed him on the cheek. "Looks like we're in for it this time."

Jack got control of his emotions and wiped his face with the back of his hand. He looked at Mark and saw him the most glum he had ever been. Jack stepped over to his best friend and put his hand on his shoulder. "Chin up buddy, this is what you've been trained for. I'm counting on you."

Mark sighed deeply and nodded. "Never fear, I'm just preparing myself for this battle.

The Captain of the Russian Police asked, "You only knelt a few seconds ago, what has transpired so quickly that sounds so bad?"

Mark grinned at the man. "Time doesn't run at the same rate where we were. Prepare yourself, the main battle is about to happen and it will be THE battle for Russia."

CHAPTER THIRTY-EIGHT

Jack used his cell phone to call all the flying squads together near the Kremlin's onion domes.

All of the Crossfire Team and all of the Russian soldiers and policemen gathered in front of a makeshift stage where Jack stood. He looked at the assembled international team. "Ladies and Gentlemen, God has informed us that the enemy is going to wage an all-out battle for the control of Russia near here, very soon. There will be many demons, major demons, and probably a lot of noise. Don't let their visages or their cries frighten you. They will kill you if they can. Our job is to kill them first.!"

"Because many of them have not been given permission by God to invade our dimension they can be killed with bullets or explosives. Do not hesitate to use your weapons or grenades. The ones that are immune to your weapon fire you may ignore as they are for us to handle."

Jack sighed deeply, "I don't know that we will be victorious or if we will all survive this battle. If you are a servant of the most high that is not a problem as your spirit will live on through eternity with God. If you're not walking with God in a personal relationship I recommend that you leave now and do not take part in the coming combat."

Jack waited and was pleased when only ten or twelve men put down their weapons and walked away from the assembled troops.

"All right, team leaders meet with Mark and myself to determine our battle orders."

The bleak light blue skies over Moscow had a few wispy clouds and the already cold temperature dropped considerably as the sun began to set. The troops arranged themselves to meet an unknown quantity and quality of enemy.

Two hours later it was dark with a few lights to dispel the gloom. There was a icy cold breeze that ghosted through the troops waiting quietly on the large open expanse outside the walls to the Kremlin. They kept a vigilant watch as the evening progressed. Their breath formed a fog before their eyes and shivers weren't uncommon at all.

When Laura came to full attention, Mark spoke into his combat microphone and alerted the rest of the two hundred people who were prepared to fight the enemy.

Jack looked to his right and saw the far group that was headed by Stan and Debbie. They were arranged in a free fire arrangement that would allow each of them to bring the most guns to bear on the enemy. That was, assuming the enemy actually came at them from the chosen direction.

Next to Jack and Laura's team were two groups also in free fire positions, one led by Alexis and the other by David.

Then there was his own team which was more prepared for hand-to-hand with demons that had a legal right to be in the human dimension and couldn't be destroyed by gunfire. Laura took the point with Jack to back her up. To their left was a similar group led by Sarah and Mark.

Demitri and Su Li commanded the next free fire group to Mark's left, with Charlie and Linda Wu holding down the last free fire group to Jack's left.

Sarah had also become alerted and moved forward to stand next to Laura. They were looking thirty degrees to the left of front and center for the teams. Mark spoke into his mic and the entire set of teams to their right wheeled forward while those to their left backed up to form up facing the direction that the two women were facing.

This waiting period was the hardest. Then the area in front of the teams suddenly became populated. Rushing at them were dozens of horrible-looking demons screaming or howling. Some came on all fours with terrible fangs, claws, and grunts. Others lumbered forward on two legs yelling and roaring. There were even some that had more than four legs.

The golden armor and the swords of the Word exploded into existence on Laura and Sarah as they prayed and waited for the ugly horde to reach them.

The fire teams began to fire into the ranks of the demons. Most of the first shots missed due to nerves or the movements of the demons but when they hit they ripped big holes in the demons out of which poured rancid red or black smoke with the demon vaporizing quickly.

Gunfire didn't stop four of the larger demons who advanced at Laura and Sarah. Jack and Mark moved up closer to the women with Japanese Samurai swords. No one knew if they would have any effect on these demons but they didn't have any other way to support their wives.

More and more demons appeared and between their screaming and the gunfire the roar of battle was deafening. The entire battle scene was sporadically lit by the rifle fire which gave a strobe-like effect.

Laura and Sarah stepped into the leading demons and battled them. Laura finished off her demon with a rapid sword block to the demon's blade and a reverse under her right arm plunge directly into the demon's chest. She stepped back and another large demon came around the first to attack her. She went to high guard and faced the second demon without fear.

Sarah had more problems with her demon but finally beheaded him with a sudden reversal in her attack. She went forward at the second demon with fire in her eyes.

The rush of the lesser demons was overcoming the American and the Russian rifle fire and quickly closed with the other teams. Only the area in front of the center teams was still in the hands of Laura and Sarah.

More demons entered into the fray and the battle scene dissolved into chaos with hand-to-hand fighting at all quarters. The Russian troops and police used bayonets and pistols to decimate the demons. As ammo ran out the Russian troops started suffering major defeats.

Jack took on a third demon and managed to cut it down by superior swordsmanship. A heavy blow to his left leg spun him around and dropped him to the ground. He looked at his left leg and saw a large black arrow that had entered his thigh just below his buttock with a large, bloody, sharp end sticking out the front of his thigh. The pain washed over him and almost knocked him out.

A second arrow struck Mark in the back and slammed him to the ground face first in a spray of blood. He laid there, unmoving, with his eyes open and fixed.

Several arrows smashed into Laura and Sarah but bounced off of the golden armor. A large demon smashed Stan to the ground with a club and two smaller demons jumped onto his unconscious form only to be blown away by rifle shots from Debbie's Russian AKS. She stepped over her husband's inert form and cut down any of the lesser demons near them. Debbie had a cut across her face and blood running from an arm wound on her left arm. The look of righteous anger on her face caused several demons to veer off and head toward other targets.

Out of the melee of demons stepped a twelve foot tall bronze demon looking like a heroic human man. He had a large black arc-shaped sword and he rushed to attack Laura. The two dueled for several series before Laura's blazing chrome blade sliced through the demon at the waist and then she whirled her blade and beheaded the wounded creature.

Sarah encountered a second bronze giant and became an imitation of a helicopter blade. The speed of her sword work outran the bronzed demon's ability to defend against the attack and she drove the blade through the demon's throat and out the back of its neck. It fell away from her.

As she stepped away from the last demon, Laura's heart jumped into her throat when she saw Jack fighting from the ground against the smaller demons that were crowding around him. She stepped back and hacked eight of them to pieces before facing back to the front.

There was a major commotion at the back of the pack of demons and screams and moans reached her ears. She saw an even larger bronzed demon clad in silver armor and wearing a purple cape. He was striding through the crowd of demons and was either smashing or slashing them to either side with his huge black sword.

He reached the leading edge of the battle with the humans and came up against Laura.

The demon swung a powerful stroke from his right to the left and Laura countered with a vertical block. The black blade knocked the gleaming blade out of Laura's hands and it disappeared as it left her hand and flew into the air. The giant demon swung his blade backhand and the side hit Laura in the right side. The blow knocked her five feet into the air and slammed her to the ground near Jack.

Sarah attacked the huge demon and was smashed backward into the ground. Her sword and armor disappeared as she fell to the ground barely conscious.

The big demon spoke a command and the rest of the lesser demons stopped attacking and backed up until they were behind the major demon, even though they snarled and complained about having to desist. The demon looked at the smashed and broken people making up the Crossfire Team and the few standing Russian soldiers that supported them. There was no one able to stand against him at this time.

His deep bass voice was nasty and oily. "Kneel before me and worship me or die now!"

Laura's right arm was hanging useless, her left ankle didn't want to work, and she felt like she'd been run over by a truck. But, she forced herself to a standing position and spoke in a strained voice to the imposing demon. "We will never bow or worship a piece of Satan-slime like you. You can kill our bodies but you will never touch our souls. We are servants of the Most High Yahveh Elohim and His son, Yahshua..."

The demon roared, "You will not speak those names in my presence! I am in charge here you worms, and your God does not care about you nor does he tell me what to do!"

He raised his black sword to strike her down but couldn't bring it down as she stood there defying the demon waiting for the blow. The muscles in his arms bulged and strained but the blade would not descend. The demon started to shake and dropped the sword. You could tell he wanted to turn and run but could not. The roar of screams and grunts from the lesser demons quit suddenly as they all disappeared.

A silence fell over the combat area and a wave of peace filled everyone. Laura wanted to collapse and sleep but couldn't do it while she faced the large demon with the silver armor. A man dressed in white linen walked slowly from behind the humans. His bare feet bore scars as did his hands. He was darkly Caucasian and had black ringlets of hair descending from his head. He had eyes that one could only describe as filled with love.

He walked up and stopped next to Laura. He looked at the giant demon with sadness. He said, "Qixalpaq, you have broken your promise to Yahveh to remain in the second heaven. You are thereby guilty of defying Yahveh. You are to go to the pit until you are judged at the end of time."

The huge demon slowly knelt to one knee and said, "Yes Master". He faded out of sight with a look of incredible sorrow.

Yahshua turned to the defenders and looked with compassion on the dead and broken warriors. He put his hand on Laura's shoulder and looked in her eyes. He spoke with such love that it was palatable to the other people. "Good and faithful servant, you have served well, be healed and give thanks to Yahveh."

He turned to Jack and squatted down next to him. Smiling at Jack he said, "I'm truly sorry that you all had to go through this battle but it was needed to draw Qixalpaq out of the second heaven as was foretold by the prophets."

He waved his hand to include all of the warriors. "You have all served in the highest order of heaven's servants. You each were willing to lay down your lives for others and did not try to save your lives but offered them up willingly. My Father wishes the injured to be healed and the dead restored to life. You have proven that your love for Him is stronger than your love for life in this world. Stay strong in your faith and whatever you ask in my name will be done." Jack somehow knew that the Son of God was with each of them at the same time.

Yahshua faded out of sight and Jack lost consciousness Unseen, the angels tended to each person and then left. A wonderful peace settled over the area. In minutes, each of the warriors, stirred and sat up looking around at the others.

CHAPTER THIRTY-NINE

The Captain of the Russian Police walked up to where Jack was hugging Laura and waited until they broke the clinch. "General Malone, could you explain what happened here to me and my men? I really don't understand it. I, for one, know that those "things" killed me, and many of my men, as well as some of your team. Yet, we are still here alive. Was it all a dream that we all had?"

Jack prayed for the right words and waved all the Russians to form up around him. When they were all close enough to hear he started. "Warriors all, as General Connelly told you before, you now serve a loving God that is concerned with everything you do. What happened here tonight was not a dream. It was real. Many of us, including your Captain here, were actually killed by the demons. The Son of God, Yahshua walked among us and after banishing the main demon to the pit to be held until the end of time, restored all of us to life and health. Remember, God designed each of us and authorized our births. What he makes, He can repair. He is the source of all life and He can restore life to a dead man as easily as you can refill a Vodka glass. Give praise and thanks to Yahveh for your restoration and your health."

One of the Russian Spetznaz troops asked Jack, "If He was going to restore all of us why did we have to go through the battle?"

Jack smiled at the man. "Because He needed us to battle the forces of evil so that all things would be done that were needed to be done by mortals to achieve heavenly results. We "facilitated" God's will tonight. He will not forget any of us. I want to commend each and every one of our Russian brothers and sisters tonight who fought against overwhelming odds and evil beings without running in terror or fainting." Jack stepped back one step and raised his right fist into the air. "I salute your bravery and ask that you continue to stand tall against any form of evil on this earth."

Mark came up next to Jack, "I second that salute and will see that your superiors know of your sacrifice for the Motherland."

The entire mass of soldiers and policemen raised a fist and shouted, "Long live Russia!"

General Gennadiy came over to Jack and Mark and shook both of their hands. He had a strange look on his face. He stared at both Americans and then looked at the other members of the Crossfire Team. He shook his head slightly. "I think I know now how you Americans can be so humble after what just happened here. I too, was overrun and killed. Yahshua, as you call Him, restored my life to me and restored me to full health. Next to Him my life, my career, everything I have ever done was like dirt on the floor. I felt so unworthy to be near Him. But he told me that I was His brother, the child of Yahveh. I doubt that I will be "command material" for the Motherland after this. I have been shown a wider world with the truth now rejecting much of what I thought I knew. I want to thank you all for your efforts for our country. I have never seen such sacrifice. If there is ever, anything I can do for you, you have but to ask."

Laura stepped up to where her husband was. Her body was clean, pure, and healthy again. She spoke up so that all two hundred people could hear her. "Our Father in Heaven has informed me that the criminal element no longer has any contact with the demon world and demons are forbidden to come into our world here in your nation for now. Therefore, our work is done and thanks to all of you, we can leave victorious. I'm glad I've had a chance to meet all of you and stand alongside you in combat."

General Gennadiy got a cell phone call and answered it. He stepped up to Mark and Jack and told them that a special flight was being prepared for the team to return them directly to the United States as a gesture of the government's thanks for ridding the country of the "abnormal" plague.

As the team collected what little things they had brought with them, General Gennadiy silently motioned

Mark to come near to him. After Mark sat down and leaned close to the General he heard, "Mark, this thing with the politics in the Russian government sickens me. I was told by a friend in the Kremlin that in their convoluted logic the secretary has ordered the Air Force to shoot down your plane after it leaves Russian air space."

When Mark jerked back, the General put his hand on Mark's arm and glared at him. "Remember we are being observed right now."

Mark settled down and asked the General, "If they were watching what happened out there, how could they think we are a threat to Russia?"

The General laughed loudly for the watchers. Then he whispered, "They don't think you are a threat. They are extremely grateful for your efforts against the demons. They are afraid of your team after what you did. I don't think they trust any of the men who helped you, especially me. I don't expect to last very long after your flight leaves the ground. They want the whole thing excised from the collective memory. It apparently makes sense to them. Oh! Be assured they will mourn your untimely deaths after your efforts and they will be very solicitous to your country. But, it is all an act of frightened men."

Mark thought for a few minutes and then told the General, "Look, I've got a plan. Just go along with what we're going to do. Da?"

The General sat back and looked at Mark like the thought of not dying for the Kremlin was a new thought. He pursed his lips and nodded his head.

Mark got up and went over to some of the Russian troops that were preparing to leave. They looked over at the General who nodded his head to do what Mark said.

Mark then called the team together and outlined the problem and his plan. Jack grinned. He'd seen Mark pull off major schemes before.

Mark pulled out his cell phone and put it on scramble. He called General Miles at the Joint Chiefs of Staff in Washington, D.C. Ten minutes later he circled back to General Gennadiy. Leaning over the General's shoulder he whispered, "Do you think you can get that flight stalled for a couple of hours?"

The General thought about it and nodded. Then Mark added, "And for all our sakes make sure that the plane isn't wired to explode." The General smiled and nodded again.

Four hours later the Russian General announced that they were ready to leave. Mark asked if the troops that had fought with them could come aboard the plane for the trip so they could discuss the battle and get more information. The General shrugged and made a phone call. He hung up and nodded.

The entire group trooped out to the flight line and boarded the Antonov AN-124. Since this was one of the largest cargo aircraft in the world there was plenty of room for everyone.

After they were all aboard the General told Mark and Jack. "Good move. The addition of two hundred of our people forced them to replace the original plane with a much bigger one. My troops secured it as soon as it was decided which one they would use. This one is not "wired" and if we aren't shot down it shall be a comfortable but nerve-racking trip." He said it with a smile so it took the sting out of the thought.

Mark just smiled. He wasn't about speak of his "plan" until they were out of the Russian sphere of influence.

One hour later they left that sphere as they were heading for the trans-Atlantic trip. The plane didn't have windows in the cargo bay and there were many edgy people waiting for their fate to be played out for them.

Mark got up and used a microphone and speaker system to address the men and women over the drone of the plane's engines. "Ladies and Gentlemen, you are all confessed children of the most high and therefore we will make the entire trip to America without interference. Yahveh will protect us. And the fact that there are twenty five U.S. F-22 Raptors and an AWACs aircraft pacing us will help ensure that we are not bothered on the trip."

There was major cheering and dancing in the cargo bay. When that settled down Mark continued. "As General Gennadiy has told you, your government wants the entire operation erased which unfortunately means you get erased to ensure their fears. I have an agreement from the U.S. State Department that each and every one of you will be offered asylum in the United States if you want it. If you do not want to stay you can return with the plane. I told you that I saluted you and I mean it. I don't want you to come back and be removed. As far as your loved ones and family members they will be allowed to come to the U.S. to live with you if we can get the Russian ruling council to agree. You will have plenty of opportunity to use the military skills you've shown and to go to school and develop other skills if you feel like it. Think about the offer and let me know before we land.

One of the troops asked if they could live in Hollywood, California.

Mark grinned, "If you want to and if you can afford it."

Another troop looked troubled. "General Connelly, what if the pilots of this plane are ordered to crash it to kill all of us?"

Mark smiled again. "I sincerely doubt that Su Li and Charlie Wu who are flying the plane will agree to do that. The regular pilots are taking it easy and riding as guarded passengers on this leg of the trip.

There were more yells and dancing as the troops realized that they were truly safe.

General Gennadiy came over to Mark and shook his hand. "Congratulations, you just outsmarted the Kremlin."

Jack, who was standing there, said, "Just another day in the life of the Crossfire Team." They all laughed at that.

Back in Russia the Secretary sat in his chair mad enough to spit bullets. The team he wanted to destroy was flying away from his justice in his aircraft and there was nothing he could do about it. The Air Force fighters didn't even get a chance to destroy the plane. They had tried but four of them had died trying. The accursed American Raptors were even better than they were supposed to be. The demon running his mind tortured him non-stop for his failure to do his duty as ordered.

A thought occurred to him and he grimly smiled. Picking up the telephone handset he commanded military communications to connect him to a special number.

CHAPTER FORTY

Fifteen hundred miles from England over the mid-Atlantic Ocean, U.S. Navy fighter flight Delta, was comprised of two F-18 "Hornet" naval fighter jets The flight was patrolling eighty miles west-north-west of the aircraft carrier "Ronald Regan" CVN-76.

Delta flight leader contacted carrier air operations. "Mother One, I have an unknown surface bogey on a bearing of 032, seventy five miles out. We are going to investigate and report."

Switching to his wingman's frequency Ted Mitchell said, "Let's go check out this character." He got a "Roger" from his wingman and curved his flight path around to intercept the location. His wingman matched his maneuver and they dropped down from angels fourteen to just four hundred feet over the ocean.

The two aircraft approached the location of the unknown radar image and Ted called it into carrier operations. "Mother One, we have a large Russian Boomer (nuclear missile submarine), probably an old Typhoon class on the surface moving northward at approximately five knots. They are conducting some kind of operations on the deck."

The jets overflew the submarine and Ted continued the report. "It looks like they are preparing a SAM missile and... HOLY COW! Mother One, the crew on the deck has just fired two MANPAD SAMs at us. Attempting to disengage, firing chaff and flares . . . LOOK OUT!"

The sounds of explosions came over the speakers at the carrier and then silence. The flight controller called the XO and reported that apparently a Russian nuclear submarine had just shot down two of their aircraft without warning.

The XO called the Commander to flight operations. When he was apprised of the situation the Captain ordered the three plane reserve flight to launch and head for the area at full speed. He had the rescue chopper prepared and turned the ship towards the last known location of their aircraft. Then he called ATLADCOM and reported the situation to Naval Operations.

Admiral C. P. Owens talked to the carrier commander. "Captain, we feel that this submarine is attempting to attack the special aircraft flight from Europe flying in your area at angels 35. Their attack on our aircraft is an act of war which the Russians will deny. But, since we have been ordered by the Office of the Joint Chiefs to prevent any attacks on that aircraft at all costs, have your aircraft revisit the area. If our planes have actually been shot down then I order you to attack the submarine if it is still on the surface. I will contact fleet operations to handle it if has submerged. We feel that it cannot submerge until it has fired it's SAM. Time is of the essence gentlemen and we need to get on top of this situation immediately."

The aircraft carrier Commander relayed the orders to flight operations who contacted the three plane Alpha flight on its way to the area of the action. "Alpha flight, you are ordered to confirm downing of our aircraft and if the submarine is still on the surface you are to sink it. Repeat, you have authorized weapons release to sink the submarine."

The Commander looked at the XO and shook his head, "There is probably two hundred and ninety men on that boomer along with twenty nuclear missiles. This could be the start of World War Three."

The XO shook his head, "I agree that there may be that many sailors but I seriously doubt that old boat has any missiles. They only had ten for it fifteen years ago. That boomer and it's missiles were supposed to have been destroyed ten years ago."

In the Russian Cargo aircraft Su Li got a heads up from the Fortress in Colorado about the ongoing action and the probability of a SAM attack on the aircraft they were flying.

Su Li got Mark up to the flight deck of the giant cargo plane and explained what was happening. Mark thought for a second and went to the seats where the Russian pilots were being held by one of the Spetznaz troopers.

He spoke in Russian and told the pilots the situation. Then he asked, "Are there special transponders operating on this plane that the missile could home in on rather than using radar or heat seeking?"

It finally dawned on the pilots that they were simply being thrown away by their government and they agreed to help. Both of them ran to the area behind the flight deck and opened a floor compartment. Crawling into the tight space they used flashlights to look for the correct components.

On the sea, Alpha flight was approaching the submarine that was still on the surface Alpha flight leader got a low power call from the Delta Flight Commander. Ted Mitchell was bobbing in the ocean in a small emergency raft and using the handheld emergency radio. "Be warned that this submarine will attack you without warning and I think they're using U.S. made "Stinger" missiles. I have had no contact with my wingman and I think he bought it when they blew him out of the sky."

Alpha flight Commander told his flight. "Shoot down of our aircraft is confirmed. We will go in hot with "Mavericks". He lit up the submarine on his attack radar and began his run.

On the Russian submarine there was frenzied activity and there were more men coming up with MANPAD launchers.

At two nautical miles out the Alpha flight Commander launched two AGM-65A "Maverick" missiles at the submarine. The electro-optical homing devices in the heads of the missiles locked onto the submarine and they flew true and hot. Both of his wingmen also fired two missiles at the sub.

All three planes immediately began evasive maneuvers to avoid any Stingers that might be launched at them. As the Mavericks sped to the hull of the submarine there was a large flare of light and the surface-to-air missile launched into the air and rapidly climbed into the air away from the ship.

Two by two the Mavericks struck the submarine. The first two hit the conning tower or sail and literally blew it completely off of the hull along with the officers and crew on it and in it. The following four missiles struck the hull right at the center of mass and the explosions blew the submarine into two parts which sank immediately out of sight. Even though the aircraft circled the scene of the debris marking the sinking they saw no survivors.

Alpha fight Commander radioed in to the carrier. "Alpha fight engaged the Russian submarine with six Maverick missiles. The submarine was completely destroyed but they were able to launch the SAM before being sunk. We will fly cover for Captain Mitchell until the helicopter arrives."

Having a solid radio signal to home in on the SAM flew unerringly upward toward the speck speeding to the west. The missile was an order of speed faster than the plane and would overhaul it in thirty seconds.

Mark yelled at the Russian pilots, "The SAM is on the way!"

In the electronics bay the Command pilot realized that they didn't have time to follow the procedure to remove the transponders and he just grabbed the wires running to the transponder circuitry and ripped them out physically.

Suddenly the missile lost its homing signal. Following its programming it switched to infrared tracking. It found a hot source and homed in on it.

The Air Cap pilot of the F-18 "Hornet" the missile was homing in on rotated to the left and fired off flares to distract or confuse the missile tracking circuitry. The pilot turned into the direction of the missile which removed his hot exhaust from the missile's view.

The missile homed in on one of the flares and exploded harmlessly in midair. The F-18 rejoined the sky cap for the Crossfire Team's aircraft.

Su Li blew out a big breath. This lead goose would never be able to get away from a missile and she was very relieved that the threat had been neutralized.

The Russians climbed out of the electronics bay and shut the hatch. They walked back to the people on the cargo deck and spotted the Russian General. Walking up to him they showed him the transponders they had ripped out of the circuitry and asked about possible asylum in the U.S. They realized they had been written off by the government and didn't see much of a future by returning to their homeland.

Jack noted the situation and added the pilot's names to the list for the State Department.

On the flight deck Mark told Su Li, "I think I could really use a stiff drink right about now!

Su Li laughed a little too loud even in her ears as the tension broke. She told Mark that there was thirty bottles of Russian Vodka chilling in the aft galley. The Russian pilots had told her about the "celebration supplies". Mark headed aft and grabbed six of the troopers to help him distribute the drinks to everyone.

Laura was sitting in one of the wall-mounted seats looking very much at peace with the world at the moment. Jack thought back to the garage they had been in and the look of fire on her face at that time. He shook his head and sat down next to her. She leaned over and laid her head on his right shoulder. She asked, "Well, is this mission finally over?"

Jack laughed, "I certainly hope so."

Mark walked over and squatted down in front of them. Sarah and David walked over and stood near them. Mark grinned at the pair. "Well, according to General Miles we continue to create real messes for him. The old nuclear missile submarine that fired that SAM was sunk by our Navy. I'm not sure how that is going to play on the political scene. We may have just started WWIII."

Jack thought about it and shook his head. "No, I doubt that the Russians will even make a scene about it because that would necessitate their telling the whole world about the action we just left and their attempts to repay us by downing their own aircraft. I'm pretty sure that the Navy has tons of evidence of the sub's firing of the SAM and probably on their unwarranted attack on the Navy jets. The whole thing would be way too messy. They'll just act if it hadn't happened."

Sarah laughed, "I thought the day when I was in deniable actions was over. Well that is obviously not true."

Laura stretched and stood up. She swatted her husband on the shoulder. "Go get the practice swords, I think our newbie and I could use some more training. I saw how you completely out classed that demon in Moscow. I want to be able to handle my sword that way."

Sarah smiled, "Touché!"

CHAPTER FORTY-ONE

The rest of the trip was uneventful and even a lot of fun for the troops. When the Antonov AN-124 landed at JFK airport it was taxied to a private hanger which was a good idea since it was so big anyway. The amount of brass and politicians was only exceeded by the number of State Department Staffers who manned a temporary immigration facility for the two hundred plus Russians requesting asylum and eventually, citizenship.

General Miles was there himself to see to the debriefing of the Crossfire Team. It was thorough and detailed as benefitted a group that prevented world chaos and almost started a new world war.

After they had finished all the paperwork the State Department had released the Antonov to the Russian team who had been sent to the airport by the Russian consulate to secure the plane. The pilots that decided to stay in America had taped the ripped out transponders to the inside of the electronics area with duct tape so that they couldn't be accused of "stealing" the devices.

Eventually the General had the team to himself and he took them to a suite at a luxury hotel. He had them fed a wonderful dinner and then gathered them into the large living room in the suite. He stared at the eleven team members for a second and then scratched his head. "I had really decided to have a parade for you guys. I didn't do it because the Russians would deny you were ever there and the majority of people in New York don't believe in demons anyway. So I decided to feed you and tell you that what you've done is way, way, way, above and beyond the duty we could have asked of you. Trying to determine what we could do in way of a thank you I think the President came up with a solid plan."

Mark stared at the General with one eyebrow raised. "Will this "plan" involve anything that will embarrass us?"

The General smiled, "Probably."

Mark frowned, "Will it make us wish we were somewhere else?"

The General nodded, "Definitely!"

Laura stood up and said to the General. "I believe everyone here trusts you and is fairly game, but, I would choose my entertainment carefully. The General could see golden flecks in her eyes, the same color as the golden armor. Mark wondered if they had just threatened the highest ranking member of the U.S. military and if there were any charges for something like that.

The General sat back a bit and laughed, "Never fear, I wouldn't think of irritating anyone on this team, especially you. Remember, I've seen you in action."

Jack put his hand on Laura's arm, and laughed "I sure hope you know she's pulling your leg."

General Miles grinned, "Not a problem, we have the same boss. Anyway, what the President wants to do is have a full-out state dinner in your honor. Everyone on the team is asked to come and celebrate what is probably President Bollen's last state dinner and it won't be advertised. There will be just a few hundred of his closest allies and friends, mostly military. He has commissioned a new medal in your honor and wants to present them to each of you."

Mark shook his head, "Does that mean I have to wear formal wear? You know I don't like wearing a tuxedo."

The General turned serious, "I've heard that. But six of you will be attending in full Military dress as befits General Officers in the U. S. Military and as befits your military ranks. There will be a few other surprises but they will be nice ones. I'm telling you the truth when I say that President Bollen really wants to do this for you. Can I count on your being there?"

Mark nodded and thought to himself, "Full dress Two-star General's formals. Oh well, I can take it for one night," The others agreed to attend and then Jack asked, "When does he want to do this?"

The General smiled, "This evening" He looked at his watch. "Actually in about twelve hours from now. That way you don't have to go to Denver and back again."

After that everyone was assigned to a room and most of them went to bed at five a.m. pretty well exhausted.

Regardless of the hour, the next day started early with fittings and people rushing around preparing for the dinner. Carol Moffet showed up from the Fortress to attend the dinner and Demitri made his appearance with some evening wear. He tried on the outfit and looked very handsome and distinguished. He and Carol would be watching from the table of honor.

CHAPTER FORTY-TWO

That evening, when the whole team gathered in the lobby of the hotel Jack counted noses to make sure no one was left out. He and Laura along with Mark and Sarah, and Stan and Debbie were replete in General Officer's uniforms with all appropriate ranks, badges, ribbons, and medals. They made a very solid image as officers of the U.S. Air Force. David and Alexis were in formal dinner dress as was Su Li, Charlie, Linda, Carol, and Demitri.

A Marine Sergeant and a Lance Corporal escorted the entire crew to two limousines and they were transported to the white house. Instead of going to one of the entrances they were driven into an underground garage and used the little-known underground tram system to travel over two miles to the reception. When the small train pulled up to the reception hall there was the Marine Corp Band that broke into a beautiful rendition of the Air Force song the "Wild Blue Yonder". The team gave them an ovation when they were done.

Entering into the reception hall Mark softly commented, "Hard to believe this is over a hundred feet underground, huh?"

The reception was well attended by many of the military and some of the Congress. Jack noted that there were no liberal members in sight. The dinner was an excellent meal with squab and steak as choices.

When the meal was over and the dishes cleared away the President stood and called for attention. He looked at the team at the first table and then spoke to the entire assembly. "I am honored by all of you who attended this celebration. As most of you know, this is probably the last state dinner that I will hold as the election is upon us next month. I have had a great eight years serving as your President and Commander in Chief. One of the reasons that this last eight years has been successful is the team of people seated to my right."

The President waved his hand to include the entire team. "Most of you are in the military and are aware of the dangers and perils of combating the enemies of our country. Many times you fight and die for something that will never be known or honored due to national security." He waved his hand to include the members of the team. "They have long labored unknown and unthanked by the majority of people in the world. I want to present this group of people to you tonight and I want to thank them for putting their lives on the line many times over the years for our country, our way of life, and the God we all serve. I also have a personal reason for honoring this group." He motioned to his left and a beautiful young woman stood up. As many of you know, this is my niece Tracy. At one time she was kidnapped by a very evil individual named Max Lister. This team of people rescued her and a hundred other children he was going to kill. I owe them a large debt of gratitude for that."

Tracy waved at the team and sat down. Laura grinned and waved back at her.

The President recounted several of the events in the team's history including the Believer's Prophets attempt to destroy the world and the challenge in Zyngola where Yahveh showed his true power over the false religion of Zultar. "There are many other services they have rendered the people of this country including saving the cities of Dallas and Denver from destruction. Two of those times were by preventing nuclear holocausts. It is unfortunate in the extreme that while this team was able to stop a major riot in the city of Houston, Texas several years ago that we now mourn all those lost in the nuclear holocaust of several months ago. As you know the majority of that area is lost to us for the next generation until the nuclear radiation can be eliminated. But, it was this team that was able to allow us to strike back at the people who did that. There is so much that the Crossfire Team has done for America that I cannot even tell this select group about. We are all dearly in their debt."

The President paused for a second. "I have been asked to allow two other people to speak to the honor of this team." The President waved to the woman on his far left. The woman stood up and there was a collective gasp from the audience. The President introduced the Prime Minister of Israel to the people.

The Prime Minister waved to the crowd and turned toward the team. She bowed, and In lightly accented English told them, "My country owes many debts to this small band of courageous warriors. We do not forget our debts. I am not at liberty to reveal all the times they have prevented the destruction of our land, our way of life, and our lives. You all are aware of the poisoning that the ASF attempted against both of our countries. In conjunction with our security forces, notably the Mossad, these people alone stood for our country and prevailed. We especially want to thank Mrs. Sarah Connelly, nee Cohen who obeyed God and led a prayer for the healing of all the poisoned people. God heard her prayer along with millions of other prayers and healed us all. Millions of people in both of our countries owe their lives to these people. I have travelled here tonight to honor them for their service to America and to Israel." The Israeli President sat down and the next person stood up.

A tall, distinguished African-American smiled at the team. Victor Chamberlain cocked his head a little and spoke to the assembled people. "I met this team at a very low point in my life. I had lost everything to a group of terrorists who I thought were members of my management team. They wanted my money and my island to assemble a missile and a nuclear warhead to attack Israel. Members the Crossfire Team prevented that and rescued me. More than that they led me to Jesus and changed my life forever. I owe them more than my life and I too want to honor them tonight."

Victor sat down and the President asked the team to stand up and form a line behind him facing the assembly. After they were in position the President turned back to the audience. "In one of the last acts of my Presidency I have had a new national American medal created, the "Supreme Valor" award. This will only be presented to a highly select set of people who have selflessly offered their lives in defense of our great country. Tonight I want to present one of these new medals to each of the Crossfire Team standing here."

There was a hush over the entire assembly. A large photograph of the new medal was shown on a huge video screen behind the podium. An aide brought out a stack of boxes and walked behind the President. The President took the first medal and took it out of the box and had Jack Malone bend down so he could place its ribbon around the warrior's neck. He smiled at Jack and told him. "This country owes you so much and hopefully this will be only the first payment on that debt." He shook Jack's hand and softly said, "Thank you."

The President repeated the ceremony with each of the team with the exception of Carol and Demitri who were sitting in the audience grinning so much their faces might have split.

The President stood to one side and the Prime Minister of Israel presented each member with a unique medal that hadn't been seen in over a half of a century. The Prime Minister told them that the "Hero of Israel" is an Israeli military decoration that was awarded during the War of Independence. Only twelve of these medals were ever awarded to the greatest heroes of the brand-new nation of Israel. When she had pinned the medals on each of the team members she pointed out that the number twelve was very significant to the Israelis. It represented the twelve tribes of Israel.

She then pointed out that there were only eleven members of the team standing on the platform. That left one of the medals still to be awarded. She turned to the audience and asked U.S. Air Force Colonel Michael White to join the team on the platform.

Mike White was very surprised but rose and walked up to stand by the team. When the Prime Minister pinned his medal on his uniform Mike quietly asked, "Why me? I didn't think anyone knew anything about my participation with the Crossfire Team except the U. S. Air Force and the CIA."

The Prime Minister smiled at him. "You forget that we also have an intelligence agency and they remember your part with this team ever since the attack at Ben Gurion Airport and," She then pointed out David Zahavy and Sarah Connelly. "We also have our private sources of information." The smaller woman then shook Mike's hand. "We want to honor you in the service of your country and your future service to the world with the Crossfire Team."

The Israeli Prime Minister walked up and offered her hand to President Bollen. "I have heard about the team's offer to you and your family. I know what you've done to support these people in their efforts that have saved our country. I also offer you safe haven after you leave office."

President Bollen got choked up on that one. He smiled and shook the woman's hand again. It crossed his mind to wonder how Israel knew about the Crossfire Team's offer which was made in private.

Victor Chamberlain walked up to Jack and told him, "I don't have any medals to award to you and your team but I do have something I can give. You know I have and will back your team financially in any effort because I know that you are serving Yahshua as I try to do. Well then, in the event of my death, I recently executed papers that make you, and by extension, your team, as the sole beneficiaries of my personal fortune and all my world-wide businesses."

Jack realized the trust and the honor the billionaire had given them and he could only stand in awe of the honor. He shook Victor's hand and thanked him from his heart for the whole team. He also told Victor that they would protect his assets and his name.

Victor stepped over to the podium and the President stepped back to let him speak to the crowd. Victor was a handsome and refined man who commanded attention for his billions of dollars if not for his eminence. He looked out at the crowd. "I want to tell you all about one event in my life that speaks loudly about the faith of these people." He motioned back to the team. "During the battle to regain my business empire from the evil people who had taken it, and me, hostage, Jack Malone, Mark Connelly, and I were deemed unworthy and were to be executed in an extremely cruel fashion."

Victor saw that he had everyone's rapt attention. "The evil men who had captured us cast us into the nuclear reactor they had developed to refine the weapons grade fuel for their missile. They told us that we would be irradiated and our cells would quickly break down, our hair would fall out in clumps, and we would go blind. Then we would quickly die a horrible, screaming death. I had just become a believer in Jesus Christ but these two men were like solid rock in their belief and convinced me that we would be all right. I couldn't understand how and now realize that they meant we would be fine whether we lived or died. We walked bravely into the nuclear furnace and met our Savior there. He led us in a dancing, and singing celebration of His Father's power over all things evil. After thirty minutes in the furnace where we were not supposed to live over ten minutes we walked out praising the Father and the Son without a damaged hair."

There was absolute silence in the room. Victor ended his tale with, "All of the evil directors who decided our fate left the island just prior to our being thrown into the furnace. They left to go to secret places and savor the destruction of Israel. They had no way of knowing that Mark Connelly had reprogrammed the missile to head for the sun rather than the Jewish homeland. Each one of these vile men died of acute radiation sickness in the next four hours regardless if they were in the air, on the sea, or driving away. Our Elohim, Yahveh, promises that if we walk with Him, He will destroy those who attempt to destroy us. I saw that very clearly that day and I realize that it was Yahveh's will to have these wonderful people come into my life." Looking at the whole team he smiled. "I'm so glad I have had the chance in front of all these witnesses to thank for you all for everything."

Victor turned to the audience. "And I want to thank you all for listening to me."

CHAPTER FORTY-THREE

President Bollen spoke to the audience. "I would now like to have Jack Malone say a few words for the Crossfire Team." He stepped away from the podium and started clapping. To a person, everyone in the room rose applauding. The roar of applause continued even as Jack stepped to the dais. The applause went on for three minutes even after Jack held his hands up to get the audience's attention. Finally it quieted down and everyone sat down and paid attention to Jack.

Jack was an accomplished speaker as the President of his own company. He had presented before tougher crowds than this. But, this time it was hard not to be emotional.

"Ladies and Gentlemen of the military, Congress, and civilians, speaking for this team I want to thank President Bollen for using this state dinner to celebrate the success of our team. I would also like to express our deepest thanks to the Prime Minister of Israel and Victor Chamberlain for their gracious honors to our team. But, we don't deserve all the credit for these impressive victories."

There was a collective intake of breath on the part of just about everyone. Jack continued. "I don't know the depth of the understanding or personal relationship any of you have with Jesus Christ. We refer to the Savior as Yahshua because that was His name in Hebrew and Aramaic. But, I can confidently tell you that each and every one of this team have a daily, on-going personal relationship with both Him and the Father Yahveh, the Creator of the universe. I tell you truly that we did the things we have been recognized for tonight in the service of Yahveh, and, we are more than grateful for having had the chance to do them."

Jack judged the audience's mood and pushed forward. "Yahveh is our Commander and we do as He asks. Some of this team have been killed at least once, only to be restored by a supernatural miracle. The reason isn't because we are special. or because we bring unique talents to the team. It is because we are obedient to a loving God who has a loving plan for everyone on the earth. Let me explain what most of you don't know. The reason that Yahveh created this team is because this "age of the Gentiles" is in its last minutes of the last days before the return of Yahshua, and the enemy of mankind is taking liberties outside of God's laws. Satan knows that the time is short for him to steal all of the people away from God. He has his minions, the demons, physically entering our world and that is something that God has forbidden them to do. Essentially it gives them an unfair advantage against mankind that they are not entitled to. We are one of the balances to those excesses which is why we are always in the middle of the battle against Satan's demonic plans to destroy our world. As I've heard it said, "God is our shepherd and we are His sheep. As long as there are wolves around God will anoint some as sheep dogs to protect the rest."

Because Satan and his demons are stepping over the boundary between the spiritual world and our world the Father has evened the odds by giving us the tools we need to compete in the battle to protect the innocent."

Jack prayed out loud. "Father Yahveh, the people in this room are the core of hope for most of the innocent in this country. I ask that you allow the team to show your unique weapons to your esteem and to honor what you have put in place to compete with the evil one."

Laura looked at Sarah and took a deep breath. She tipped her head towards the audience and stepped forward praying the 23rd Psalm.

The golden armor, shields, and the swords of the Word flared into existence and lit up the room. Both women stepped into a basic defensive stance with their swords in high guard over their right shoulder. The audience went wild with yells of encouragement and applause. Jack prayed, "Thank you Father Yahveh."

The armor faded from view and the women stepped back into the line. Jack waited until he could be heard again. "Laura and Sarah have been anointed by Yahveh to do battle with demons. We also are not alone in our spiritual battles. Besides the immense amount of help we have received from President Bollen, General Miles, NSA, CIA, the U.S. military branches and many others we also have heavenly help that is represented by two angels who call themselves Rose and Caleb". Jack looked back at the team, "Father?"

With a sudden swirling of gold and white Rose flashed into existence on one end of the line and Caleb appeared in his youthful shape at the other end. Caleb's appearance as a warrior was more than impressive. The people in the room were silent in the presence of God's messengers. Caleb moved forward and stopped next to Jack.

His eyes of flaming steel looked over the crowd and he nodded. "Many of you are men and women of integrity and faith. I am honored to be here with you."

Silent was too mild a word for the audience. Rose moved forward and spoke in that beautiful voice. "Yahveh be with all of you." She swirled out of sight and Caleb turned to Jack. "We will meet again, soon." He vanished leaving the room darker.

Jack turned back to the silent audience. "As I said, we use our talents for Yahveh in His service. The fact that most in America honor His will for a life of love, peace, and duty as it's foundations should tell you that this country has been on the right path. Although some of you might dislike what I have to say I have to tell you. The wanton abandon by abortion, homosexuality, and the efforts of some to eliminate the name and reverence for God are sinful. God cannot abide where there is sin. If these trends are not reversed or eliminated we, as a country, will lose our protection from evil as God has to draw back."

Jack honored the audience by finishing with, "We are committed to protecting the innocent of the world and our great country and will continue to as long as Yahveh gives us the ability and the time to do it."

Jack turned to President Bollen, "Thank you for this honor and accept our thanks for all the support you and General Miles have given us in the name of the Father." Jack looked out at the still stunned audience. "Yahveh bless each and every one of you."

Everyone in the room stood and applauded non-stop until Jack motioned the whole team forward and had Carol and Demitri join them. They bowed to the crowd and held their hands in the air as a sign of victory.

The team moved out into the audience where they met and talked with as many people as they could on a one-on-one basis.

Jack and Laura were talking to Mrs. Bollen when a gasp caught their attention. Jack walked over and found Carol on her knees with the white diamonds glowing white hot at her forehead and throat. He calmed the people around her. "It is all right. That is another sign that the Father has blessed Carol with to show her talent is in operation. She is praying and is spiritually in heaven right now. She can see the heavenly operations in eleven dimensions. Her ability to interpret the enemy's plans really helps us to define our operations and warns us when Yahveh needs our abilities.

To a person the people around Carol stood in awe of her. A minute later the white diamonds faded and Carol opened her eyes. Jack was shocked by what he saw. Carol's look at him was way more mature than he had ever seen before. Carol got carefully to her feet with Jack's help. She locked eyes with him and confidently moved close. She told him in a friendly but no-nonsense voice, "The whole team has to move now! Yahveh needs us at the Arctic circle in the next twenty four hours. Satan's demons are on the move and they are about to change the history of the world unless we stop him."

There was no doubt in Jack's spirit at this news was true and reliable. He pulled out his cell phone and hit Team Recall. In less than twenty seconds all fourteen members of the team were by his side. He repeated Carol's message and stepped aside to speak to General Miles. "General, we are going to need some very fast transportation to the Arctic Circle. What have we got?"

The sudden change from conversationalists to warriors was not lost on the people in the audience. One of the President's staff asked Mark to let the President know what was going on.

Mark walked over to a small group which included President Bollen, his wife, the Israeli Prime Minister, and

General Miles. Mark had moved into his no-nonsense mode. He saluted the President and reported the input from Carol and the sense of urgency the summons generated caught fire with the listeners.

CHAPTER FORTY-FOUR

The Chairman of the Joint Chiefs of Staff can get things done when there is a need, especially when his Commander-in-Chief tells him to not spare the horses.

General Miles called the command center for the U.S. Marine Corp. He talked to a Colonel who transferred him to another General. General Miles detailed his request and was put off. He handed the phone to the President.

The President didn't cut corners. "General, I understand your need for secrecy but this is a national emergency I can assure you. Yes, I am President Bollen. All right, stand by." The President gestured for his aide who carried the Presidential Command Phone. He told the aide to contact the Marine Commander at Alpha Prime base. The aide punched in the number like he had it memorized. He handed the phone to the President.

The President listened and said, "General Hays, this is the President of the United States of America and as your commander in chief I am ordering you to grant all assistance to General Miles in this matter. Are we now clear on this?" He listened for a minute and motioned General Miles to step near to him. He muted the microphone and asked, "Who is this man's direct commander?"

General Miles thought for a second. "Three star General Joseph Tolliver."

The President activated the phone and told General Hays to wait. He selected the second line and looked at his aide. The aide reached over and typed in a new number. In less than ten seconds the President had General Tolliver on the line. "General Tolliver, this is President Bollen, can you confirm the authenticity of this communication?"

The General on the other end confirmed the authenticity.

The President was getting up a head of steam at being stonewalled by the base commander. "General Tolliver I am giving you a direct order as your commander in chief. I want General Hays arrested for insubordination and placed in the base stockade. I then want you to get the next in command to prepare the X-76 for immediate flight and send it to the JFK airport. I want it here in less than four hours. The CJCS will handle the security arrangements so that we keep the nature of the X-76 secure. The aircraft is to take fourteen members of the Crossfire Team to an undisclosed area of the Arctic Circle. I want no lolly gagging on this or I will have the hide of everyone involved. I will not tolerate being told by a one-star General that I can't use the X-76 because it is classified. General Tolliver, I hope we're clear on this matter or I will have your pension and your guts for garters if it doesn't happen!"

He listened for a few seconds and responded, "General the need for the public use of this development project is critical to our national security and all I can tell you is that it involves defeating demons from hell or losing the freedom of the world."

"Yes, I said "demons" as in Satan, Hades, and the end of the world. Snap to it man. I will tolerate no delays and if General Hays defies you. Let me know and I will have the rest of the Marine Corp up his backside in less time than it takes to bake a cake!"

The team was having their combat clothes and weapons sent to them from the hotel and it would take thirty minutes to get to them. Jack was talking to the President and General Miles when Laura and Sarah walked up and asked to interfere with the conversation. Jack focused on his wife, "Okay, what up?"

Laura didn't look happy. "Mr. President, General Miles, Jack, I have been praying since Carol's message and it doesn't look good. Apparently a splinter group made up of some renegade ASF types and thoroughly ticked off Russian Mafia personnel have hi-jacked two Russian MIRV ICBM missiles or had already hi-jacked them and they are planning to launch them from a base on the Arctic Circle. Yahveh doesn't say what they want to destroy but I think we can guess what the enemy wants to destroy, us. I think the loss of Qixalpaq has ratcheted us up a notch in the enemy's estimate."

Jack said, "Then again it might be aimed at Israel. Most of his attacks have been in that direction."

The President of Israel shook her head. "I think it might be both. If they launch soon I think it will be Tel Aviv and New York City."

General Miles snorted, "With those multi-megaton MIRV warheads it could be every city in Israel and the whole eastern seaboard of the United States. I have already ordered the Twenty-fourth Regiment of the Sixth Marine Division to move toward the Arctic Circle. Is there anything even resembling a country as a more specific target?"

Laura shook her head. "Sorry, nothing specific as yet General. But, I'm sure we'll get more information as we head north..." Jack's cell phone rang and he answered it. "Jack Malone." He listened for a few seconds and rang off. Turning to General Miles he said, "The computer center at the Fortress has pinpointed the probable location of the missile launch area. It is on Banks Island in the Canadian Arctic Archipelago. NSA's satellite coverage shows multiple Russian nuclear signatures at that location and our computer center has spotted demonic activity there also. The island has a total population of less than two hundred and is basically deserted. It lies very close to the Arctic Circle and that location puts the east coast and Israel both well inside the effective range of the Russian ICBMs."

The General nodded his thanks and punched in a number on his cell phone.

Two Marines came in with the clothes and weapons from the hotel and the team members were taken to a small conference room off of the main assembly area to change. The women changed first and then the men. The M-8s brought from Denver by Carol were bagged along with ammo and handguns. The team left them that way until they were out of the White House area as a courtesy to the President and the Marines providing his security.

As the team headed for the exit to make their run to Banks Island, the people in the assembly area made a corridor between themselves so that the team could leave without having to make their way through a crowd.

Someone started to applaud and it rapidly became a thunderous ovation for the Crossfire Team as they left to contend with American's enemies, again. Laura shook her head slightly as she smiled.

As they were driven to JFK in a military transport, driven by a Marine and guarded by armed Marines, Jack asked Carol what she could tell them about the on-going operation.

Carol gave Jack that new maturity look again. "The demonic element has been aiding the terrorists since last month. They covered the highjacking of the missiles from the Kazakhstan arsenal. In fact, until last week no one was aware that there were any missiles missing. They also covered the transportation of the missiles to Bank's Island which is equally far away from Russia and their chosen targets. They are still trying to hide the operation from most observation but their coverage is fading. We will be able to locate their base."

Jack decided to satisfy his curiosity. "Carol, your demeanor has changed since the ceremony, how come?"

Carol smiled a small smile and looked him in the eye. "How long do you think I was praying while I was on my knees at the reception?"

Jack thought back. "Less than ten minutes in our time."

She laughed quietly. "I was in the heavenlies, primarily with Hugo and Rose, for exactly seven years. I was trained in the finer points of interpretation of the multidimensional matrix as well as the meaning of intent on both human and spiritual entities. It was quite a life-changing, eye-opener for me, especially the studies and hands-on practices I had to go through. Even though I only aged ten minutes in our time this activity probably aged my mental processes by over twenty years. My attitude is different because I had years to mature. So, I have become much more comfortable in my abilities and talents and my interpersonal relationships. Remember I was barely out of college when God drafted me into the Crossfire Team. The training showed me how little I actually knew and how immature my attitude was at the beginning of this evening."

Carol smiled at the others in the vehicle. "To serve the team correctly in Yahveh's eyes I had to expand my vision and expertise. To do that I had to expend that much time to mature and that's why Yahveh invested so much of Hugo's time in my training. One confusing concept was the urgency of this message and the slow even casual passage of time during the training before I could give the message to you. I now realize that I would of given you the wrong message if I hadn't had this training."

She looked a little taken back. "I now have the understanding of how little I know compared to the newest angel let alone one like Rose. It was a very humbling experience and I needed that to set my feet on the right path to serve Yahveh and the team."

She reached over and put her hand over Jack's much bigger one. "Forgive me for being so prideful when I first got this job. I've had to do so much repenting and prayer that it is a wonderful thing to have you all as friends and, now I see that. So, you can see why I lost my starry-eyed, teenager attitude."

Jack had to clear his throat before he could speak because in his spirit he felt the full weight of her burden and her sacrifice and it caused an emotional reaction on his part. He reached over and hugged her. "Welcome to the war, Carol. We are all proud of you and the vital role you play in our lives."

Laura scooted over and put one hand on Jack's and the other on Carol's. "Jack is speaking for all of us Carol. We love you and we really appreciate your sacrifice to this team. Hang tough and keep Yahveh's will in mind as well as His directives. I now know what Hugo meant when I was training with him and he said, "Even the youth will give their all to the success of our mission." We didn't even know you then, but they did in the heavenlies."

The vehicle pulled out of the chilly late evening air into a private hanger set off from the main area of JFK's operations. As they exited the bus the driver got Jack's attention. "General Miles said to tell you that your ride is fifteen minutes out and should be ready to go as soon as you are all on board."

CHAPTER FORTY-FIVE

Jack stood on the tarmac outside of the hanger waiting for the X-76 to land. Suddenly, the whole airport went dark with the exception of the blue outline lights for the runways and taxiways. As his eyes acclimated to the darkness he saw a shape drop lightly onto the active runway and execute a quick roll out. The plane wasn't using its landing lights and unerringly made its way through several intersections and came up to their hanger. The plane made a tight U-turn in front of the hanger and the engines dropped to an idle.

In the dark Jack made out a craft that was probably sixty feet long and had four wings set in an X shape with a thirty-degree separation between the wing angles. There were stubby Canard wings at the front under the pilot's area and there were no tail surfaces at all. The whole shape of the craft was stealthy with the engine exhausts buried in the fuselage above a wide horizontal direction vane to hide the engines from the ground much like the B-2 bomber. In fact, the impression Jack got was that the plane was a stretched and widened B-2 without the humps at the front where the engines were.

A hatch opened in the left side and a soft light lit up the stairs and the interior. Jack called the team and they all got on board. There were about forty-five seats available for passengers. The stairs and the hatch retracted as they found seats. The plane unerringly retraced it's path back to the active runway and without hesitation accelerated rapidly down the runway. It transitioned into the air quietly and smoothly. As the plane left the area Jack saw that all the airport lighting was coming back on. He thought, "Nice trick General. I'll bet no one saw this thing coming or going."

After they climbed above a layer of clouds a voice came over the speakers. "General Connelly, would you please come to the cockpit and give us some idea where we're going?"

Mark got up and went forward. The hatch to the pilot's area slid silently aside for him and he stepped into the cockpit. The door slid shut behind him. The only problem was, there was no one there. Mark looked at the pilot's position and realized that there was no seat or any provision for one. The only seat available was a jump seat set at the back of the fully automated cockpit. There weren't any controls either.

The voice came over the speakers in the cockpit. "Sorry to break this to you without warning but this is an autonomous vehicle. I am Captain William C. Maxwell and am based in the U.S. Air Force base at Minot, North Dakota. You are the first passengers we have had the honor to help disappear from one place and suddenly appear at another. General Connelly, where exactly is our destination? I don't get to do too much other than monitor, but, I can tell the X-76, where to go."

Speaking conversationally, Mark commented, "Pleased to sorta meet you Captain Maxwell. Our ultimate destination is the Canadian Island called Bank's Island. How close can your autonomous stealth aircraft get us to that island?"

The Captain chuckled, "General, you ain't seen nothing' yet. This baby will take you exactly where you and your team want to go and deliver you to any flat spot it can fit in."

Mark grinned, "Good! I want it to get us to Bank's island as quickly as possible and by then we should know where on the island we need to go precisely."

The Captain was quiet for a few seconds. "Okay, your distance is roughly 2263 miles and you should reach your island in roughly fifty-five minutes. When you get an actual destination on the island come back up and let me know. There is a button on the edge of the cockpit door to announce your presence. Have a good flight. Control out."

The cockpit door opened and Mark exited the cockpit to find Su Li standing outside the door which slid shut again. "What's the flight deck like? I'd like to see it."

Mark thought for a second. "Actually it's not a place a pilot like you would want to see. But, I've got to come back in about an hour and you can see it then." He headed back to his seat.

Su Li was a bit upset and followed him. "Why can't I see it and talk to the pilot?"

Mark put on his seat belt and looked up at the irritation in her eyes. "Because there is no pilot. Can you say Autonomous?"

Su Li at first though Mark was pulling her leg. Then she saw the honesty in his eyes and she said, "Oh." Then she went back to her seat and told everyone in the area, "There's no pilot up there. What's the world coming to?"

Mark looked over at Jack and said, "It's over twenty-two hundred miles and we're supposed to be there in less than an hour."

Jack nodded wisely. He then indicated the Mach meter in the bulkhead above the door to the cockpit. It read Mach 4.5. Mark was amazed because he hadn't felt any acceleration after the takeoff. To reach these hyperspeeds the X-76 must have shifted into a Ramjet or even a Scramjet configuration like the SR-71. He looked out the window and realized he was seeing a derivation of Jack's viewport. The hull didn't need any windows to weaken it.

The ground below did not look much different than in a normal commercial airplane except it was changing quicker. Mark looked up and saw the moon come out of the clouds. Then he noticed the clouds zipping by and dropping downward as the craft moved upward toward thinner air.

True to Captain Maxwell's prediction they were almost to the area of Bank's Island in forty-five minutes. The plane had slowed down and dropped almost to the ground. It was going a lot slower but it's proximity to the ground made it look like it was going even faster. It was essentially doing nap-of-the-earth navigation to reduce its radar image to any hostile forces.

Jack knew about the autonomous plane project and knew that Captain Maxwell wasn't flying the craft from a remote control panel. The plane was flying itself and doing a great job.

Jack's satellite phone chirped and he answered it. He got the precise latitude and longitude for the terrorist base. He gave it to Mark and then called the CJCS to pass the information to General Miles.

Mark got up and tapped Su Li on the shoulder. She got up to follow him and went to the cockpit door. He pushed the button and the door slid aside. He stepped in followed by Su Li. She gasped when she saw the arrangements. Mark spoke into thin air. "Captain Maxwell, here are the coordinates of the target. Be advised this is a terrorist base with nuclear missiles they are planning to launch and we really don't want to just show up uninvited. We need to survey the target area while remaining unseen and then we can determine a landing spot."

The Captain acknowledged the new requirements and told Mark, "Roger that. We will instruct the aircraft to observe your requirements. Why don't you and Commander Su Li wait in the cockpit until you can make that determination?"

Mark chuckled, "Ten-four."

Su Li asked Mark, "Commander?"

CHAPTER FORTY-SIX

The X-76 dropped even closer to the ground and Mark thought it would amaze most pilots with the dexterity it negotiated the landscape. It certainly had Su Li mesmerized.

The speed of the craft dropped rapidly to almost a hover as they neared the suspected location of the base. Mark told Captain Maxwell to open the door to the cockpit. When it was open he called Jack to the front with Laura. They entered the cockpit area and Laura's left eyebrow went up a notch at the absence of pilots.

Mark said, "The location that Crayton identified is about two miles to our left." Mark looked at his watch. "We've got about two hours until first light. What do you want to do?"

Jack pulled out his cell phone and leaned back into the passenger compartment. Calling Charlie Wu to the front, Jack related Mark's comments and gave Charlie his cell phone. Charlie dialed the computer center at the Fortress and asked for Shirley. Once he got her he asked the correct question. "We are at the location minus two miles. What have you got?"

Shirley came back with, "I see you and the base. They are under camouflage and the readings that Crayton is detecting indicate that they are in stage two fueling for at least two ICBMs. Our suggestion is that you bomb the stitching out of everything there."

Jack shook his head, "Too many unknowns. We need to see it before we destroy it."

Mark told Captain Maxwell to tell the aircraft to set them down in the closest location it could find.

The plane immediately moved a mile closer to the suspected base and dropped down vertically into a clearing behind a rise of the land that covered it's position from the view of the enemy.

Mark shook his head, "I think we need to get one of these."

Su Li pouted. "I think a pilot is still needed. Although, I wouldn't mind letting it do all the things it has already done."

Laura smiled, "I agree that it needs local oversight by a competent pilot but it has met all our mission parameters precisely and with no wasted effort."

Mark got up as the craft settled to the ground. "Captain Maxwell, can the X-76 wait for us here?"

The Captain's voice came back quickly. "As long as it isn't detected by a scouting party or air search. It will take defensive and offensive measures as it deems necessary."

Mark shrugged, "Good enough. I'll stay in touch by cell phone. Give me your number."

Mark watched as the entire crew put on the cold weather gear they had been given by the Marines when their destination was first determined. The area wasn't called Arctic for any reason. They prepared their weapons and trooped off the silent aircraft into the frigid landscape. Once they gathered at the front, Mark told them, "Lock and load, this will be a hot mission."

They all set off at a quick pace directly towards the supposed base with Crayton advising them as to any obstacles or spiritual disturbances they would run into.

Twenty minutes later they were just outside the base proper. Mark was checking out the operation by binoculars. He whistled quietly. "Well, there are two Russian ICBMs on launchers and third-stage fueling is being readied. I don't see any other explanation as to what this could be."

Jack's phone vibrated and he answered it. "What? Who? When? He hung up the connection and said, "Crayton has two major military forces closing in on this location. One is the Marines that General Miles dispatched. The other seems to be a Russian force launched from a Russian aircraft carrier."

Mark shook his head. "That's not good. They will be detected and these hotheads will accelerate the launches." He looked at the base again. "How long before the Spam hits the fan?"

Jack was also studying the base with binoculars. "Crayton thinks about thirty minutes for the Marines and forty for the Russians."

Laura had been praying with Carol and said, "We have to defuse this situation or we will see the beginnings of world war three."

Jack said, "Okay, Mark how can we accomplish that?"

Mark frowned, "With our usual delicacy."

Sarah said, "Go in and kill everyone and destroy the missiles?"

Mark nodded, "Pretty much."

Jack said, "Okay three waves. Laura, Mark, Su Li, and myself in first. Then Sarah, David, Alexis, Stan, and Debbie next. Everyone else stay behind us. Keep your eyes open to the rear too. Remember there are demons here too. Let's move it. Mark get hold of the Marines and warn them of the potential conflict and our intentions."

Alexis put her hand on Jack's arm. "Don't forget that the Russians are seldom constrained by caution and they may just bomb the place while we are in there."

Mark listened and shook his head. "Not this time. They would of have just sent planes to do that. Troops mean a ground assault."

The three groups moved quickly toward the missiles. Jack added, "Mark, you, David, and Sarah shut down those missiles. Laura, you and I will handle any demonic problems, and the rest of us will attend to the human enemies."

Mark took a priority call from General Miles. "Yes, Sir!"

"Mark, I've got a company of Marines coming at you right now. They are less than ten miles away. It is a reinforced company with about two-hundred and fifty troops and mechanized transport plus two Bradley fighting vehicles. They can't locate the base you indicated was there. Can you help them find it?"

Mark answered back, "Yes, Sir! It's the demonic covering. It's probably playing havoc with the Russians too. I'm eyeballing the base and the two ICBMs which are venting LOX right now. Use my cell phone as a GPS locator for the troops."

The General passed the information to the Marines along with the warning that the Russians were in the area also. He then called Mark back. "Mark, I want your team to handle the demonic aspect of this raid. Leave the missiles to the Marines. They should be there in time to handle the enemy troops also."

Mark replied, "Sir, those missiles are only minutes away from being launched. The Marines need to hurry. We'll see if we can avoid contact until they get here."

CHAPTER FORTY-SEVEN

Jack moved cautiously forward with Laura to his right and Mark to his left. As they entered the outer area of the base Laura's golden armor flared into bright visibility along with her flaming sword. She stepped forward in a fore-and-aft stance with her sword held at high guard over her right shoulder.

Out of the dark stalked a hideous demon with pin-point red eyes and a jaw full of ugly teeth. He was about six foot two inches tall and very stocky. He had a large shield on his back and an effective looking club. He made straight for Laura.

The last several steps he broke into a clumsy run with his club held high in both hands. As he reached striking distance he swung the club down with all his might. Laura rotated to her right by swinging her left leg around. This brought her facing the same way as the demon and on his left side. The move allowed her to avoid the club. She swung her sword down to her right side. The demon stepped back to bring his club up again. Unfortunately for him his arms ended between his hands and his elbows. Laura's sword had cleanly amputated both of the demon's hands and the club.

The demon looked at his missing hands long enough for Laura to backhand her sword across his throat. His head followed his hands to the ground. The body fell to the ground and started dissipating into red smoke.

Laura stepped back and waited because her armor didn't disappear. Two more demons appeared out of the darkness from the camp and spread apart to attack the golden woman from two sides. Laura stepped between them and executed a fast left-right stroke causing both of the demons to jump backwards.

Jack engaged one of the demons with his Katana sword. The demon blocked the first cut which turned out to be a fake anyway. Jack's second swing cut through the demon's right arm and chest. The demon stepped back again looking confused. His arm and chest were leaking a brownish-black smoke and he dropped his sword and then followed it to the ground.

Relieved of a dual attack Laura closed with the second demon. with her blade at mid-guard. Dodging his first strike Laura stepped into the space between them and drove the pommel of her sword into the jaw of the bigger demon. She followed this with a direct strike downward and managed to split the head of the demon, ending his life.

Laura's armor faded out of sight and Jack picked up her M-8 from where it had dropped and tossed it to her. They turned to continue towards the base and the missiles.

The first bullet hit Charlie Wu in the chest and slammed him to the ground on his back. Everyone went to the ground or sought cover as more rounds flew by them or hit the dirt. They had just made contact.

Alexis and David were the nearest to Charlie and they crawled to his inert form. Each one grabbed his ammo harness above a shoulder and they began dragging his form behind a boulder.

David pulled open Charlie's shirt and the bullet dropped out into David's hand. He reached in and started rubbing the smaller man's chest under his body armor while Alexis checked for a pulse.

Charlie started suddenly and jerked up from the ground. Alexis grabbed his shoulders and held him down behind the boulder. Charlie's wild-eyed look quickly settled down as he realized the situation. Charlie moaned, "Not again". David pulled his hand out from Charlie's shirt. Charlie reached in and rubbed the same place while looking at David. He coughed twice and cleared his throat. Then he looked at Alexis. "Why didn't you let her rub my chest?"

David grinned, "I'm just glad you're alright. That was a solid round that took you down."

Above them the rest of the team was seeking targets and firing back at their assailants. Suddenly there were six clear shots of a much heavier caliber than the ones that were firing at them. Then there was silence. Debbie walked out from behind a high boulder with an XM110 sniper rifle chambered in the NATO 308 caliber. The men shooting at them had all been eliminated by one small female in less than twenty seconds.

The missiles were boiling off their evaporative fuel and the outside of the missiles were frosted. The noises indicated that they were about to launch.

Mark used his night glasses and studied the base. He shook his head. "There's got to be a hundred troops in there and we can't go any closer.

Jack's phone vibrated and he answered it. He listened for a few seconds and said, "The Marines are still ten minutes away."

Jack's phone vibrated again and he listened. He waved Mark over. "The Russians are also only about ten minutes from here. The Major in charge of the Marines is aware of them but suggests we fade back so that we don't get hurt if there is a major misunderstanding that ends in a battle.

Carol and Laura had been praying. Laura got their attention. "There are no more demons in the area. We can move out and let the Marines do their thing."

Mark was studying the missiles. "No time! Those things are going to lift off in less than two minutes. I can see the preliminary hoses disconnecting!"

Mark grabbed Jack's cell phone and hit redial. When the Colonel answered Mark told him, "Colonel, This is General Connelly. I am ordering you to come to a halt and wait for my orders before moving towards the base."

He shut off the phone and handed it to Jack. "Debbie!" He shouted as he ran past her. She looked up, "What?"

Mark started running to his left. "Grab that Barrett M-107 and come with me now!"

Debbie grabbed the huge rifle in its case and ran after Mark up an incline. Reaching the top she dropped to the ground next to the ex-Navy SEAL. She quickly stripped the case off the rifle and snapped the large .50 caliber round magazine into the rifle and chambered a round. Flipping the lens caps up she looked at Mark for direction.

Mark said, "Line up on the missile to the right. It's a liquid fueled Russian "Satan" missile. I want you to see where the frost is the heaviest near the rear end. Put a round into the missile at that point now!

Debbie didn't question Mark. She lined up her shot in the 20-power scope on the dark rocket and was about to squeeze the trigger when there was a tremendous roar and a intensely bright flare of light as the missile launched off its base.

Debbie didn't flinch. She tracked the slowly accelerating missile and pulled the trigger on the Barrett. The huge rifle rocked her back but she used the time to lever a new round into the chamber. She raised the angle of the rifle and fired a second 1500-grain round into the missile.

The missile was almost fifty feet up and starting to accelerate more quickly when a spider's web of fiery lines spread out from where she'd hit the missile. The cracks widened for a few milliseconds and then the entire bottom of the missile exploded with tremendous force.

Since the team was over a half-mile from the missile the effects were only immense. The explosive blast washed over the base and destroyed everything in the area. The second missile was just launching when the fireball and the explosive force hit it. It added it's full fuel load to the continuing explosion. The second blast killed everything again.

Mark and Debbie tried to bury themselves into the dirt and shrubs of the hillside as the flame front washed over them. The rest of the team was doing the same farther back from the hill. Fortunately the hill deflected the majority of the blast and fire above the team members. The distance from the explosion was the saving grace for the team though.

After the flame front burned itself out and the land stopped shaking Mark ventured a glance over the top of the hill and shook his head. "Looks like hell on earth out there."

Mark's phone chirped and he answered it. "Connelly."

The Colonel was totally astonished by the immense explosion. "General Connelly, what did you do? It looks like there's nothing left but burning debris where the base was."

Mark replied, "The missiles were launching so we had to stop them. Mission accomplished. I apologize that we had to act without waiting for you but there was no time."

The Colonel stared at the destruction and said, "That's perfectly all right. We'll be right along to see if there's anything to investigate."

Mark shook his head, "I wouldn't do that Colonel. I think the Russians will take umbrage at a U.S. military presence near the damage done by their missiles. I suggest that we extract and join up with you."

The team made haste to reach the X-76 which was waiting quietly for them. They boarded and it lifted off and skimmed the ground until it was several miles away from the island. It climbed and closed with the troop transports for the Marines which Mark noticed had reversed course and were now flying away from the island. The early dawn glinted off the body of the experimental aircraft as they paced the lead jet. Mark told the Colonel they would meet him back in New York and they could debrief then.

The Colonel stared at the unreal aircraft near them and watched as it accelerated rapidly and rising upward out of sight heading south.

CHAPTER FORTY-EIGHT

The X-76 returned to its base and was safely hidden in its hanger by the time the team gave their impressions of the aircraft to the designers.

Jack asked one of the design team how the plane could travel so fast and still not need to refuel for the trip back to New York.

The designer smiled. "It's not quite that super General. While you were gone the 76 lifted off and met with a refueling tanker at 20,000 feet. It got a full set of fuel tanks and returned to wait for you. It did that on its own by the way."

Even Su Li gave the autonomous aircraft high marks especially in an unexpected combat role.

The whole team took a MATs flight back to JFK and was ferried to a base headquarters by military transport. The team had some good down time while they waited for the Marine Colonel to arrive

After a good long shower and some food the team then kicked back and relaxed. The women discussed their plans after their return to Denver while the men watched a Monday night football game.

About a half an hour after the game was done Colonel Haskins made his appearance. He brought with him several legal types and a two-star General. General Duncan was a rather dour specimen who didn't like rebels in his army. And that was the way he thought about it. It was HIS army!

Convening what looked to be an ad hoc Kangaroo court the Colonel asked Jack and Mark to give their rendition of what had happened on Bank's Island.

Jack explained the circumstances of their being called to the island to handle the demonic element and the events that happened there. Mark filled In with technical details up to the downing of the missiles by Debbie's rifle.

The Colonel described the efforts of the Marine company to reach the island in time only to have the site destroyed just before they arrived.

General Duncan played with a pencil while he contemplated the reports. He threw the pencil to the table and sat up straight. "General Connelly, your rank is primarily ceremonial. Where in God's name did you get the audacity to give a command to Colonel Haskins to stop our forces from advancing on the base?"

Mark's smile didn't fade as he looked at the General. "In the first place, General Duncan, my two-star rank was conferred by the President of the United States and carries the same weight as your more polished stars. Secondly, I was the only commanding officer in place at the base. Colonel Haskins was miles away. Thirdly, one of the demonic ploys was to get our forces into a full out firefight with the Russians. Fourthly, I didn't want to lose our troops in the fireball that we had to create to stop the MIRV war-headed Russian missiles from destroying the east coast of our country."

Mark stood up and stared at the General. "I also resent your insinuations that we usurped your operation. If you are worried about possible repercussions from the Russians, please note that the two missiles we destroyed were reported destroyed by the Russians ten years ago in the SALT treaties. If you want to take this up the line then I suggest you do that because you don't have jurisdiction over us or our operations."

Mark sat down and waited for the explosion he was sure to happen after the General digested all the information he had just been given.

That General Duncan was going to explode wasn't even debatable. He was turning red in the face and one could actually believe they could see steam coming out of his nostrils and ears.

The General told several of the troops with him to place the entire Crossfire Team under arrest and take them to the brig. He would file charges on them the next morning.

Ten of the troopers moved in but Mark said in a loud voice. "Belay that action troopers,. I'm ordering you to stand down."

General Duncan stood up and screamed for the men to do as he ordered. Jack shook his head and stood up. The entire Crossfire team jumped into action and in less time than it takes to tell there were nine soldiers unconscious on the floor of the room.

Sarah smelled a rat and had really had enough of this misguided officer's actions. She dropped the tenth and last unconscious trooper she had just knocked out to the floor and walked past Mark to the General. Mark noted that no one said anything or moved.

General Duncan was beside himself with anger. He looked at the woman coming toward him and he grabbed his sidearm out of its holster. As he swung it up he was amazed at the speed of the woman. She closed with him in a heartbeat and disarmed him. She then lifted the shorter but heavier man off the floor and leaned into his face. "General Duncan, I am not pleased with your attitude. It smacks of insurrection and some form of evil. Shall we find out if your evil is real?"

The General started to complain when Sarah started to pray. Her golden armor flashed into sight with the shield and her sword at her sides. The golden helmet was directly against the General's forehead and there was something like a golden spark between the two.

The General wailed hideously for a second and then passed out.

Sarah placed him back into his chair and said in a very commanding voice, "In the name of Yahshua Ha Meshach, come out of him, NOW!"

Her sword was in her hand and the power flowing off of the sword blade washed the General's body. With an even more hideous shriek a semi-transparent demon emerged from the man's slumping body and rose into the air. It solidified into a nightmare shape and flew at Sarah. Sarah timed out the approach and swung the fiery sword in a cross body chop.

The blade hit the demon and cut it into two pieces. The top of the demon floated in the air as it started to vaporize when it spoke in a grating voice. "We will beat you!"

Sarah slashed the sword through the upper part of the demon's body and out its head. As it disappeared she said, "Not today, slime ball!"

Several more troops rushed into the room with weapons which they aimed at the Crossfire Team. Sarah stepped between the troopers and the team and raised her sword.

Jack told everyone to just calm down. He stood there ignoring the weapons and the actions behind him. "The reason that you're all excited is because that demon was deliberately trying to get us to fight. Just like the ones on Bank's Island."

Everyone settled down and the Marines lowered their weapons. Jack walked over to General Duncan and checked his condition. The man slowly came to looking twenty years older than before. He looked around the room and asked. "Is it gone for good?"

Sarah's armor had faded from view. She squatted down next to the General. "Yes, Sir, I destroyed it completely."

The General smiled at her. "Thank you, that spirit has been slowly killing me and taking over my life." He looked around the room with bleary eyes. "I haven't been myself for a while and I don't want the weight of command anymore." He tried to stand and Sarah helped him up. He looked at Mark and said, "General Connelly, I pass command of this action over to you. I think I'm going to go home and sleep for a month."

Laura moved up to the General and Sarah. "Let's pray for angels to keep him safe and free from Satan's works."

After the whole team prayed for General Duncan's protection, the General departed with an escort. Mark declared the debriefing session at an end and dismissed everybody.

The next morning they left by commercial air to Denver International Airport.

After suffering through the rigors of commercial flying and the airport hassles the team was still tired when they arrived at DIA. The one bright spot in the trip was the mistake made by a news team in the main terminal. They thought the team was an ensemble of actors from a new action adventure film and tried to interview them on the spot.

David Zahavy stepped up to the interviewer and asked him not to take videos of them because it was a mistake that would prove very detrimental for his career. When Jack and Mark came over and towered over him the man decided he didn't want to bother them anymore.

Mark was relieved when at long last they arrived back at the Fortress and after a good long sleep everyone found time to get back into their normal routines.

CHAPTER FORTY-NINE

Several days later Charlie called Jack and Mark from the computer center. He asked them to come up for a visit. After they arrived he put some data up on one of his big monitors. Charlie looked much better after a few days of rest. He used a laser pointer to indicate the various information on the screen. "After an analysis of several secret Russian communications from Banks Island I discovered three things I thought you would like to investigate. First, see here? The Russian unit that investigated the ruins of the terrorist's base found a couple of survivors."

Charlie shook his head, "After some cordial interrogation which apparently was fatal to the interviewees they came to some worrisome conclusions. It seems that there were four more ICBMs stolen from the breakaway satellite nation and it wasn't discovered until these revelations from the Banks Island torture sessions. The Russians performed a hard physical search and were able to penetrate the demonic covering hiding the four additional MIRV thefts. They are now doing the same type of inventory everywhere their missiles are located. I recommend we have the same thing done on our inventories."

"Second, the terrorists revealed that the other four were transported to the Middle East or Africa. They weren't sure which and that probably cost them dearly. The Russian interrogator felt that they may have been transported to Zyngola."

Charlie switched files. "Thirdly, the remaining four missiles were taken by a group headed by a man only known as "The Serpent". That sounds demonic to me but I ran a real time search for this "Serpent" and came up with a bunch of references and suppositions. No facts or provable data on his background, location, or MO. I will continue to seek information about him but I think we need to let the administration know about these new threats."

Jack and Mark looked at each other. Mark asked Charlie, "Do you know how long ago these missiles were taken by this "Serpent"?

Charlie shrugged his shoulders, "Best guess is about two weeks ago."

Mark frowned, "You're right Charlie, we'll spread the word. Keep looking for a possible location of the missiles."

After they got back to the War Room Mark put in a call to General Miles. When he was finally connected he greeted the CJCS. "General Miles, this is Mark Connelly. Is this line encrypted?"

The General said, "Hold one."

He came back a few seconds later, "Okay, Mark, we're secure. Why do I feel that this won't be good news?"

Mark agreed with the man. "Yes, Sir, I hate to be the bearer of bad news after the action on Banks Island but we've intercepted some Russian communications that indicate that four additional MIRVed ICBMs were taken at the same time as the two on Banks. The Russian communications indicated that two, now deceased, terrorists coughed up the information and it was confirmed by a hard physical search of the missile inventories. Charlie suggested that we might do the same type of inventory to make sure that there is nothing missing from our inventories."

The General was quiet for a few minutes. "Are we sure that this isn't just a ruse by the Russians? They are well known for that type of disinformation to cause us trouble."

Mark laughed, "I understand, General. I doubt that is the case because the communications about the additional missing missiles came from lower level types which shows a large number of people involved in the search and discovery. The Russians would have buried the information if they could have and since they haven't it seems that they are headed for a major egg-on-their-faces event. Remember that the two Banks Island missiles were part of an announced and supposedly verified SALT destruction. If the other four missiles were also part of the hidden cache then they are going to be hard-pressed to explain them on the world scene. I would think that they will secretly contact us for help again."

There was a significant pause on the General's end. "Good call, Mark. It seems that just such a communication came through the Russian embassy this morning. We are just gearing up to locate the missing weapons. This is completely hush-hush per the President. We will definitely need your expertise again if we get a hint where these missiles are. I think that the demonic covering will still be in place."

Mark nodding as he told the General. "Yes, Sir. We'll be available whenever you need us. There are so many wackos in that part of the world I would guess we'll find out where they plan to use them soon.

The Crossfire Team will return in ***"Nuclear Crossfire"***

If this story has awakened your spirit or moved you to seek the love of Christ and His power for your life, whether you've never accepted Jesus as your savior or you've fallen away, repeat the following prayer and begin a most wonderful journey into eternal life with Him today.

Father God in heaven, As You said in Your Holy Word, (Romans 10:9) that if we confess the Lord our God and believe in our hearts that God raised Jesus from the dead, we shall be saved.

(The prayer on the next page is a sample prayer when asking Jesus into your heart as your Savior. You can also pray this in your own words.)

Salvation Prayer

Dear God in heaven, I come to you in the name of Jesus. I confess to You that I am a sinner, and I am sorry for my sins and the life that I have lived; I need your forgiveness. I believe that your only begotten Son Jesus Christ shed His precious blood on the cross at Calvary and died for my sins, and I am now willing to turn from my sin.

Right now I confess Jesus as the Lord of my life and my soul. With all my heart, I truly believe that your Holy Spirit raised Jesus from the dead. Today I accept Jesus Christ as my personal Savior and according to Your Word, right now I am saved.

I thank you Jesus, for your unlimited grace which has saved me from my sins. I thank you Jesus that your grace that never leads to license, but rather it always leads to repentance. Therefore Lord Jesus, transform my life so that I may bring glory and honor to you alone and not to myself.

I thank you Lord Jesus, for dying for me at Calvary and giving me eternal life.

Amen.

If you just said this prayer and you meant it with all your heart, believe that you are now saved and have been born again.

You may ask, "Now that I am saved, what do I do next?" First of all you need to get into a spirit-filled, bible-based church that teaches the Scriptures, and you need to study God's Word.

Once you have found a church home, you will want to become water-baptized. By accepting Christ you are baptized in the spirit, but it is through water-baptism that you publically announce your obedience to the Lord Jesus. Water baptism is a symbol of your salvation from the dead. You were dead but now you live, for Jesus Christ has redeemed you for a price! The price was His atoning death on the cross. May God Bless You!